W9-BCJ-445

THE DAY THE RABBI RESIGNED

Rabbi David Small, the most unorthodox rabbi ever seen in or out of temple, wants to leave. Although his years at Barnard's Crossing have never been dull, he is bored with clerical duties and wants to teach. But before he can say *alma mater*, the rabbi is enlisted by Police Chief Hugh Lanigan, to set his scholar's mind to a drink-driving accident that looks like murder. Chief Lanigan and the wise rabbi discover that there were quite a number of 'innocent' citizens driving down the seldom-used road on that rainy Saturday night. And any one of them could have had it in for the victim. But it is Rabbi Small, combining the wisdom of Solomon with an analyst's understanding of his fellow man (and woman), who ingeniously lays out all the answers like a delicious holiday feast.

JAMES PRENDERGAST LIBRARY
509 CHERRY STREET
JAMESTOWN, NEW YORK 14701

THE DAY THE RABBI RESIGNED

Harry Kemelman

CURLEY LARGE PRINT
HAMPTON, NEW HAMPSHIRE

Library of Congress Cataloging-in-Publication Data

Kemelman, Harry.
  The day the Rabbi resigned / by Harry Kemelman.
    p.   cm.
  ISBN 0–7927–1414–8
  ISBN 0–7927–1413–X
  1. Large type books. I. Title.
[PS3561.E398D3   1993]   92–35645
813'.54—dc20   CIP

Published by Curley Large Print, an imprint of Chivers North America, by arrangement with Scott Meredith Literary Agency, 1993.

U.S. Hardcover ISBN 0 7927 1414 8
U.S. Softcover ISBN 0 7927 1413 X

Copyright © 1992 by Harry Kemelman
All rights reserved

Printed in Great Britain

TO
STEPHEN R. VOLK,
WELCOME TO THE FAMILY!

CHAPTER ONE

The evening at the Bergsons' had been pleasant, even gay at times. But as Rabbi David Small, both hands clutching the wheel, drove the short distance home, he was aware that his wife Miriam was annoyed with him. It was not that she did not speak—she was always careful not to distract him with casual conversation when he was driving—but he could detect it in the set of her chin and in the way she sat upright, her back barely touching the back of the seat. As always when he reached their house, he let her out and then drove into the driveway to park the car in the garage. Normally, she would wait for him to rejoin her and they would walk up the steps together and he would unlock and open the door. But tonight, when he let her out at the curb, she used her own key and entered the house alone.

'Something bothering you?' he asked when he came in a couple of minutes later. Although of average height, he looked shorter because of the scholarly stoop of a man who had spent his life poring over books, an effect heightened by his tendency to thrust his head forward as he peered at the world nearsightedly through thick-lensed, wire-rimmed glasses.

1

She was slim, with the figure of a young girl, but there were fine lines at the corners of her eyes. Her heart-shaped face, though youthful, showed its maturity in the set of her firm chin. Her blond hair, now occasionally tinted, or as she would say, 'touched up' at the hairdresser's, was piled on top of her head as though to get it out of the way. She stood very straight and looked at him accusingly.

'You weren't very sociable tonight,' she said coldly. 'In fact, you were positively hostile.'

'Only to that idiot Ben Clayman,' he said. 'And maybe to his friend, Myron Levitt, the G.E. fellow who came from Rochester a couple of years ago.'

'But why? What did Ben Clayman say or do?'

'He asked me if I had visited Morris Fisher at the hospital. I told him I hadn't got 'round to it yet, and when he looked disapproving, I asked him if he had been. He admitted he hadn't, and then added, "But I'm not his rabbi," and that really annoyed me. So I explained to him that visiting the sick was enjoined on all Jews, and was not a special rabbinic function.'

'You lectured him.'

The rabbi smiled. 'Yes, I suppose I did.'

'I heard you,' she said, and then added, 'from the other side of the room.'

'I guess I did raise my voice a little. Several

2

others had joined us, and Arnold Robbins kept bleating, "But you're our spiritual leader." Now that really ticked me off, and I told him if it was a spiritual leader the congregation wanted, they should have got a Protestant minister or a Catholic priest rather than a rabbi.'

'You didn't!' She was shocked, but she couldn't help smiling.

'I certainly did.' He nodded in smug satisfaction. 'And then this Levitt person said his rabbi in Rochester, who had married him, was a veritable saint, and he was sure it was responsible for the success of his marriage. Now, how do you respond to that kind of idiocy? So I said that no doubt it was the reason for the low divorce rate in the Jewish community of Rochester.'

'Oh, David, you didn't.'

'I did, and I don't think he even realized I was being sarcastic. When I asked Clayman if he had any complaints about *his* marriage—at which I had officiated, if you remember—someone said he wouldn't dare say so if he did, and that broke it up.'

'Ben Clayman is one of your most loyal supporters. I don't know why you'd want to antagonize him.'

'Oh, I didn't antagonize him, just kidded him a little.'

'Well, then, Arnold Robbins. You know, David, it seems to me that lately you've been

3

awfully short-tempered with a lot of members of the congregation.'

He grinned at her. 'You think they might fire me?'

'Of course not, but—'

'Because as you know very well, the Board of Directors has tried to fire me a dozen times. They tried the very first year I was here. I had to fight to keep my job. Each time I justified it on the grounds that the congregation as a whole wanted me, and that it was only the board that was hostile. But maybe that was only a rationalization for what was actually plain stubbornness on my part.'

'That was then, but now the board is behind you, a hundred percent. You've won them over. Now they like you, and you're presuming on it.'

He shook his head. 'No such thing. It's just that I got older and they got younger.'

'What do you mean?'

'I mean that when I came here I was under thirty and the board members were in their forties and fifties, even a couple in their sixties. When I disagreed with them on something, they regarded it almost as an impertinence because in their eyes I was a youngster, a kid. But now I'm fifty-three, and I'm older than most of the members of the board. The older ones either died off or moved to Florida, out of the area anyway. I've officiated at the weddings of most of the present members of the board, anyway, all those who married local girls. One or two of them I even prepared for the Bar Mitzvah ceremony. Ben Clayman for one. So now I'm the old man, and they, even those who are about my age, are the youngsters. I suspect that even when I appear harsh and unyielding, they take a kind of pride in my being a crusty, irascible old curmudgeon who won't compromise the least bit on principles.' He grinned. 'If you're worried about my antagonizing Ben Clayman, I overheard him later explaining to his G.E. friend that it was my modesty and humility that led me to deny my spiritual leadership.'

'And if they do think of you as their spiritual leader, is it so bad?'

'Miriam!' He sounded shocked. 'It's not our line of work at all. We make no pretensions to having an inside track to the Almighty. A rabbi, unlike a Protestant minister or a Catholic priest, has not received a call from God. I got my call from Jake Wasserman, the chairman of the Ritual Committee at the time. I studied for the rabbinate as I might have for any other profession, the law or medicine. I chose the rabbinate because of my fascination with the Talmud. As a rabbi, my function is to sit in judgment on disputes that are brought before me, to advise on all matters relating to our tradition, to teach our tradition and guide the

5

congregation in it, and to be the resident subsidized scholar of the community. I don't bless people or things, and I have no special role in our service. I don't know what spiritual leadership involves, but it suggests trying to be more than human. And I suspect that trying to be more than human, you are apt to end up being less than human.' He chuckled as a thought occurred to him. 'Do you suppose the children of ministers are frequently on the wild side because they've been disillusioned by seeing their fathers as they really are, as ordinary human beings who are annoyed when the toast is burned, and downright angry when their wives scratch the fender of the car backing out of the garage, rather than the unworldly, spiritual beings seen in the pulpit by the congregation?'

'All right, so you're not a spiritual leader, but you give sermons.'

'Yes, because the congregation expects it, perhaps to relieve the tedium of our long services, or maybe'—he grinned—'to assure them that I'm doing something to justify my salary. Traditionally, the rabbi's contract called for him to deliver only two discourses during the year, and the discourse was not a sermon, not an exhortation, but rather a scholarly dissertation.'

'You do a lot of counseling.'

'Only because I'm available. They come to my study at the temple because I'm usually there during the day. They tell me what's troubling them and I listen. I suppose just unburdening themselves helps some of them. To some I give commonsense advice, and maybe that helps. And I know about various social agencies that they can apply to for help, say, for the care of an elderly parent. But I have no special expertise in the field.'

'You want to know what I think, David? I think you need a vacation.'

'The trouble with a vacation is that what you leave is no different from what you have to come back to.'

'Yes, but *you're* apt to be different. Would it be any different in another congregation?'

He shrugged. 'Who knows? This was a new congregation when I came to it. Maybe an older congregation, in a city, perhaps, where they were more knowledgeable about their religion, might be different. Or maybe it was because I got off on the wrong foot with this one and there's been a sort of tradition of doubt and suspicion about me ever since.' He canted his head to one side and eyed her speculatively. 'You know, Miriam, thinking back, the most enjoyable time I had in the years that I've been here is the year I taught the class in Judaic Thought at Windermere. I wouldn't have got the chance to give the course if I hadn't been the rabbi here.'

'Are you saying you wish you had gone into teaching instead of the rabbinate? That you'd

7

rather be a teacher than a rabbi?'

'Well, as a rabbi I am a teacher. It's just that the class I've been given to teach, these youngish, successful, professionals and executives who by and large make up the Jewish community of Barnard's Crossing, don't seem to profit by my teaching. I was far more successful with the younger people in college, and it was more satisfying.'

'David,' she said accusingly, 'this isn't something that just popped into your head because of what Ben Clayman said tonight.'

'No,' he admitted, 'I've been thinking about it for some time.'

'How long?'

'Ever since my birthday.'

'But—But why then?'

'Because I'm fifty-three, and it occurred to me that in a few years I'd be too old to be considered for a teaching job. Maybe I'm too old now, but I'd like to give it a shot.'

'And have you done anything about it?' she asked quietly.

'Well, I've written to my cousin Simcha.'

'Simcha the Apicorus? You wrote to him because you thought as an atheist he would approve of your leaving the rabbinate?'

'I wrote to him because he's been a professor at Chicago for over forty years, and I thought he might be able to help me. And an Apicorus is not necessarily an atheist. We use the term very loosely and are apt to apply

8

it to anyone who doesn't observe some regulation we do.' He looked at her curiously. 'You don't appear to be particularly upset at my wanting to leave the rabbinate.'

'I'm not,' she said flatly. 'Do you think it's easy being a rabbi's wife?'

'Why? What do you have to do? Oh, you mean you feel you have to go to all the Sisterhood meetings and the Hadassah meetings.'

'Oh, I don't mind going to those. I'd probably go even if I weren't the rabbi's wife. I mean, I have to be nice to everyone. The Bergsons are good friends of ours, but would I ever say to Rachel that I thought Janice Slobodkin used too much makeup? Or that Nancy Bersin spoils her kids rotten? Or that I didn't think the other Nancy, Nancy Goldstein, was much of a housekeeper?'

'You mean Rachel Bergson would tell them?'

'Of course not, but in talking to her good friend Debbie Cohen she might mention it. And Debbie Cohen is friendly with both Nancys, and *she* might mention it to them.'

'I don't hesitate to tell Al Bergson what I think of various members of the congregation.'

'Of course not. You've been fighting with one segment of the congregation or another ever since we came here. Sometimes you've opposed the entire Board of Directors.

9

Besides, men don't talk.'

'How do you mean we don't talk?'

'I mean that a man doesn't call another man on the telephone unless he has something specific he wants to tell him, but women talk on the phone for hours even when they've got nothing to say to each other. It's a form of visiting, of keeping in touch. So things get said that you hadn't planned on saying. I've got to smile and be friendly all the time, and it's a strain. Janice Slobodkin calls me 'Mimi.' I hate the nickname. But if I ask her to call me Miriam, she's apt to think I'm stuck-up, or that I want her to keep her distance. Let's get out, David. Find another job in teaching or editing—'

'But it's not easy for a man of fifty-three to get a job, especially in an entirely new field. I can't very well give up this job until I get another.'

'But you can, David. There'll be just the two of us. Jonathon goes into that big law firm at the end of the year, and Hepsibah is getting married in September.'

'That's going to cost a pretty penny.'

'But we've saved for it.'

'We have?'

'I have.'

'Still, we've got to live. What if a job doesn't come along? Do you expect me to ask our children to support us?'

'Heaven forbid! But we'll manage. In a

10

couple or three weeks, in June, you will have been here twenty-five years. And you are eligible for your pension, which pays seventy-five percent of your present salary. And there's a cost of living increase included. Seventy-five percent of your salary for just the two of us. We'll be rich, David. Even if you don't get a job right away, we won't suffer. We can travel. We can go to Israel without having to worry about getting back in time for the High Holy Days, or because you have to officiate at someone's wedding.'

A slow grin spread across his face. But then he shook his head. 'No, I've got to have a job, even if it's just one to come back to.'

'Why?'

'Because I've got to have something to do. I have to know that something has to be done, to give structure to my life. It's different for a woman. She always has a job—preparing meals, running a household. But if a man has nothing to do, he disintegrates. You know what happens to men who retire, men who have nothing to do? They're with their wives all the time. They go shopping with them and carry their bundles. The big decision of the day is where they'll go for lunch or what to prepare for dinner. No, thank you. I won't give up this job until I get another.'

★   ★   ★

11

Later, as they were preparing for bed, she asked curiously, 'Why didn't you see Morris Fisher, David? Didn't you make your regular visit to the hospital? And don't you see every one of the congregants when you go?'

'And any other Jew who happens to be there at the time,' he said. 'As a matter of fact, I did go Tuesday. That's my regular day at the Salem Hospital. I asked about him, and the nurse said he was down in X-ray, so I didn't bother to stop in at his room. I'll catch him next Tuesday, if he's still there.' He sighed. 'And if he's not, I'll stop in and see him at his house.'

'You don't sound very enthusiastic. Don't you like him?'

'Well ... he's not a very cheerful fellow; seems to be in a perpetual state of mourning.'

'But that's because he's lost his wife.'

'That was five or six years ago, before he came to Barnard's Crossing. And I've heard from those who know him that he's always been that way.'

'Well, maybe your visit will cheer him up.'

'What do you suggest, that I tickle him with a feather?'

'Oh, you. Go to bed.'

12

CHAPTER TWO

Whenever Mark Levine, short, stocky, and balding, came up to Boston from his home base in Dallas, he always made a point of seeing his old friend Donald Macomber. They had been classmates in college, and in their senior year they had roomed together. After college, Mark Levine had gone to work in an insurance office in Dallas, had branched out for himself after a year or two, had made some shrewd investments, or as he would say, had been extremely lucky, and was now a very, very rich man.

Donald Macomber, tall and slim, with piercing blue eyes and silvery gray hair, had gone on to take a doctorate in history, to a professorship in a good university, to a deanship where he had shown considerable administrative skill, and finally to the presidency of Windermere Christian College in Boston. When informed of the appointment, Mark Levine had written facetiously, 'It was only a question of time; people who look like you are bound to become college presidents.'

They had maintained contact over the years by an occasional letter or phone call, and on the occasion when business brought Mark to Boston, he always made a point of leaving one

13

night free so that he could have dinner with his friend.

It was after such a dinner that Macomber had asked, 'How about joining our Board of Trustees, Mark?'

'You want me on the Board of Trustees of Windermere Christian College? You must be joking. Just what denomination is it?'

'I'm not joking, Mark. And it's no denomination.'

'I mean originally.'

'It was never denominational. It started out as a ladies' seminary back in the middle of the last century. You know what those places were: a place for girls to mark time for a couple of years after high school until they managed to get married. They couldn't go out to work because in those days the only acceptable job for women of good family was teaching school. So the wealthy girls were sent to finishing schools with large campuses out in the country, with tennis courts and horses, where girls learned the things that aristocratic gentlewomen were supposed to know. But Windermere was for girls of the middle class. It was in the city, so the girls could live at home. It was called the Windermere Ladies' Christian Seminary, not because it was religious in any sense of the word, but to convey the idea that it was a moral place, strictly supervised, and that no high jinks were permitted.

14

'Then at the turn of the century, it became Windermere Christian College for Women because ladies' seminaries and finishing schools were going out of fashion. It became a four-year college of liberal arts because—because, I suppose, things were beginning to open up for women and there were other things they could do besides teach school.'

'Or perhaps because two years was not enough time in which to catch a husband,' Levine suggested.

Macomber chuckled. 'You may have something there,' he conceded. 'In any case, they kept the Christian in the name, maybe with even a little more justification since the four-year girls' colleges were a lot less supervised than the two-year seminaries had been. I don't think anyone thought of it as a school with any religious orientation. In going over the names of some of the graduating classes, I noted a number of names that were almost certainly Jewish.'

'It doesn't prove anything,' said Levine. 'In Catholic countries like Ireland and Poland, I understand Jewish youngsters are enrolled in the religious schools with a dispensation from attending the religious services.'

'I suppose so, but I would think that after the school had been in existence for so many years, its general orientation would be pretty well-known, at least in the area.'

'All right.'

15

'Then after World War Two, with the G.I. bill enabling large numbers of veterans to go to college, it became coeducational, the way many schools did. Women's Lib had something to do with it, I imagine.'

'But you still kept Christian in the name,' Levine insisted.

'Yes, it became Windermere Christian College of Liberal Arts. As I understand it, they kept the Christian in the name because it had always been referred to as Windermere Christian. It's not easy to give up a name. The company is still called American Express even though it hasn't engaged in the business of delivering parcels for years. And then, too, it was argued that there were a number of scholarships and gifts of one sort or another that had been made out to Windermere Christian, and that these might have to be given back if they changed the name. At least, that was one of the arguments that was offered me when I took over as president. I didn't push it because I sensed that the board wouldn't go along with me. But I did do something to indicate that the school was nondenominational. I hired a Rabbi Lamden to give a three-hour course in Judaica. He is the rabbi of a Reform congregation in Cambridge. He's not much of a scholar, but he's popular because it's a snap course and anyone taking it is sure of an A. You see, the school had become a fall-back school—'

'Fall-back?'

'Yes, you know, as it got harder and harder for kids to get into the prestigious colleges like Harvard, Yale, and Princeton, they'd apply to those and then to some less prestigious school, like Windermere, to fall back on if they were refused admission to their first choices. Well, because Windermere had become a fall-back school, it had begun to get students from outside the Boston area, especially from New York and New Jersey. The student body had been pretty much local until then. Quite a few from the New York and New Jersey area were Jewish, and I thought the Judaica course might allay whatever suspicions their parents might have of the name.'

'I see, and you think my name on the Board of Trustees would add to the effect?'

'No, believe me, Mark, that's not what I had in mind.'

'What then? An endowment, perhaps?'

Macomber smiled. 'A college can always use some extra money. But that's not what I was thinking of either. Look, the board meets only four times a year, and the agenda is set beforehand. If you can't make it to one of the meetings, there's no harm done. Many of the out-of-state trustees come only once or twice a year, although the college picks up the tab for the trip. There are twenty on the board. When a vacancy occurs, I nominate the

17

replacement, and although they vote on it, my nomination is tantamount to election. There's a vacancy right now, and I'd like to put your name up. And by the way, it's for life.'

'Really? So someone has to die before—'

'Well, there are resignations, and once one of the trustees was involved in a rather smelly bankruptcy. The board called for his resignation, and it was understood he would be voted out if he did not offer it. But that was before my time.'

'Well, I'm clean, but why do you want me?'

'Because I want people on the board I can be sure of'

'But if you're the president, don't you automatically get the backing of the board?'

'It's not like taking over a corporation where your people hold the majority of the stock. In a nonprofit institution like a college, the members of the board aren't there because they own a certain number of shares. They're there because they are presumed to be important people or to come from important families. Some of them even inherit their places on the board.'

'Come, come, you mean their fathers will the seats to them?'

'Of course not, but what frequently happens is that when John Whatsis the Second, the president of the Geewhiz

Corporation dies, and John Whatsis the Third takes over, he's apt to be offered his father's place on the boards of the various charitable institutions that his father had held, at least the smaller ones. Right now, I have a majority, but it's a bare majority.'

'And with me, you'd have a comfortable majority?'

'It will be better, but not yet enough to give me full control. Because for certain things—and changing the name of the college is one of them—I need a two-thirds majority.'

'You realize, Don, you can't count on me to make a financial contribution, not while you're Windermere Christian. Every Jewish organization would be on my back for donations or to increase the sums I've already given.'

'Believe me, I understand.'

'All right, as long as you understand, I'll come aboard. Will that give you your two-thirds majority?'

'No ... It would have, but you see, sometimes you make a mistake. When we were expanding by buying up all the old brownstone front houses on Clark Street, I found a Cyrus Merton, a very knowledgeable realtor who proved to be extremely helpful. He had entrée to any number of banks for mortgage money, and he's a genius at financing. So I asked him to serve on the board. He was very pleased and accepted.'

19

'And he didn't work out?'

'Oh, he became one of our most active members. He is semiretired and has plenty of time for us. He's chairman of our Faculty Committee and spends a lot of time around the school.'

'But?'

'He backs me in almost everything, except the name change. He's a very devout Catholic, fanatic, according to Charlie Dobson, another Catholic on our board. It is the Christian in our name that attracted him to the school. And from his point of view, the fact that we're not denominational made it all the more important that we retain the name.'

'And my coming on the board?'

'Will probably please him,' said Macomber promptly. 'To him it will signify that while all faiths are represented, the institution is essentially Christian.'

'But the two-thirds—'

'With you on the board, we're close, but not there yet. He's the leader of the opposition, and as long as he keeps his troops in line, he can stop us. But they're not all as adamant as he, and if we can detach just one, we'll be home free.'

CHAPTER THREE

At sixty-five Cyrus Merton was a wealthy man. Shortly after graduating from high school, he had got a job in a small real estate office in Dorchester, a suburb of Boston, where he had grown up, as a typist/file clerk, which included whatever else had to be done in the office, such as sweeping and dusting, running out for coffee and doughnuts, and delivering documents to banks and the Registry of Deeds. By the time he was twenty-two, however, he was showing properties to clients, and he even received a percentage of the commission when he occasionally succeeded in closing a deal. By the time he was twenty-five, he had a broker's license and had opened his own office.

He was not too successful, was struggling, in fact, until by chance he met a high school classmate who had gone on to a seminary and was now Father Joseph Tierney, a curate at St. Thomas's in Barnard's Crossing. It was through him that Cyrus was brought in contact with the pastor who was engaged in building a parochial school. There were problems with acquiring the necessary land, and Cyrus was able to help out with the negotiations for the financing and with various real estate transactions involved in the purchase of several of the needed lots.

The pastor was grateful and reciprocated by recommending him to parishioners who were interested in buying or selling property. Quite suddenly, Cyrus began to prosper, and closed his Boston office and opened one in Barnard's Crossing.

It was a fortunate decision, for Barnard's Crossing, which had been largely a summer resort separated from Boston by an arm of the ocean, was fast becoming a suburb of the city by reason of a tunnel under the water and a bridge over it, and property values were beginning to climb. Cyrus bought or secured options on as much property as he could, and within a decade he was rich.

From the time he had moved to Barnard's Crossing, he had attended Mass daily, not merely because he was a devout Catholic—formerly he had been devout but not all that devout—but because it was good business. After all, the pastor of the parish was recommending, indeed pressing, his name on his parishioners. Then, as his success continued in increasing volume, he began to feel that perhaps it was due to his being so faithful in his attendance.

He had not married; he was too busy. When he thought about it, he reflected that the Mertons always tended to marry late. But now, forty-five and rich, he decided he ought to look around for a wife who would cook for him and manage the fine house on the Point he had acquired, one whom he could confide in and discuss his business deals with of an evening, who would keep an eye on the staff in his office on those days when he didn't go in, and most important, who would bear his children to continue the Merton line. Sex did not really enter into it. He had no great need for it, and when the need did arise occasionally, he had no difficulty in satisfying it, although he was always careful to mention his fall from grace when he made confession.

For a bachelor as rich and successful as Cyrus Merton, there was no paucity of young and attractive women who would have given him the rather limited sexual gratification he needed and would have borne him the children he wanted, but none of them quite fitted his requirements for housekeeper/ confidante/ office manager. And then, quite suddenly, there was at least a partial solution to the problem: his younger sister, Agnes, was notified that her husband, Army Captain Ronald Burke, was missing in action in Vietnam. She had married late, at thirty-nine. She was a long-time civil servant, a clerk-supervisor working in a federal office where she had first met her husband. It was not difficult for Cyrus to persuade her to come and keep house for him while she awaited news of her husband, which never came.

There was a third Merton, a half brother, James, quite a bit younger. Neither Cyrus nor Agnes had much to do with him, or he with them. They had resented his mother because their father had married her shortly after the death of their own mother, and this resentment had increased when James was born, and she had neglected them in favor of her own child. What little family feeling they might have had for him was dissipated when he disgraced himself, and they felt, them, by marrying a Puerto Rican, or as Agnes put it, 'a dirty little spic.' The derision inherent in their receiving a wedding invitation several days after the wedding did nothing to improve relations. They debated whether or not to send a gift, and finally decided not to. And when, three months later, they were notified of the birth of a daughter, Margaret, they came to a similar decision. Occasionally they exchanged Christmas cards: that is, when they received a card from Mr. and Mrs. James Merton, Cyrus Merton and Agnes Burke jointly sent one in return; otherwise not. They did not see Margaret until they were notified that James and Theresa Merton had both drowned. From what they were able to learn, James had suffered a cramp while swimming, and Theresa, in trying to rescue him, had also been pulled under. Margaret was twelve at the time.

In addition to the grief they thought they

ought to feel over the loss of a brother, even though they hadn't seen him in years, they felt guilty over the death of the wife who had tried to save him; Agnes especially, since she had been most scornful of their sister-in-law. The very sight of the little girl when they brought her to Barnard's Crossing to live with them was a reproach. This feeling was assuaged somewhat when Cyrus suggested that the report of the double death might have been wrong.

'It could have been the other way around, you know,' he remarked.

'How do you mean?'

'Well, those reports, you never can trust them. It could have been James who tried to rescue her. He was a pretty good swimmer as I remember. Nobody actually saw her try to rescue him, just that somebody thought he saw him go in the water first.'

'And so he could have drowned, trying to save her.'

'It could have been that way.'

'Yes, it could.' And she felt better about it.

CHAPTER FOUR

If Margaret had come to them when she was two or three, they would have had to hire someone to take care of her, to be sure, but she would have been cute, and they would have played with her and loved her. But she was twelve, an awkward and ungainly age, and she was not a pretty child; even worse, she resembled her grandmother, their stepmother. She was thin and pale and sad, the last at least understandable, but nonetheless upsetting to Cyrus and Agnes. Frequently, at night they could hear her crying. Never having had any experience with children, they did not know what to say to her or how to comfort her, and she spoke to them only in answer to direct questions. Father Joe Tierney, now the pastor of the parish, naturally expected she would be enrolled in the parochial school Cyrus had helped establish, but when Agnes explained to him that there was no one to take care of her when she got out of school, he suggested sending her to a boarding school in Ohio that was operated by the same order that ran the school in Barnard's Crossing, Sisters of Mary of the Mount.

'That way, you see, there'll be no trouble when you decide to bring her back and transfer her to our school.'

'But won't she feel sort of, you know, abandoned?' Cyrus demurred when Agnes explained the plan to him. 'Here, she'd just lost her folks, and then we, the only kin she's got, send her off to strangers.'

'But we're like strangers to her,' said

Agnes, 'and there she'll have a lot of girls her own age, and the Sisters will keep her busy so she won't have time to mope around.'

*   *   *

She wrote to her aunt and uncle once a week—the Sisters saw to that—a page long, as required, and signed 'Your loving niece, Margaret'—anything less affectionate would have elicited inquiries. She told about the weather—'It snowed all night and after class we made a snowman and threw snowballs,' and of what she was studying—'We are studying about the New England states in geography, and I had to tell them about Massachusetts. I told them about Boston, and Barnard's Crossing, which they had never heard of. And I told them about the ocean and the lighthouse on the Point, and the sea gulls. And Sister Anne said it was very interesting.'

She came back to Barnard's Crossing at the end of the school year for a round of shopping in the Boston stores, and then she was shipped off to the school's summer camp. And this became a pattern: school, summer camp—first as a camper and later on as a counselor—and then school again. In between she would spend a week or two in Barnard's Crossing. Her uncle and aunt were kind to her, but distant and impersonal. They were merely another set of authority figures to her, like the school principal and the camp director.

★   ★   ★

Of course, they intended to go to the graduation, but an important deal was impending and Cyrus felt he just couldn't get away.

'Then perhaps I ought to go alone,' said Agnes. 'Somebody from the family should be there. It'll look funny if she has no one.'

'Look, Agnes, I'm going to be out of the office most of the time, and I've got to have you there to keep an eye on things. The Ralston thing is coming to a head, and I can't trust anyone but you to manage it.'

'But the Sisters will think—'

'They won't think a darn thing. It's a boarding school, and lots of the girls—their folks are away in Europe or just can't get away, like us. Margaret herself told me so the last time she was home. As for Margaret, she may feel kind of neglected that day, but she'll forget all about it when she gets home and sees the present I'm planning to get her.'

'What are you planning on?' asked Agnes curiously.

'What do you say to a real snappy roadster? She took Driver Education, so she should be able to get her license right away. And it will be awfully handy when she goes back to camp for the summer, and when she goes on to college next year.'

'I don't think she cares too much about going to college.'

'Well, she's going. And you know why? Because she'll be the first Merton to go to college. She's got to go.'

'She might not be able to get in. Her marks were not very good.'

'Oh, I'll get her in someplace. I've got contacts with colleges through Macomber. Don't worry, I'll manage it.'

When Margaret came home, she assured her uncle and aunt that she had not minded their not coming to her graduation. Cyrus was pleased that she concealed her disappointment, and resentment perhaps, from them. Agnes thought perhaps she really meant it.

She was of course delighted with the car they had bought her, and it seemed to Agnes that for the first time she felt close to them. Nevertheless, Margaret was vague when they questioned her about her plans for the future. Later, however, when Agnes pressed her in private, she explained that she was certain she would not be able to gain admittance to a college because she had taken the general course rather than the college preparatory course.

When Agnes transmitted this to Cyrus, he said, 'She's just a child—'

'She's eighteen.'

'She's still a child, and doesn't know what's good for her. Of course she'll go to college. I'll get her in.'

A few days later he announced triumphantly that he had made all arrangements and that she had been admitted to a Catholic women's college in New Hampshire. 'She'll have to go up there and take the summer course, but then she'll be admitted to the regular course when school starts in September. Too bad, she won't be able to go to camp this year, but college is more important.'

'Was it through Macomber you were able to arrange it?' asked Agnes.

'No, through Father Joe,' he replied shortly.

Margaret made no objection to their plan for her future. How could she when she had just received so munificent a gift as a roadster? But she showed no great enthusiasm either.

'She's an obedient child,' Cyrus observed.

'And very religious,' said Agnes. 'I've seen her on her knees several times, clutching that watch of her father's. Do you suppose she still mourns him?'

'No.' Cyrus shook his head vigorously. 'She holds the watch while praying because of the relic on the dial. When she went away to school—'

'She took it with her. At least she didn't leave it in her bureau drawer.'

'Well, that's a good thing. I understand they do a lot of praying at the college.'

They drove her up since the college did not permit freshmen to have cars. 'We'll see you Christmas vacation,' said Cyrus after they had seen her ensconced in her room and they were ready to depart. But they did not see her at Christmas. Word came that she was in the infirmary with a touch of pneumonia, and it was thought best not to move her. They thought they ought to go up to see her, but by the time they found a convenient day, she had called to say that she was out of the infirmary and was up and around. She came home for the April vacation, however.

Margaret felt closer to her aunt than she did to her uncle because she was a woman and she saw more of her. It was her aunt who went into Boston with her and got her outfitted for the coming school year. So it was in her aunt that she confided, and left it to her to tell her uncle.

'She says she has a vocation and wants to enter a convent.'

'You mean after she graduates?'

'No, right now. She doesn't want to continue at school.'

'That's ridiculous. We can't have her doing anything like that. It means turning away from the world before she's ever experienced

31

it. Maybe we made a mistake in sending her to a women's college. We should have had her go to a coed college where she'd have had a chance to meet boys. I'll get her to transfer to Windermere. If there's any problem of credits, I ought to be able to fix it.'

'But if she feels she has a vocation, Cyrus—'

'Well, if it's a real vocation, it'll keep for a couple of years. Lots of girls think they have a vocation when they just want to get away from their folks, or a love affair has gone sour, or maybe she just doesn't have any friends at her school. I guess it was a mistake to send her there. She ought to meet some boys. That's what she ought to be thinking of—boys and dates and parties and getting married—'

'Getting married? At her age?'

'Sure. Why not? She's nineteen and will be twenty soon. It's a good age to marry. That's been the trouble with us Mertons. We've always married late, and that's why there were so few of us. Maybe in the old country we had to wait because we just couldn't support a wife and family until we were pretty well along in years, and then there was no push behind it. Like me and like you. I got caught up in my real estate business and you in your civil service job. But she's not involved in anything, not in any profession, or even in her studies. She's got nothing to do except mope around. She should be married and have kids, lots of kids. She's the last of the Mertons. If she goes into a convent, it means the end of us, the end of the line. The Merton genes or chromosomes or whatever they are will end. It's a terrible thought. And this estate I've built up, what happens to that after we're gone?'

'But let's face it, Cyrus. She's pretty plain.'

'So what? Plenty of plain girls get married. If they didn't, where would the plain kids come from? She's a good girl, a sensible girl, and will make someone a good wife. So she's plain. So what? She has expectations. She'll inherit from us, and there's enough to make her beautiful in plenty of men's eyes. Dammit, I'll get her a husband, I've got contacts at the college and through my business. I could have her married off within the year.'

CHAPTER FIVE

Weekdays, the morning service at the temple began at half past seven—providing, of course, the necessary ten showed up, which was by no means certain in bad weather. On Sundays, however, the service began at nine, and there was never any trouble getting the ten needed for a minyan, for classes in the

Religious School began at that hour. Fathers brought their children and then could be prevailed upon to come to the minyan since they had to wait until classes were over anyway to drive them home.

The weekly meeting of the Board of Directors of the temple was held at ten o'clock. The room set aside for their meeting was in the vestry in the basement of the temple, as was, indeed, the Religious School and the small chapel where the morning prayers were said. The members drifted in after the prayer service, those who had attended, and sat around talking, arguing, shmoosing as they were joined by those who came straight from home.

At ten o'clock the president, Al Bergson, rapped sharply on the table with his knuckles. He had a gavel, but he rarely used it. He liked to keep the meetings informal. 'This meeting will now come to order,' he announced.

'Ron Berlin said he'd be along a little late this morning,' said Aaron Schneider.

'So he'll be along,' said Bergson. 'We have a quorum and I'm calling the meeting to order right now. If we waited for everyone who said they'd be here to show up, there'd be no time to transact business. The secretary will now read his report of the previous meeting.'

The secretary, Bill Leftow, dutifully rose

34

and read, 'The meeting was called at 10:05 ... House Committee reported on measures required to repair leak in roof ... Discussion on whether new roof needed ... Ritual Committee ... Entertainment Committee ... Discussion during Old Business ... Motion to set up committee to investigate costs ... Norman Rath appointed a Committee of One to report by April fifteenth ... Meeting adjourned 11:47. Respectfully submitted...'

'Discussion on the Secretary's Report? If not—'

'Seems to me, someone made a motion on starting a lecture series.'

'That was in Good and Welfare.'

'No, I'm sure someone made a motion.'

'Yes, Arthur Edelweiss made a motion that we start a lecture series, but it was two weeks ago,' said the secretary. 'You weren't here. Last week he mentioned it in Good and Welfare.'

'Well, I think we ought to discuss it.'

'It was discussed two weeks ago.' The secretary leafed through his book. 'And it was put to a vote and was defeated seventeen to three.'

'Well, I think we ought to discuss it some more.'

'You can move for reconsideration, or make another motion.'

'Just a second. I don't think anyone can move for reconsideration two weeks after a

35

motion is defeated, and I think it has to be made by someone who was on the winning side, that is, one who voted to defeat.'

'All right, so he can make another motion.'

'Not in Old Business, he can't.'

'So, he'll make it in New Business.'

It was almost noon when the meeting ended. Since the day was mild, the rabbi had walked to the temple, and now refused all offers of a lift home. Bergson, the president, lived only a couple blocks beyond the rabbi, and he, too, had chosen to walk.

As they walked along together, Bergson said, 'Do you ever wonder, David, why you bother to attend the board meetings every week?'

'I attend because at the beginning of the year you invited me to attend.'

'You mean, because having been invited, it would be ungracious not to.'

'No ... not really. Not just for that.'

'But you must be bored out of your mind, as I am most of the time. Why do we have them every week? We don't transact any business to speak of most of the time, maybe once every five or six meetings. Why don't we hold them once a month, instead of weekly?'

'I suppose,' said the rabbi thoughtfully, 'it's because it gives us, some of us, a chance to get together and ... and just be with each other. You see, it's not like living in a big city where there are apartment houses and there are clusters of Jews living near each other and seeing each other regularly. Here, in Barnard's Crossing, there are only one-family houses and we Jews are scattered all over the town. Sure, we see each other at parties like yours the other night, but then they're all people who know each other and are of the same general class. It's different from living in the Jewish section of a large city where you are aware that all your neighbors, all the people walking along the street are Jewish. They may disagree with you on politics, on—on morals and ethics, on all sorts of things, but on certain things—like the safety of Israel, like their pride in a Jew who has done something meritorious like win a Nobel prize, or the unease when one of us is guilty of some crime that is splashed all over the newspapers, you know they feel as you do.'

'But all the talk—'

'Oh, that's only the human way of maintaining contact. Apes and monkeys do it by touching and grooming each other, we do it by talking—of the weather, of politics, of baseball, of almost anything. All that business at the meeting this morning, the arguing whether something should be brought up in Old Business or New Business, the very subjects: should we set up a lecture series? a book fair? a summer camp? That's all just human grooming.'

'And is that why you attend the meetings

regularly, David?'

The rabbi grinned. 'Certainly not for the business that's transacted.'

CHAPTER SIX

Assistant Professor Victor Joyce, a tall, handsome Irishman with light blue eyes at curious variance with his mop of jet-black hair and the bluish jowls he showed even after the closest shave, was one of the two candidates for the one tenured position vacant in the English Department of Windermere Christian College. The other candidate, Assistant Professor Mordecai Jacobs, was presumed to have the edge because he was from Harvard and his field was Linguistics, which was considered more scholarly than Modern Literature, in which Joyce had taken his degree; and most of all because he had published in the prestigious JML, *Journal of Modern Languages*.

But just how one secured tenure was something of a mystery and differed from department to department. According to the scuttlebutt in the faculty lounge, it was wise in any case to make contact with the chairman of the Committee on Faculty of the Board of Trustees.

'Who is it?'

'A guy named Merton, Cyrus Merton.'

'What do I do? Call and make an appointment? Go to his house?'

'Nah. He's sort of retired, so he hangs around here a lot, usually in Prex's office, in the outer office talking to the secretary while waiting to see Prex.'

'So what do I do? Go up to him and introduce myself?'

'You don't have to. If you go to Prex's office, and you see this little guy, around sixty, with rimless eyeglasses sitting there, that will be Cyrus Merton. You sit there, and unless the secretary sends you in to Prex right away, he'll begin talking to you. Then you tell him you wanted to see Prex about your chances of getting tenure, and that'll do it.'

So in the next few days, whenever he had a free period, Joyce made a point of looking in the president's office. Finally, one Friday afternoon, he saw the little guy, around sixty, with rimless eyeglasses. And that's how Victor Joyce got to meet Cyrus Merton. He didn't get to see the president that day, and neither did Cyrus Merton. In fact, within minutes after Joyce mentioned that he had got his doctorate from Boston College, a Catholic college, and that he had written his dissertation on Lady Gregory and the Abbey Theatre, Merton said, 'Look, I happened to be in town for the day, and I thought President Macomber might care to go out for a beer, but it looks as though he's going to be tied up for a while. Do you drink beer? You don't have a class now, do you?'

Over beer—and Merton encouraged Joyce to have several—the younger man told of his problems getting a job and his fears that he might not get tenure at Windermere, 'because my degree is from B.C. and they think because it's a Catholic college, their standards are not as high as those of Harvard, or Tufts, or B.U. But let me tell you, the guy who supervised my dissertation at B.C., a Jesuit, was as good a scholar as anybody they've got at Harvard, and...'

And Merton talked about how he had got started, about his present situation and his real estate holdings, about his sister who ran his household, and about his niece, the only Merton left besides him and his sister. 'She's a very spiritual girl.' From which Joyce immediately deduced that she was plain. 'In fact, she wanted to become a nun.'

'I thought of taking orders myself,' said Joyce, and then with a smile that just avoided becoming a leer, 'but I knew I wouldn't be able to keep the vow of celibacy.'

'I'm sure your wife is happy about that,' said Merton.

'Oh, I'm not married,' said Joyce, and added, 'Can't even think of it without tenure.'

'Maybe something can be done about that,'

said Merton, his eyes twinkling roguishly behind his rimless glasses.

Their meeting lasted a couple of hours and ended with an invitation from Merton to Sunday dinner. 'Or better yet, come out tomorrow afternoon, and I'll show you around the town. You don't know Barnard's Crossing, do you? Lovely old colonial town. Stay the night, and you can join us Sunday morning for Mass and dinner afterward.'

When Joyce climbed up to his fourth-floor room in the brownstone house on Commonwealth Avenue, he was quite drunk, not from the beer he had consumed, but with the prospects that he saw opening up before him. Later, he went out to a local restaurant for a meager dinner; and then, to celebrate, he went to a single's bar where he let himself be picked up by a woman a good ten years his senior and to be taken back to her flat to spend the night. She was short and plump and cuddly, with a mop of blond curls. Her name was Marcia Skinner, and she said she was a buyer for Consolidated Stores. When she thought he appeared doubtful, she gave him her card, which did indeed say, Consolidated Stores, Marcia Skinner, Buyer of Junior Sportswear, and her office telephone number. She was not displeased when she saw him copying down the number of the telephone in the apartment.

41

*   *   *

Although she had hoped to keep him with her
for the weekend, he managed to extricate
himself a little before noon, pleading an
important engagement. He hurried home,
where he showered and shaved, going over
his face twice, followed by after-shave lotion
and then patting on talcum powder to reduce
the blueness of his jowls. Then, in accordance
with the instructions he had received from
Merton, he took a train to Swampscott and
from there a cab to the Point of Barnard's
Crossing. As they drove along the Point,
Joyce could see that the houses were large and
commodious and suggested money, lots of
money. All had large well-kept lawns with
patches of carefully tended shrubbery. The
Merton house was no exception. It was a
two-story frame house with a broad veranda
on the side facing the ocean.

Cyrus himself opened the door to him and
then called out, 'Aggie, Peg, company.' The
two women came down from the upper floor
together. Cyrus's sister Agnes looked to be
just a few years younger than her brother.
But it was on Margaret that his attention was
focused. He decided that his original surmise
had been correct: she was plain. Her hair was
thin and straight, and she had an overbite
which in combination with a long, thin nose
gave her a sad look. But her skin was white

42

and clear and free of blemish. She reminded him of Sister Bertha, his sixth-grade teacher, whom he used to dream of.

'Have you had lunch?' asked Agnes anxiously, and appeared relieved when he assured her that he had. He'd had a sandwich and a cup of coffee at the railroad station while waiting for his train.

'Well, that's fine,' said Cyrus, rubbing his hands. 'Now, I said I'd show you the town, but I'm going to be tied up for a while. If you don't mind waiting...'

'Oh, sure,' said Joyce.

'Or tell you what. Peg could take you around. That be all right? Do you mind, Peg?'

'Oh sure. I'll just get my scarf. I won't be a minute.'

It was a warm April day, and they rode in her roadster with the top down. Behind the wheel, with her head raised against the breeze coming over the windshield, he thought she looked quite attractive. She drove out to the lighthouse and they got out and stared down at the harbor with its hundreds of small sailboats. Then they got back in the car, and she offered commentary as they drove along. 'That's the Carlson Yacht Club. They don't have Catholics or Jews.' A little farther on, 'That's the North Shore Yacht Club. They have Catholics, but no Jews. And just beyond, that brown house, is the Barnard's

Crossing Club. They allow anyone to join.'
She showed him the Catholic church and told
him that the pastor, Father Joseph Tierney,
was an old curmudgeon and that his curate
was Father Bill. She thought perhaps Father
Joseph didn't care too much for his curate.
'We make a point of going to Father Joseph's
Mass because my aunt and uncle think Father
Bill is too modern.'

They drove down to the center of town and
parked once again, so they could walk along
the narrow streets where many of the houses
had little mounted tablets giving their date of
construction and who had built them
originally. Most of these houses had been
built in the eighteenth century, but some as
early as the seventeenth.

'None of the houses are particularly
attractive,' she pointed out, 'but the net effect
is quaint. Which is why the town has begun
to attract a lot of artists. Uncle Cyrus doesn't
approve of them and won't rent to them. But
he'll sell them. He says if they've got enough
money to buy a house, they're probably
pretty stable, but if they only want to rent,
you can't trust them not to have wild parties
and do damage.'

As it began to grow dark, he suggested
dropping in at one of the numerous cafes for
coffee, but she explained, 'We have supper
promptly at seven. Mrs. Marston—she's the
cook and the housekeeper—kind of expects

us to eat then. She's apt to get annoyed if we're late.'

'What does she do? Break dishes?'

'No, but she somehow manages to show it.'

'Well, how about a movie afterward?'

'I'd like that,' she said. 'There's a good movie at the Criterion. I've wanted to see it, but neither Uncle Cyrus nor Aunt Agnes cared to go, and I don't like to go alone.'

Supper was served by Mrs. Marston in the large paneled dining room. Conversation was concentrated on their afternoon excursion. 'Did you see ...' 'Did you show him ...' 'Why didn't you take him to ...' And he was called upon to give his impressions, of course approving of what he had seen.

When they finished the meal, Margaret announced, 'Victor is taking me to the Criterion.'

'I hear it's a good picture,' said Agnes.

'Don't bring her home too late,' said Cyrus with a twinkle, from which Victor deduced that he expected them to go someplace afterward rather than come home immediately after the movie was over. Then he added, 'We go to the early Mass, you know.'

The movie ended shortly after ten, and this time they did go to a cafe. He could have had a cocktail, and he wanted one, but he forebore because he thought it might be politic not to, and ordered beer instead. They

45

sat and talked about themselves mostly. She told him about her school, about the teachers she had liked and those whom she did not care for.

'Your uncle said you had thought of entering a convent,' he said at one point.

'Yes, I thought I had a vocation, but my uncle felt that perhaps it was just that I had been in contact with the Sisters all my life, and it was that rather than a real call. He wanted me to experience the secular world a bit before making up my mind. He's been so kind to me, I thought the least I could do to reciprocate was to do what he wanted me to do.'

'And has your experience of the world changed your mind?'

'I haven't experienced very much of it, so I can't tell.'

They got home just before midnight.

*   *   *

After church they spent the morning watching the various political programs on TV and reading the Sunday papers, and dinner was served after the last news program was completed. It was a lavish meal with Cornish game hen as the main course, and Victor enjoyed it, but he was also beginning to get fidgety. If he could have gone off for a walk, or if Cyrus had taken him into his study for a talk, the situation would have been tolerable. But he sensed that Sunday was the day they were supposed to be together, and that to split up in any way at all would be taken in bad part. He wondered how long he was expected to stay, and whether he might not plead the necessity of having to prepare his lectures for the next day as an excuse for leaving early. Fortunately, Cyrus was called to the telephone, and when he hung up, he said, 'I've got to run up to Revere. I can take you to the Swampscott station, where you can make the three o'clock into Boston.'

'Oh swell, I'll get my things.'

When he dropped him off at the train station, Cyrus said, 'I hope you had a nice time.'

'I had a wonderful time, Mr. Merton. You were all so kind.'

'How about next week? Agnes asked me to ask you, and I know Peg would like to see you again.'

'I'd certainly like that.'

'Look, I have an idea. I'm coming in to Boston Friday. Why don't you plan on coming out Friday instead of Saturday. Bring your things to school, and I can pick you up after your last class and we could drive out to Barnard's Crossing together.'

'Well—I had sort of a date to go to a driving range and hit a couple of buckets of balls. It's the only exercise I get.' He had

47

actually planned to see Marcia Skinner if she was free.

'Golf? You play golf? Then bring your clubs with you Friday. There's a golf course in Breverton, the next town north of Barnard's Crossing. Maybe half an hour's drive. Bring your clubs and Peg can drive you out there Saturday morning, and she can walk around with you. And you can have lunch at the club afterward. They have an excellent dining room.'

*   *   *

In the half-hour ride from Swampscott to Boston's North Station, Victor Joyce thought about the weekend he had just spent. He felt certain that the reason for the invitation was not so that Cyrus Merton could judge his candidacy for tenure, but as a possible husband for his niece. Pretending some business so that she could substitute for him in showing him the town was pretty obviously an attempt to throw them together. He suspected that if he had not invited her to go to a movie, Cyrus or Agnes would have suggested it. Maybe all that questioning about what they had seen and what they had missed in the tour of the town was intended to justify a suggestion that they make another survey of the area. And the invitation for the following week, that clinched it, didn't it?

48

Well, why not? He was thirty-two and she was, what? Nineteen? Twenty? It was time he got married. True, she was not what he had pictured as the kind of girl he would marry. He had rather thought in terms of someone beautiful and voluptuous. And she was certainly not that. On the other hand, they had made it plain that since she was their only relative, she would eventually inherit what they had indicated was a very considerable estate. That was in the future, to be sure, but on the immediate question of tenure, surely there could be no doubt.

In some departments the tenured members voted on who was to be granted tenure and thereby included in their number. In other departments, and the English Department was one, the chairman of the department decided. He would then notify the dean, who would pass on the recommendation to the Committee on Faculty of the Board of Trustees, whose chairman, Cyrus Merton, would notify the president, who made the final decision. Well, if he were an in-law of Merton's would Arthur Sugrue, chairman of the English Department, dare to nominate someone else? With all that Merton had to say about salaries, allocation of funds, even courses of study and subjects to be taught?

But the girl was plain. On the other hand, she exuded a kind of virginal purity that was—his mind fished for a word—

49

challenging, even exciting, sexually exciting. The train pulled into the station. He made his way to the subway station to go home. He fished in his pocket for change for the turnstile, and found Marcia Skinner's card. He considered for a moment, and then went to one of the public pay stations.

When she answered, he said, 'Marcia? Are you free? I'd like to finish the weekend.'

'Oh, it's you. Where are you? You want to come over, is that it?'

'Yeah. I could be there in half an hour.'

'All right.'

When she opened the door for him, she was wearing a long silk dressing gown. She glanced at the bag he was carrying. 'You plan on moving in?' she asked.

'Just for the night,' he said, and took her in his arms. His hands stroked her back as he held her close to him. Then he reached for the zipper tab at the back of her gown. 'And I thought we'd make it an early night,' he said as he pulled it down.

CHAPTER SEVEN

Tuesday, the rabbi made his usual trip to the Salem Hospital. He stopped at the front desk to get a list of the Jewish patients, and then repaired immediately to Morris Fisher's room, so that if he were absent again, he could see the others and then double back to Fisher.

Fisher was a man of seventy, short and fat, with a bald head surrounded by a fringe of grizzled white hair. He had suffered a small stroke from which he had largely recovered, but was being kept at the hospital for further observation. When the rabbi came to see him, he was out of bed, sitting in the one chair in the room, in his pajamas and bathrobe. For a few days his left side had been partially paralyzed, but he had now recovered motion and feeling in both his leg and his arm, and all that remained was a slight twisting of the left side of his mouth, which gave him a sardonic look.

When the rabbi entered, Fisher greeted him with, 'Hello, Rabbi, I bet you don't recognize me.'

Since he was one of those who rarely appeared in the temple except on the High Holy Days, the rabbi might very well have failed to recognize him, but obviously that was not what was intended by the remark. The implication was, rather, that his physical appearance had changed so radically by reason of his illness that intimates would fail to know him.

But the rabbi rejected the gambit and asked innocently, 'Lost a little weight, have you?'

'That, too,' Fisher conceded. 'I've been

51

here a week now. You can lose a lot of weight in a week.'

'Don't they feed you well?'

'Oh, you pick your own menu. And when do you pick it? You pick it for the following day when they bring your breakfast. How can you tell what you want to eat tomorrow when you've just finished eating? And they serve it at set times, all on a little tray. So you eat faster so your ice cream won't be all melted by the time you're ready for your dessert. And your coffee waits there on the little tray getting cold before you can get to it. Now I like a cigarette with my coffee. I'm not a heavy smoker, but I like to smoke while I'm having my coffee. But here, a cigarette is regarded like you're perpetrating a gas attack on the entire hospital.

'They wake you up in the middle of the night to take your blood pressure and temperature. And somebody comes around to take samples of your blood. And then an intern or the resident comes in to examine you. He listens to your chest, and he squeezes your belly, and taps your knees and elbows with a little rubber hammer. And it's usually a different one each time.'

'But your doctor—'

'Who sees him? He might come in once during the day, or in the evening to say hello, but everything is done by the interns and the nurses. It used to be that your doctor sat with you and talked with you. No more. You see him like a private sees a general.'

'Things have changed quite radically in recent years,' the rabbi remarked, 'not least among them the practice of the professions.'

'You can say that again,' said Fisher. 'Your own profession, for example. My father was sickly, and was in and out of hospitals for a good portion of his life, and not once did a rabbi come to see him. And we were living in Boston at the time, where there were any number of rabbis.'

The rabbi nodded. 'But I'm sure he had plenty of other visitors. Visiting the sick is enjoined on all Jews, but here in Barnard's Crossing where Jewish practices have largely lapsed, the rabbi of the congregation is expected to do it because he's engaged, in part, to be the one practicing Jew. We also have a Visiting Committee who are supposed to—'

'Oh, yeah, some of them have been.'

'And family?'

'I don't have any family, Rabbi.'

'No children?'

Fisher shook his head vigorously. 'My wife was a career woman and never got around to having any. Not that I was anxious for children at the time. I was—'

A young woman, wearing a white coat and a stethoscope draped around her neck, entered the room. 'Mr. Fisher? I'm Dr.

53

Peterson.' She looked at the rabbi. 'If you don't mind—'

'I was just going,' the rabbi said. 'Good luck, Mr. Fisher.' As he walked down the corridor to his next appointment, he wondered if he had benefited Fisher in any way, or had he merely obeyed the injunction to visit the sick?

CHAPTER EIGHT

The next Friday, Victor brought his golf clubs in to school, along with his spiked golf shoes, slacks, a sport shirt, and a windbreaker, in addition to the pajamas, slippers, and bathrobe he had brought the first time. To the questioning looks of his colleagues in the English Department office, as he placed his clubs and suitcase against the wall behind his desk, he said only that he was going away for the weekend. He did not say where he was going.

When he came back to the office at two o'clock, after his last class, he found Cyrus Merton there waiting for him. None of his colleagues was present, however—there were not many classes Friday afternoon—for which he was grateful. Although aware that a special connection with Cyrus Merton might be to his advantage, he did not want them to know just yet.

Cyrus Merton was a slow and careful driver, and it took him almost an hour to drive the thirty miles or so to Barnard's Crossing, even though traffic on the road was light. It was after three when they arrived at the house on the Point, too late to do anything except sit around the house, watch TV, and wait for supper.

The next morning, shortly after breakfast, Victor in his golf clothes loaded his clubs into Peg's roadster and the two set out for Breverton. The Point, a long fingerlike promontory extending into the harbor, was connected to the rest of the town by Abbott Road. Peg drove slowly, and Victor, anxious to get to the golf club, asked, 'Do we have to crawl along like this?'

'It's a populated area, speed limit twenty-five miles an hour,' she explained, 'and it's patrolled, but after about three miles we come to the state highway.'

'And how far is it then from the Breverton Country Club?'

'Oh, about twenty miles. Once we're on the state highway, we should be able to make it in about twenty-five minutes or half an hour.'

'Your uncle said it was about half an hour from his house.'

'Oh. He was probably thinking of going by way of Pine Grove Road.'

'So why don't we go that way?'

'I don't like to drive it. It's the old road connecting the two towns. It goes back to colonial times, I suspect. It's narrow and rutty and curves in and out between ledge and swamp, and there are trees on both sides so that you can't see more than fifty feet ahead. We can take it back if you like.'

'Yeah, let's plan on it.'

'All right.'

A thought occurred to him. 'Look, are there shops in Breverton? I was thinking you might care to go shopping while I play, and we could meet around noon for lunch.'

'I thought I'd go around and watch you.'

'It's apt to be a long walk,' he said doubtfully.

'Oh, they have these little carts, and we could rent one of them and ride around together.'

'They have electric carts, have they? Swell, then you can be my caddy.'

'What's a caddy do?'

'Normally, he carries the clubs. But since we'll be going around in a cart, all you'll have to do is watch and see where my ball lands.'

'I guess I can do that.'

★   ★   ★

There were not many on the course, and he was able to finish the round shortly after noon. They repaired to the spacious dining

56

room and he ordered a scotch and soda. He drank it while they studied the menu, and then when they gave their orders, he asked for another. Because he thought she looked askance, he explained, 'The first one is customary after finishing a round of golf, and the one I just ordered is an appetizer for the meal to come.'

They drove home by way of Pine Grove Road, and when they reached Abbott Road, he marveled at how little time it had taken. 'Gosh, you'd think they'd fix that road up. It's so much shorter.'

'I suppose they don't because there's not too much traffic between the two towns, only those headed for the golf club would be apt to use it.'

'That Pine Grove Road looks as though it's probably used as a lover's lane,' he suggested.

She colored slightly and said, 'I suppose it is.'

Several times on the golf course when no other players were in sight, and in the car as they drove along Pine Grove Road, he had thought to make a move, to put his arm around her shoulder and then perhaps accidentally let his fingertips rest lightly on her breast. Each time, however, he was able to overcome his impulse, fearful that she might take offense.

As in the previous week, he was taken to the train Sunday to catch the three o'clock train to Boston, but on Cyrus Merton's suggestion, he left his bag and golf clubs behind.

'You'll be coming out next week, won't you? I can pick you up on Friday again.'

Once again, when he reached North Station, he called Marcia Skinner. And once again he went to see her, and once again she got the benefit of his frustration of the two preceding days.

★   ★   ★

This became the pattern for the next few weeks. Cyrus would pick him up on Friday, and he would be brought to the train on Sunday afternoon, and then spend the rest of the day, and sometimes the night, with Marcia.

Then he caught a bad cold. He managed to get through his classes Thursday, but Professor Sugrue, the head of the department, suggested after a particular fit of coughing and sneezing that he go home and go to bed and plan on not meeting his classes on Friday. He nodded his agreement, and even took a cab home rather than take the usual longish walk entailed.

Mindful that he was expected in Barnard's Crossing for the weekend, and that Cyrus would be coming to the English office the next day to pick him up, he called the Merton home. Cyrus answered. wnen Victor, in a hoarse voice interrupted by coughing and sneezing, explained the situation, Cyrus asked, 'Have you seen a doctor?'

'No.'

'Do you have temperature?'

'I don't have a thermometer.'

'Now you listen to me, Victor. I'm coming to your place tomorrow morning. I'll get there about nine. I want you to bundle up warm, and when I ring your bell, you come down and I'll take you out to Barnard's Crossing where you can be properly cared for. There's a lot of flu around, and we don't want you catching anything serious.'

Sure enough, the next morning, a little before nine, Cyrus rang his bell. He had a couple of blankets in his car, and after Victor entered, he put a blanket around his shoulders and one across his lap.

'Have you eaten yet?' Cyrus asked.

'No, I just didn't feel like it.'

When they got to the house on the Point, he was immediately put to bed. A few minutes later Peg came up with his breakfast, which she fed him as he sat up in bed, his back supported by several pillows which she had brought up before and which she tucked behind him.

'The doctor will be coming to see you soon,' she said.

'Really? I didn't think doctors made house

59

calls anymore.'

'I guess they do when my uncle calls them.'

Dr. Riley came, examined him, and suggested he stay in bed for a day or two. Victor did not mind. He was comfortable and he enjoyed being waited on. Peg brought him his meals and sat with him while he ate. It was after dinner Sunday, as she was removing his plate, that he seized her hand and kissed it. Then, to show that it was not merely out of gratitude, he turned it over and kissed the palm. He felt her stiffen momentarily, but then she relaxed and smiled and took away the tray. When, a little later, she brought up the Sunday paper, again he kissed the palm of her hand. This time she responded by kissing him on the forehead. He was sure if he were to kiss her on the mouth, she would not object, but of course he did not make the attempt for fear of giving her his cold.

In the evening he felt well enough to get out of bed, and came down in his bathrobe to join the family for supper. Cyrus wanted him to stay the week, but he insisted that he had to be back for classes. He did, however, call in Monday morning to say that he would not come in that day but would be in Tuesday, when he had only one class, and that in the afternoon. Cyrus drove him in Tuesday morning.

Back in his own apartment, it occurred to him that Marcia Skinner might have expected

60

him to call Sunday afternoon, as he had on previous Sundays, and he felt he ought to call to explain, if only to ensure their future relationship. He dialed, quite prepared for the phone to ring several times, indicating that she was not at home, in which case he would call the next evening a little earlier. He was not prepared for the operator to inform him that the phone had been disconnected.

The next morning he called her office number. 'Miss Skinner is not in,' he was told.

'When do you expect her?'

'Oh, she won't be back here. She's been transferred to the New York office.'

'Until when?'

'Indefinitely. It's a permanent transfer.'

He felt, unhappily, it was an omen that meant that his future would be with Margaret Merton.

CHAPTER NINE

Peg had gone off with Victor, and Cyrus was alone with his sister. 'Well, Aggie, what did Dr. Riley say?'

'He said she was underweight and a little anemic. He prescribed iron pills and said he wanted to see her again in a couple of months. But then I spoke to him privately, while she was dressing. He thought it might be a good idea if she didn't get married right away. He thought she ought to build herself up first.'

'He did, did he? Well, maybe I ought to have a talk with him. These doctors—you come to them for some medical advice, and right away they want to run your whole life. So what did she say to that?'

'Oh, he didn't tell *her*. He said it to me. He said that if the woman is anemic, it's apt to affect the child. Children of an anemic mother are prone to all sorts of birth defects. And from what he knew of her background and education, he rather thought she wouldn't be apt to practice birth control.'

'Because she's a good Catholic? Well, she could use the rhythm method, couldn't she?'

'I suppose.'

'We ought to arrange to have Dr. Riley explain it to her.'

'Oh, she knows about it. It was in her course of sex education at the seminary.'

Cyrus was aghast. 'They taught that in a Catholic seminary?'

'Of course. They taught it when I went to school, although I guess they were less explicit than they are now.'

'Have you ever spoken to her about—well, about how she feels about getting married, and you know, about Victor?'

'Yes. She said she was grateful for all we've done for her but that she wanted a family of her own. She said Victor felt the same way,

62

that he was a kind of orphan, too. I asked her what she meant by that, but she didn't want to talk about it. And you know how she is when she doesn't want to talk about something. She just clams up like she hadn't heard you. Do you know anything about it? You said you were going to make some inquiries.'

'Well, I wondered about his folks coming to the wedding. I thought maybe they might not be able to afford to make the trip. They're in California, you know. I thought if that were the case, I would arrange something. You know, offer to advance the money for their plane fare. I'd call it a loan, but I wouldn't expect it to be repaid. Victor told me they wouldn't be coming. So I made some inquiries on my own. I have contacts through the bank.'

'And?'

He hesitated. He was reluctant to answer, although he had known for some time. 'Nothing to brag about,' he said at last. 'His mother and father were separated when he was about four years old. For 'separated' you might read abandoned. Then the courts took control because she couldn't or wouldn't take care of him. Given to drink, I understand. Then foster homes until he finally ended up in a sort of orphanage run by the Christian Brothers. He showed aptitude, and they pushed him. They even encouraged him to take a classical course in high school. Then college by way of scholarships, and ended up at Boston College Graduate School on a fellowship.'

'And with that kind of background you want him to marry our Peg?' she demanded.

'Sure. Why not? He's big and strong and handsome, what Pa would have called a 'big broth of a lad.' And she's small, and from what Dr. Riley says, not very strong. All the Mertons have been runty. Well, with someone like Victor, there's a chance that the kids will be big and healthy. And he's a college professor, too. And he did it all himself. He teaches evening classes a couple of nights a week. That shows character. What's wrong with that? For that matter, what sort of background did we have? Pa was a sweeper for the streetcar company. And Ma did housecleaning. All of us Irish who came over a couple of generations back were of much the same level. The same with all the other immigrants, the Italians and Poles. That's why they came to America. The doctors and lawyers and big farmers, they stayed in the old country. It was mostly the riffraff that came over. But given the opportunity, we made something of ourselves. And so did Victor. So I'm all for him. The only question as far as I'm concerned is, does she want him? Is she in love with him?'

'Sure she loves him. He's the only man who ever paid any attention to her. In fact, he's practically the only man she's ever known. He's thirty-two and she's a very young twenty. She's been in girls' schools all her life. Yes, they had dances that were arranged by the school, and boys were imported. But I doubt if any of them ever got a crush on her. She's no raving beauty. And we, the only other people she has ever been close to, we approve of him and encourage him. And to top it off, he is a big broth of a lad. She'd have to be pretty perverse not to like him.'

'Fine, so let's get them married off as soon as possible so we can sit back and await the arrival of grandchildren.'

'Shouldn't we have some sort of engagement party?'

'What for? We'd have to invite some of the local people, and why bring in competition? I bought an engagement ring for Victor to give her. I figured he might not be able to afford anything decent and I didn't want him to go in hock for it.' He reached into his pocket and brought out a velvet ring box. He opened it and passed it to her. It contained a gold ring with an emerald flanked on either side with two small diamonds. 'What do you think?'

'Oh, it's lovely.' Then anxiously, 'Do you think I ought to get her some kind of gift to give him?'

'No, that's not necessary, not necessary at all.'

But Margaret did have an engagement gift for Victor, a wristwatch. 'It was my father's,' she explained. 'It's not very expensive, but my father treasured it. My mother bought it for him when they went to Rome on their tenth anniversary. She had the Sacred Heart painted on the dial, and do you see that little silver tube right above the twelve. That's a relic of Saint Ulric. Dad always wore it inside the wrist so it should be right next to the blood vessels and sort of that way connected to his heart.'

'Then that's the way I'll wear it.' He adjusted the gold-colored metal band to fit his wrist and then put it on and snapped the catch. 'And you know, dear, these days our lives are governed so much by the time, that it's a wonderful thing to have it done by a holy watch.'

CHAPTER TEN

Agnes arranged for the wedding to take place at the beginning of Victor's April vacation, and Cyrus treated the couple to a week in Bermuda for their honeymoon. Peg had mentally prepared herself for the trauma of the wedding night by telling herself it was a sacrifice that she must make. She had expected it to be painful, but she found that it was also distasteful. To be sure, her aunt had warned her, 'Married life takes getting used to for some women. If you find you don't particularly like the marriage duty at first, well, you'll get used to it after a while. It's different for men than it is for women, they enjoy it. In fact, they sort of need it like—like you need a drink of water when you're terribly thirsty. If you love him, and if you keep in mind that it's a need that he has to satisfy, it will help. And for his sake, if you don't enjoy it, it helps to pretend that you do.'

But Peg had no talent for pretending, and each night when he made love to her, she found the experience unpleasant even if no longer physically painful. Curiously, although at first a little chagrined at her lack of appreciation of his lovemaking, very soon he found that he did not mind, and that in fact it gave a certain fillip to the process, and sometimes when he sensed her disgust as he thrust, Sister Bertha, his sixth-grade teacher, came to mind.

For the rest he was especially kind and considerate, as if to make amends. The days were spent in lying on the beach and swimming, in cycling and in wandering about the streets and shopping. She enjoyed being with him, and even at night she enjoyed

67

having him beside her in bed; perhaps because it was the first time since she was orphaned that she had had intimate personal contact with another human being, and while the act of love was unpleasant, at least it did not last long.

All too soon they had to return. They had made no plans, but had assumed that they would be living with the Mertons for a while. They would sleep in her room because it was much larger than the guest room that he was used to. Perhaps Agnes would make some changes, if only to replace her bed with a double bed. On their return, however, when she went up to her room, she found all her things were gone, the closet empty of her dresses, the bureau empty of her underwear, sweaters, stockings.

She came down to the living room where Victor was having a drink with her uncle and aunt. 'My things are gone,' she said, 'everything. There's nothing in the closet or in my bureau or—'

Cyrus grinned. 'Sure. We moved them to your house.'

'My house?'

'You didn't think we were going to have you two lovebirds staying here with us old fogies? We thought you'd rather be alone, so we moved your things to one of my summer rentals. It's a nice house, one of the two on Shurtcliffe Circle. It's furnished plainly, but adequately. It's certainly better than a room in a hotel. You can have it as long as you like, or until you find someplace you like better.'

It was a small, frame house on a dead-end street, with two bedrooms on the second floor separated by a hallway that led to a bathroom. One bedroom, presumably the master bedroom, was considerably larger than the other and had an adjoining bathroom. It had twin beds joined together with clamps to form one large king-size bed. The other bedroom had a single bed. Their clothes, Margaret's dresses, and the extra suit that Victor had kept at the Merton's were in the closet of the large bedroom, of course.

'How do you like it?' asked Cyrus.

'It's wonderful,' said Margaret.

'Perfect,' said Victor.

'Of course, the furniture,' Cyrus began apologetically.

'Fine,' said Victor. 'It's just fine.'

'And there's dishes and pots and pans,' Cyrus pointed out. 'Even a vacuum cleaner. At least there's supposed to be one.'

'I'm sure we're going to love it,' Margaret said.

'Then we'll leave you,' said Cyrus. 'Come on, Aggie. Let's leave these two lovebirds to set up housekeeping.'

They walked them to the front door, and in parting Agnes said, 'There's bread and rolls in the bread box in the pantry, and you'll find some stuff in the fridge, nothing special, just milk and butter and eggs, and on the pantry shelf there's coffee and tea bags and sugar.'

'We expect you for dinner on Sunday, of course,' said Cyrus.

'Oh, sure.'

'And when Victor has to stay in town for his night classes, plan on coming to supper, Peg, and then you can drive home later when he gets home.'

'Oh, I'm not worried about staying alone,' said Peg.

'By the way, do you know the people next door?' said Victor.

'I don't know them. They're Jews, I understand, but all right. At least none of the people I've rented this house to have ever complained about them.'

'Jews? I don't believe I've ever known any,' said Peg.

'They're all right. We've got a few on the faculty and quite a few in the student body,' said Victor.

At the door, Cyrus halted. 'By the way, how are you planning to get in tomorrow? When is your first class?'

'I've got a nine o'clock Mondays, Wednesdays, and Fridays. I thought Peg could drive me to the railroad station.'

'If you take the eight o'clock, you'll get into North Station around half past. Then you have to take the subway to Park Street,

70

transfer, and get off at Arlington and walk down.' He shook his head. 'You could make it by nine o'clock, if you are lucky and everything goes just so. No, you'd better plan on taking the seven-thirty. And how about coming home? Do you finish the same time every day?'

'No, I thought I'd call and Peg could come and meet me.'

'Then she'd have to wait around for your call. And if you take the library job, Peg ...' He shook his head decisively. 'No, that won't do at all. Look, one of my salesmen left last week, and his car is just sitting in the garage. Why don't I have one of my men drop it off in your driveway here? It has the Merton Realty logo on the side. Do you mind? Or you can remove it; it's not painted on, just a decal.'

'But—But when you hire another salesman?' Victor stammered.

'Naw, anyone I hire will have to use his own car. I'll pay the mileage. I figure it will cost me less in the end.'

'Gee, I don't know what to say.'

'Then don't say anything, my boy. I'm only too happy to help.'

★ ★ ★

Peg got a chance to meet a Jew when Helen Rosen came over the next morning to

71

welcome the new neighbor with a plate of cookies she had just baked. And, of course, Peg invited her in to have coffee.

'It's instant. Do you mind?'

As they sipped their coffee and munched the cookies, Peg learned that Herb Rosen had a large plumbing contracting business which he had inherited from his father. 'They installed the plumbing in the Barnard's Crossing High School.' But he himself couldn't change a washer on a faucet. That he had studied at the Juilliard School of Music, but had consented to go into his father's plumbing business when he realized that he was not likely to become a concert violinist. That he conducted an orchestra in the town which rehearsed once a week at the Veteran's Hall, and if Peg or her husband could play an instrument—an orchestral instrument, that is, not a guitar or accordion—they would be more than welcome. That she did volunteer work every afternoon at the Salem Hospital gift shop. That Herb had a boat and in the summer sailed every chance he got, but she didn't much care for it. That they had a daughter, Phoebe, who was in the first year at Barnard's Crossing High.

And Helen Rosen, in turn, learned that the Joyces didn't know how long they would be living in the house, or in Barnard's Crossing for that matter, because it might be more convenient to live in Boston. That Cyrus

72

Merton was her uncle, and that she had lived with the Mertons since she was twelve, when her parents died. 'I was away at school or summer camp most of the time, though.' That she had been married little more than a week—

'Yes, I think I read the announcement of the wedding in the *Reporter*. I remember now, it said you were given away by Cyrus Merton, uncle of the bride.'

That they didn't sail, 'but perhaps we'll take it up if we continue to live in Barnard's Crossing.' That her husband was pretty keen on golf, however.

'Then he'll have to go to Breverton, to the country club there. There's no golf course in Barnard's Crossing.'

'Yes, I know. He's already gone there a few times.' That he was an assistant professor at Windermere Christian in Boston.

'Oh really? A good friend of mine teaches there.'

That he taught evening classes a couple of nights a week, but she didn't mind staying home alone. Besides, she had a job in the town library, and she was sure they'd let her work on those evenings when Victor was teaching.

CHAPTER ELEVEN

When next Rabbi Small went to the Salem Hospital, he found that Morris Fisher was no longer there; had been discharged the day after his visit, in fact. That evening, however, Ben Clayman called at the rabbi's house with news of him.

'I was over to see Fisher—'

'He's no longer in the hospital.'

'Yeah, I know. I went to see him at his house on the Point.'

'Oh, you're a friend of his?'

'Well ... Look, the guy is more than twice as old as I am, but my father knew his wife, worked with her. You might say he's like a friend of the family. That's how I got his business.'

'You sell him stock?'

'Buy and sell. Yeah, he was one of my first customers when I first went to work for the Klan.'

'The Klan?'

'That's what they call the company on the street. Kravitz, Kaplan, and Kohn—KKK, get it? He used to do quite a bit of trading with us. Not so much lately, but I make a point of keeping in touch. It's more like a hobby with him; gives him something to do. When he was better—you know,

74

healthier—he used to come to our offices in Lynn and sit for hours watching the ticker tape. That was after he retired, of course.'

'He was a teacher, wasn't he?' asked the rabbi.

'That's right. Math teacher in the Lynn schools.'

'And on his teacher's pension he could afford to play the stock market?'

'Oh, it was his wife who made the big money. When she got out of college, she wanted a career. In those days, as I understand it, a woman could either teach or go into nursing. If she became a teacher, she couldn't get married, at least, not in the public schools. Did you know that? Anyway, women like Mrs. Fisher who didn't want to have babies right away and then have to spend the rest of their lives taking care of the house, tried going into business, opening hat shops or tea rooms. That's what Mrs. Fisher did. She opened a tea room.

'She served soups and small sandwiches, but I understand most of her business was in the afternoon when women came in after shopping for a cup of tea or coffee and a couple of cookies, and to rest their feet. She'd bake the cookies at home and bring them in the next day. I guess she was doing all right; not setting the house afire, but paying her bills on time. Then she cooked up a batch of cookies she called Nutchies. See, it was after

75

Passover and she had a whole bowlful of nuts left over from the holiday. So she chopped them up and mixed them in with the dough. And then she really took off. People came in not for a cup of tea or coffee, but for a box of Nutchies. Even men would come in to buy them.

'Well, to make a long story short, she began to sell them around—to other stores and restaurants. And then Continental Cracker bought her out; gave her a wad of money and an executive-type job. That's how my old man got to know the Fishers. See, he was working for Continental Cracker at the time. He says she was good, and the company knew it. They kept advancing her, and she was getting a big salary. So now she had a real career, and there was no way she was going to give that up and stay home and have babies.'

'So they never had children?'

'That's right. I guess by the time they decided they wanted them, it was too late.'

'I see,' said the rabbi, and then to bring the visit to an end so that he could get back to the book he had been reading, he said, 'I'm glad to hear that Morris Fisher is all right now. When next you see him, give him my regards.'

'Well, he's not *all* right,' said Clayman. 'He's like what you might call stable. They got his blood pressure down, and they gave him some pills which they hope will keep it

76

down, but I guess in these cases you never can tell.'

'Well, we can only hope for the best,' said the rabbi as he rose from his chair.

But Clayman gave no indication of leaving. Instead, he leaned back in his seat and crossed his legs. 'Well, I had like an idea, which is why I came to see you.'

'Yes?' The rabbi sat down.

'See, the old geezer has no living relatives, not only no children, but no relatives, not on his side and not on his wife's side, although he thinks there's maybe a second or third cousin of his wife living in Australia. Now I figure he's got a couple of hundred thou in his stock portfolio, and his house on the Point must be worth three hundred thou in today's market. And I know for a fact that it's free and clear—no mortgage. All right, so that's half a mil.'

'So?'

'Well, see, he was awfully set up by your coming to see him at the hospital, felt you were very intelligent and—'

'I barely spoke to him. He did all the talking.'

'Yeah, I know he likes to talk. So maybe he thought you were an intelligent listener. What I had in mind was that where he has no one to leave his money to, and it seems to bother him a lot, if you was to go over to his place, spend an evening with him, maybe play a game or two of chess with him—You play chess, don't you?'

'Yes, I play chess.'

'Well then, you could go over and play chess with him a couple of nights a week. Then when he starts harping on not having any relatives and no one to leave his money to—and he's sure to because he keeps harping on it—you could suggest he leave it to the temple.'

'Oh, I couldn't do that.'

'Why not?'

'I couldn't ingratiate myself in order to get his money. From then on, anytime I went to see someone in the hospital, it would be assumed that I was trying to insinuate myself in his good graces in order to elicit a contribution for the temple.'

They heard a key grating in the lock, and Miriam came in from visiting a neighbor next door. 'Oh, I didn't realize you were here, Mr. Clayman. Will you have a cup of tea? I baked some cookies this afternoon. I took some over to Mrs. Estwick, and she loved them. They're lemon cookies, but I stirred in a bunch of nuts that I chopped up—' She stared as both men began to laugh.

CHAPTER TWELVE

On their honeymoon, Victor had not only been kind and considerate, but also most attentive. They knew no one and so they had only each other. But when they were ensconced in their new home, and Victor was back at school, the situation changed. For one thing, for the greater part of the day he was surrounded by people he knew and who had similar interests. When he came home, usually around four in the afternoon, even on those days when he had only morning classes, he had little to say to her, or for that matter, she to him.

He would ask, 'Did you have a good day?' not out of interest, nor even to make conversation, but rather as a courtesy, like saying, Good evening. And she might answer, 'Oh, I went into Salem to look for shoes to go with my beige dress.' Sometimes he might ask if she had been successful. More often, he merely grunted; question asked, answer given. Transaction completed.

When she asked about his day, he was no more explicit. He might reply, 'Just the usual.' Or, 'We had a dumb department meeting where nothing was decided as usual.'

She assumed his reserve and taciturnity were due to the difference in their interests.

She could understand that he might chafe at her idle talk of shoes and dresses. So she began to read, selecting the books she thought he would approve of, the books on the suggested reading list in her course in literature. Her attempts met with little success, however.

'I've just finished reading *Pride and Prejudice*,' she announced one evening. 'Do you like Jane Austen?'

'Not my period,' he said shortly.

'Well, it's about this awfully rich young man who is terribly stuck-up—'

'I know what it's about. I read it way back when. Look, I've a bunch of papers I have to correct and a lecture to prepare. Do you mind?' And he would repair to the little back parlor he had made into a study.

When she tried a writer who was in his period, he was no more encouraging. 'Look, I had to read so much Bernard Shaw for my dissertation that I got heartily sick of the old faker.'

So she sat in the living room and watched TV while he remained in his study. Sometimes she wondered if he was really working in his study, or if it was just an excuse to get away from her chatter. He would usually join her for the ten o'clock news, after which he would announce that it was time to go to bed, by which he meant not that he was sleepy, but that he wanted sex.

And this, too, had changed. During the honeymoon, although the act was distasteful to her, she had felt that it was due to his consuming desire to become one with her. She had thought, hoped, that she would get used to it at least, even if she never expected to enjoy the experience. But now she felt that it was not her he wanted, but it, and she felt dirty and cheapened by each episode.

When her infertile period ended, she told him that she was now vulnerable and that the doctor had recommended that she wait a while before becoming pregnant.

'Yeah, your aunt told me,' he said.

'Well, don't you think we should move the beds apart, so you know...'

'Aw, c'mon Peg, I'm no teenager. I know what's involved. I can control myself.'

*   *   *

And he did—at first. But after a week of abstinence, it was going on far too long; he knew it, she knew it. And he tried to take her. She managed to push him away and jumped out of bed.

Instantly he was contrite. 'Gee, Peg, I don't know what got into me. I'm sorry. Please come back to bed.'

She finally came back to bed, but the next day when he came home, he found that the beds had been separated and pushed apart so that there was a yard or more of floor between them.

'I suppose I deserve that,' he said, 'and it's probably best that way, but when you're not vulnerable, can we put the beds together again?'

'We'll see,' she said.

A few days later, on one of the days when he had evening classes, he called and said he would be home late. 'Some of the evening courses end tonight, and a few of the guys thought we ought to celebrate.'

'Well, what time do you expect to get home?' she asked.

'Maybe not until after midnight. Certainly not much before. Don't wait up for me. You go to bed.'

She went to bed at her usual hour, half past ten, and fell asleep almost immediately. She was awakened by hearing his car turn into the driveway. She glanced at the clock on the night table and found it was after one. She heard him humming as he came up the stairs. He tiptoed about gathering his pajamas and slippers and then went into the guest room across the hall to undress so as not to wake her. When he came back a few minutes later, she pretended to be asleep and even managed a gentle snore.

Instead of going to his own bed, however, he came to hers. She felt the mattress sag under his weight, and then, before she could make a move, he had his arms around her. She struggled, but he held her tight and pressed his mouth against hers so that she could make no sound. She writhed and twisted in an effort to get away, but she was no match for him. When he was finished and released her, she jumped out of the bed and ran to the bathroom and locked the door.

He sat on the edge of the bed for a minute or two, and then went to the bathroom and put his ear to the door. He heard her sobbing.

'I'm sorry, Peg. Please come out.'

He waited, and when there was no response except the sound of her weeping, he said, 'I know you think I'm a horny bastard, but I swear I won't so much as touch you again until you ask me. Please forgive me and come out.'

Again he waited. And then, 'Look, I'm going to the guest room. I'll sleep there.'

When she heard him cross the hall, she crept out. Before going back to bed, she closed the bedroom door and jammed a chair under the doorknob.

The next morning when he came down to breakfast, he found no place had been set for him. She had the newspaper propped up in front of her and was drinking her coffee.

'Look, about last night, I'm sorry. I had a couple of drinks and I guess I lost control.'

She did not answer and she did not look up from her paper.

'I won't be meeting my three o'clock class, so I'll be home early.'

She gave no indication that she had heard him or even that he was there. He waited for a moment on the chance that she might at least look up, and then turned and left the room and the house.

As he drove to the city, he debated the matter. Sure, I can see where she might be worried about getting pregnant right now, but hell, the chances of getting pregnant from the first shot are mighty slim. She ought to know that. I guess maybe she's just a kid and just doesn't know what it's all about. But she ought to realize that a guy is only human and that he's bound to make an occasional mistake. She must realize that where I teach, in a coed college where the coeds are flaunting themselves all the time, many of them not wearing bras so you can see the nipples against their dresses, and some with these skin-tight jeans which show everything, and this one in the front row last night with her skirt hiked up—I guess that got me going And then a couple of drinks helped matters along. Oh hell, she probably won't talk to me for a day or two, and then maybe she'll talk, but she'll be cold and distant, and then she'll forget about it.

He considered bringing her flowers as a peace offering, and then decided against it. Although admittedly at fault, he thought it would be better to downplay the incident. Later, when he could discuss it with her rationally, he would explain that these things happen, pretty much had to happen when a man lives with a woman, and that the adult thing to do is to forget about them and not let them interfere with the relationship.

She was not home when he arrived. He went upstairs to change into a sport shirt and sweater, and found that his things had all been removed to the guest room. Even worse, however, she had installed a sliding bolt on the bedroom door. This was too much. He was now the aggrieved party. What he had done was an accident, at least something done on the spur of the moment. This was a deliberate act on her part. She could not have mounted the bolt herself. She must have engaged a carpenter. There was permanence and finality about it. And it engendered in him a feeling of great indignation.

As he thought about it, he told himself that he had made a bad bargain. She could be sickly all her life. And although she was fairly intelligent, she was obviously terribly immature. True, she was certain to inherit her uncle's money. But suppose Merton were to lose it? Seemingly, all his money was tied up in real estate. Well, real estate values were high right now, but they could come down. And in any case, the money would not come to her for a number of years. Cyrus would probably leave his money to his sister, and it would come to them only after her death. But Agnes was less than sixty. She could live for another twenty years or more.

He decided to have it out with her. She was his wife and he didn't have to shilly-shally. He would talk straight turkey as soon as she got home.

But she anticipated him. No sooner had she closed the door behind her than she said, 'Victor, I want a divorce.'

He was taken aback by her bluntness. 'But—but we can't. Our church doesn't permit it,' he stammered.

'I know, but we can get a civil divorce and a Church-sanctioned separation.'

'This is because of what happened last night?'

'It made me realize that our marriage was very, very wrong.'

'You want to know what's wrong with our marriage?' he demanded. 'It's you. You're frigid. You don't want a man, not any man. You took me because—because you wanted to get away from your uncle and aunt. Maybe that's why they pushed you onto me, too. Because they wanted you out of their house. Sex for you was a few minutes of unpleasant annoyance that was the price you had to pay for your freedom.' He had raised his voice and was almost shouting, out of frustration and perhaps out of apprehension of the consequences of a divorce. And there was also the thought that he might be able to induce a real bang-up fight that could end in reconciliation.

She did not shout back, however. She remained very quiet, and when she spoke, it was calmly, with no trace of anger or of hurt. 'You may be right,' she said, 'and I'm not blaming you. All I know is that I can't go on like this.'

'All right.' He sat down, his hands on his knees, leaning forward. 'If you're sure that's what you want, let's talk about it rationally.'

'All right.'

'Have you talked to your uncle and aunt yet?'

'Not yet.'

'But you're planning to.'

'I'll have to.'

'Okay, but you ought to know all the facts before you do. I don't know if you realize it, but this was pretty much an arranged marriage. Your uncle made it pretty plain that the husband of his niece would eventually be a rich man. And in my case, for the immediate future, he practically promised me tenure at Windermere.'

'I realize that now. I think I may have suspected it from the beginning.'

'So where does that leave us? I kept my part of the bargain. But you know what will happen when you tell your uncle? When the question of tenure comes up, your uncle will see that I don't get it. I don't know how it works exactly, but I know he has a lot to do with it, and if he doesn't want me to get it, I won't. And then, maybe, I'll be notified that my services won't be needed for the next academic year. And—'

'I wouldn't want that to happen,' she interposed quickly. 'I'm not vindictive. I know you weren't trying to hurt me. It's just that—that I feel we're not suited for each other. I'll keep his part of the bargain since I suppose I was a party to it. That is, until your tenure is announced, I won't say a word to my uncle. We could go on living here, but not as husband and wife. We could live here like—like a couple of strangers living in a hotel or a rooming house. The decision on tenure comes up pretty soon, doesn't it? In a couple of weeks?'

'And we'll both go on living here?'

'But like strangers who happen to be living in the same hotel.'

A thought struck him. 'But how about Sundays, going to church and then dinner at your uncle's afterward?'

She considered. 'I suppose we'd continue that for a while. We'd have to pretend that everything was, you know, like normal between us. If you could, I guess I could.'

Another thought occurred to him. 'What if some night I decided to stay in town and didn't come home at all? Would you feel safe all alone?'

'Safer than with you here in the next room,' she answered promptly.

⋆   ⋆   ⋆

The difference in age and background between Margaret Joyce and Helen Rosen was too great for a normal friendship to develop, but they saw a great deal of each other nevertheless. Both were busy in the afternoon, Mrs. Rosen at the hospital and Margaret at the library, but frequently they would meet for a mid-morning coffee, and sometimes they would go shopping together.

For Margaret it was a valuable relationship. For the first time she could talk freely to an older woman in a way that she had never been able to talk to her aunt or to the nuns at school. Helen Rosen was a good listener, but she was troubled by the younger woman's confidences. She discussed it with her husband.

The occasion was a Sunday afternoon, quite early in their acquaintance. Margaret had come over for coffee, Victor having gone off to Breverton to play golf. When they heard Victor's car come into the driveway, Margaret had said, 'I'd better get back. He wants me there when he gets home.'

'She doesn't sound very enthusiastic about

seeing her husband,' Herb Rosen remarked as the door closed behind her.

'Oh, Herb, I'm afraid she's not very happy. I don't think that marriage is going to last.'

'It'll last all right. They're both good Catholics, and they don't believe in divorce, or allow it for that matter. What's eating her anyway?'

'She's terribly worried about getting pregnant. She's underweight and a little anemic, and the doctor advised her to wait a while before having a child. He said there was a high incidence of birth defects if the mother is anemic.'

'Well, her husband knows, doesn't he? Or has she kept it from him?'

'Oh, he knows all right. It's just that she doesn't feel that he's careful enough, especially when he's had a drink or two. I don't know what to do.'

'Well, I'll tell you what you won't do. You won't try to give her any advice. And if she asks you, you'll tell her you have no expertise in these matters, so you can't presume to advise her. Understood?'

But a few weeks later she reported in great excitement, 'Herb, she's getting a divorce.'

'Who is? Who are you talking about?'

'Peg Joyce. She's divorcing Victor.'

'But how can she? Their church doesn't allow it.'

'A civil divorce, and a Church-sanctioned

separation.'

He shrugged. 'If the church marriage didn't work, what makes you think a church separation will work any better?'

'What do you mean?'

'I think they've quarreled, as young couples almost invariably do. After all, there is quite an adjustment involved in a marriage. But they'll make up, and then settle down to the humdrum of married life. He's no youngster. He's a mature man of thirty or thirty-five. He wouldn't have married her if he hadn't wanted her. And from what you've told me, her complaint is that he wants her badly. He's not going to get over that because they've had a little tiff'

But the fact of the matter was that Victor no longer wanted her, because he had met Alice Saxon.

CHAPTER THIRTEEN

Associate Professor Alice Saxon, a tenured member of the Department of Psychology at Windermere, was tall and slim, with dark eyes, a thin, almost aquiline nose, and a pointed chin. Her dark brown hair was cut short and brushed back so that her earlobes with the gold button earrings she usually wore showed. She was thirty-five, and in the square-shouldered, conservative charcoal-gray pinstripe suits she affected, she looked like an MBA who had worked her way up to a vice-presidency in a stock brokerage firm.

Victor had seen her, of course—in the corridors, in the faculty lounge, in the cafeteria—but had never actually spoken to her. He thought she might be Jewish, if only because she appeared to be friendly with his colleague in the English Department and rival for tenure, Mordecai Jacobs.

It was at a Friday afternoon faculty meeting that he finally got to know her. She had come in a little late and taken the seat beside him because, he assumed, it was the one vacant seat in the last row nearest the door. She wrote in her notebook and slid it toward him. He glanced down, and saw that she had written, *Victor Joyce?* He nodded, and then with a lift of the chin indicated that she should slide the notebook to him, and when she did, he wrote, *Alice Saxon?* She nodded and smiled.

The main purpose of the meeting was to choose the locale for the faculty dinner at the end of the academic year. The chairman of the committee was reporting at length on the various restaurants and hotels that had been considered, and explaining the reasons the committee had turned them down, each in turn.

'How about the Turner House?'

'We used that three years ago. Those of you who were there will remember that the portions served were skimpy. The committee got considerable flack about it.'

'We had a good meal at the Central last year.'

'Yes, we did, and we thought of going back there, but their Saturday schedule was full.'

The committee had narrowed the choice down to the Madison Hotel in Lexington, the College Inn in Wellesley, and the country club in Breverton.

'Why can't we have it someplace in town?'

'Because we can get much better value for our money outside the city.'

'Yeah, but those places are a good thirty miles away.'

'So what? You can drive to any one of them in thirty or forty minutes. If you come into the city by public transport, it will take you at least that, what with waiting for buses and streetcars and changing, and—'

'But I can drive in from my house in twenty minutes.'

'And how long will it take you to find a place to park, and on a Saturday night, at that? And then how long will it take you to walk to the restaurant after you park?'

Miss Saxon opened her notebook and scribbled. She then pushed it toward Joyce. He read, *Do you find this as dull as I do?*

He wrote, *Un-huh.*

93

She favored him with a smile.

A little later she wrote, *I could use a drink.*

He wrote back, *Me, too.*

'Shall we go?' she whispered.

'Let's wait until the vote,' he whispered back.

'In heaven's name, why?'

'I'd like to vote for the country club. I know it. I played golf a couple of times there. It's a nice place.'

'All right. I'll vote for it, too.'

A few minutes later the matter was put to a vote and, to be sure, the Breverton Country Club was chosen. There was other business to transact, but after a questioning glance from her and a nod from him, she got up, and a minute later he, too, rose and left as unobtrusively as possible.

★   ★   ★

Although she claimed to be 'absolutely perishing' for a drink, she had him drive almost out of the city before she found the cocktail bar she approved of.

'What's so special about this place?' he asked when they were seated in a booth in which a tufted leather bench curved around a small oblong table. It was dark, except for the bar at the other end of the room.

'I like the decor,' she said.

'It's too dark to see the decor.'

'Right,' she said. 'It's what you can't see—or hear, for that matter—that makes this place so nice. You won't see or hear any academic types here. No students, no professors. We're away from any school—not easy in Boston—and we're away from anywhere that students or professors are apt to live, so they're not likely to drop in for a quick one. It's where I come when I have been subjected to a faculty meeting or a departmental meeting of more than usual idiocy. Can you imagine any business enterprise that would tolerate the interminable discussion by the entire staff of a place to hold a dinner?'

'Yeah, I suppose academics do like to talk,' he admitted.

'I'd like to do a paper on it someday,' she said, 'but of course I wouldn't be able to publish it, not in a journal which my colleagues would see. Perhaps, when I leave teaching, if I ever do, I could work it up in a book for the general reader. *What Makes Academics* or *The Academic Mind* or—'

'How about *Alice in Academia*,' he suggested.

'Splendid!' she exclaimed, and she clutched his hand in her enthusiasm.

He moved closer to her so that their thighs were touching under the table. She did not pull away, although she released his hand. They had a couple more drinks and then

95

decided they were hungry.

'We could get some sandwiches here,' he suggested.

'No, I'm really hungry. Let's go to a restaurant.'

'All right.'

The air was crisp when they found themselves on the street. As they headed for the car, she clutched his arm as though she was afraid of falling. He could feel her breast pressing against his upper arm. When they reached the parking lot where they had left the car, and he fumbled with his keys, she said, 'Maybe it would be better if we walked for a while.'

'I can drive all right,' he said.

'Yes, but it's so nice out. I know a place only a couple of blocks from here. We could walk there and then afterward come back for the car.'

And because he had been affected by the drinks and the coolness of the evening after, he readily agreed. It was an Italian restaurant brightly lit with checkered tablecloths. The food was good and they ate ravenously. All they had to drink, however, was a small bottle of Chianti between them. While the food was good, the service was slow. Seemingly, there were only two waitresses, and these middle-aged and matronly. So they ate leisurely and it was quite late when they found themselves once again on the street.

They walked back slowly to the parking lot, and this time she felt he was sober enough to drive without danger or mishap.

When they reached her apartment house on Beacon Street, he said, 'It's been quite a day.'

'Come up for a nightcap,' she invited.

'All right, but just one. I've got a long drive home.'

They climbed the stairs to her apartment on the third floor of the converted brownstone, their arms around each other's waists. When his hand slid down from her waist to her buttock, she giggled.

He stayed the night.

*   *   *

He woke up late the next morning and found that she had already arisen and was busy in the kitchen. When she heard him go to the bathroom, she called out, 'I've fixed us some breakfast—brunch really. There's an old robe of mine at the foot of the bed that you can wear.'

He came into the kitchen, the robe ridiculously short, belted around him, to find that she had made French toast, bacon, and sausages. 'Is it all right?' she asked. 'Or would you rather have cereal or eggs perhaps?'

'No, this is fine. In fact, it's wonderful. And where did you get the paper? Surely, you

97

didn't go out for it.'

'No, the newsboy leaves it outside the door.'

They ate in the kitchen, which was just large enough to accommodate a small table. Then they took their second and third cup of coffee into the living room and sipped as they read the paper. Around noon he suggested they get dressed and take a walk along the Esplanade or in the Public Gardens. The weather appeared to be balmy, and she agreed. It occurred to him that this was the sort of woman he should have married, handsome and mature.

'You wouldn't have a razor, would you?' he asked.

She produced the little razor she used for her underarms. 'Will this do?'

He looked at it doubtfully and said, 'It will have to, I suppose.'

He managed somehow, and then showered afterward. When he came out of the bathroom, he said, 'Remind me, when we go out, to buy a razor, and oh yeah, some shaving cream.'

'What for?'

'So I can get a decent shave tomorrow morning.'

'You won't be here tomorrow. Don't you have to go to church?'

'Sure, but there are a dozen places not far from here.'

'Aren't you engaged for Sunday dinner at the Mertons?'

He was obviously startled. 'What do you know about that?'

'Oh, I know all about you. You're married to Cyrus Merton's daughter.'

'His niece.'

'Same thing since he has no children of his own. And your marriage is a complete washout. You don't talk to each other, and she's just waiting until you get tenure before she files suit for a civil divorce and a Church-approved separation.'

'How—How—'

'How do I know all this? Because Helen Rosen, your next door neighbor is a very good friend of mine. We were at school together, and we still keep in touch. Your wife confides in her, and your situation is what first attracted me to you, or rather what led me to approach you. I was attracted earlier.'

'How do you mean? I—I don't understand.'

'I mean that there was no danger of our getting involved to the point of your trying to marry me.'

'Don't you approve of marriage?'

'It's an old-fashioned institution that no longer fits modern conditions. It was all right when the outcome was children and women couldn't earn a living on their own. But I

99

don't want children and I don't intend to have any. And I have a job which enables me to live comfortably. I want a lover rather than a husband, and a relationship rather than a marriage.'

'But—'

'I've been married, and I'd rather not repeat the experience.'

'What's wrong with it?'

'It's too confining. Two people who are always together, with each having a claim on the other, can't help getting on each other's nerves. When you get tenure and you're practically sure to get it with Merton pushing for you—and your wife gets her divorce and separation, don't think you'll be moving in with me. I'll let you keep some of your clothes here, but I'll expect you to have a place of your own where you can go or where I can shoo you to when I find you irksome.'

'You mean even if I were free to marry, you wouldn't?'

She shook her head. 'Even if she managed somehow to get an annulment. I understand you can these days even if you have cohabited. I wouldn't marry you because I'd have to leave my job, or you'd have to leave yours, since they don't allow both husband and wife to serve on the faculty.'

'And your job means that much to you?'

'It certainly does. It's the perfect job. The college is another institution that has changed. It used to be for the students, but now it's for the faculty. We get a reasonable salary in exchange for very little work. In fact, we can do just as much or as little as we please, and if you're on tenure, it's almost impossible to fire you. No, I wouldn't think of giving up my job here.'

He looked at her admiringly. 'You're-You're something else. All right, I'll go home, but no need until sometime this evening. When will I see you again?'

She smiled and patted his cheek as she might fondle a puppy. 'Maybe Monday if we feel like it,' she said.

CHAPTER FOURTEEN

In the year following her graduation from Boston University, Clara Lemer had held four jobs, not difficult in Massachusetts, where the unemployment rate at the time was among the lowest in the country. Her father and mother, both of whom were attorneys practicing in nearby Lynn, had wanted her to go on to law school after graduation, but she had refused. 'I'm tired of studying. I'd like to read a book just because I want to and not because I have to,' she had said.

The first three jobs had been relatively local, that is, within a fifteen minute drive from her home in the Charleton section of Barnard's Crossing. The first job, clerk/typist/receptionist in an art gallery, she had left after a month because it had changed ownership and she didn't like her new boss. 'He's a pig. He scratches himself all the time and he picks his nose.' Her next job carried the title of Office Manager. It was a boat company, which bought, sold, and leased boats, and whose offices were right on the harbor. Her work, however, consisted of typing, filing, and occasionally greeting customers, offering them coffee, and telling them that 'Mr. Williams will be with you shortly.' For long periods of time, however, when Mr. Williams went out to look at a boat, or to have a drink with a potential customer, she was alone with no one to talk to, and nothing to do but stare out of the window at the harbor below. 'I got sick of just looking at the ocean,' she explained.

Then she got a job as a receptionist in a doctor's office, which offered the advantage of being in the Charleton section and hence within walking distance of her house. Unfortunately, it was its only advantage, and after a few months she quit, this time to take a job in Boston. When her folks asked her about it, she replied noncommittally, 'It's all right.' But after a week she called to say she would be working late and would have dinner in town. The following week she told them

102

she was considering living in the city if she could find a congenial roommate to share the expense of an apartment. However, while she continued to live at home, she nevertheless found it necessary to stay in town late several nights a week.

'I hope they're paying you for all this overtime,' her father commented.

But it was her mother who guessed the truth. 'You're seeing someone in town, aren't you?'

'Well . . . I have been having dinner several nights a week with someone.'

'Someone from your office?' asked her mother.

'Then you haven't been working overtime,' said her father.

'No, I haven't, and no, he isn't.'

'You mean this guy has been taking you out to dinner every night—'

'It hasn't been every night. Only three times last week. And he hasn't been taking me. We go Dutch.'

Her father was aghast. 'You go Dutch. You mean—'

'He doesn't earn very much, and rather than have him take me out once a week, I'd rather we went Dutch so we could see each other more often.'

'That sounds serious,' her mother remarked. 'Are you serious about him?'

'Yes, I am.'

'And is he serious about you?'

'I—I think so. Yes, I'm sure of it.'

'What does he do?'

'What's he look like?'

'What's his name?'

'When are we going to see him?'

'Why haven't you invited him to have dinner with us so we can get a look at him?'

'He's old-fashioned about these things. He feels that if he should come to dinner here with my parents, it's like announcing our engagement.'

'Well, what's wrong with announcing your engagement if you're serious?'

'Where'd you meet him?'

'How long have you known him?'

'I met him when I was still at school and he was doing graduate work at Harvard. We met at a party and we went out together a few times. He didn't have much time. He was working on his thesis and studying for his orals. And he didn't have much money either, I suspect. Then I bumped into him in town one day, and he asked me to have dinner with him. And we've been seeing each other ever since.'

'But what does he do?' her father insisted.

'He's a teacher,' she said defensively. 'He's a professor, an assistant professor of English at Windermere Christian.'

'Windermere Christian?'

'Windermere Christian is nonsectarian, you

know. And his name is Mordecai Jacobs.'

Further questioning elicited the information that right now he was uncertain of his future; and that while it had been hinted to him by the head of the department that he would in all probability get tenure at the end of the year, he'd prefer to wait until he had actually received it.

'But we want to see him,' her mother urged. 'All right, I can understand about his reluctance to come to dinner here, sort of. But I have an idea. Why doesn't he come to Ben's Bar Mitzvah party Saturday night? The whole family will be here, but there'll also be a lot of friends of the family, so his presence won't be noticed.'

'I had the same idea,' said Clara, 'and I sent him an invitation. The trouble is that the Windermere faculty is having a dinner that same night, and it was intimated to him that he ought to be there.

It's going to be held at the Breverton Country Club. He thinks he might be able to get away early, but he can't promise.'

Later, alone with Clara in her bedroom, Mrs. Lerner asked, 'What's he like? Is he tall? Is he good-looking?'

'He is to me,' said Clara stoutly. 'He's not tall, but he's not short, either. Sort of medium. At least, I don't have to tilt my head back to talk to him. And he's not, you know, movie-actor handsome, but he's nice-looking.

He's nice and warm and friendly, and fun to be with, and I'm going to marry him.'

'Have you met his folks? Are they from around here?'

'No, he comes from a small town in Pennsylvania, so—'

'But he wants you to meet them, doesn't he?'

'Sure, but where they live so far away, it will have to wait until we can arrange it.'

'But he's right here,' Mrs. Lerner insisted, 'so there's no reason why we can't meet him. Now look, Clara, I want you to tell him that he can come to see us Saturday night, no matter how late his faculty dinner ends. There'll be people here even after midnight.'

'All right, I'll tell him.'

CHAPTER FIFTEEN

As the rabbi and Miriam dawdled over their second cup of coffee at breakfast, the mail came, and Miriam went to gather it up from the floor beneath the chute. As she came back to the table she said, 'The usual junk mail: a couple of mail order catalogues, pleas for donations from the local public broadcasting station and from—let's see—from Support the Children, AIDS research, and the Heart Fund: a chance to win a Cadillac by just going up to visit Forest Park, the new vacation homesite. We don't seem to get any regular mail anymore.'

'It could be,' the rabbi agreed. 'I remember in my course in Economics there was a theory—no, it was a law, Gresham's Law, that's it—that said bad money drives out good money. So maybe junk mail drives out good mail.'

'Oh, here's one from the University of Chicago,' said Miriam, who had continued to slit envelopes. 'It must be from Simcha.'

She handed it to the rabbi and he read it aloud for her benefit.

'Dear David:

Unless something comes up to prevent it, I shall be in your area in early June for the meeting of the Anthropological Society. The first session is on Monday, June eleventh. The next day I am to receive the Dreyfus Medal and read a paper. I will be coming in the week before, on Friday, June first, because I have to attend a wedding in Gloucester on the second. It is the granddaughter of Martha's sister Sarah, the unpleasant one. So why do I have to go? Because according to Martha, if Sarah hears that I was in the area and did not come to her granddaughter's wedding, she will be indignant and be even more unpleasant than she usually is and cause all

107

sorts of ill-feeling in the family. And how will she know that I was in the area? Because I will be receiving the Dreyfus Medal and Martha is sure it will be in the newspapers.

'Martha will not accompany me; I will be coming alone. Ellen is going into the hospital for a hysterectomy. Nothing serious, I am assured, but requiring a stay in the hospital for a week or ten days. So Martha will be taking care of Ellen's children for that week, which lets her off the hook for the wedding.

'I note, by checking the map of your state, that Gloucester is only about thirty or forty miles from Barnard's Crossing. So you could easily drive up there Sunday morning and we could spend the day together.

'I have been making inquiries about your little problem from various knowledgeable people around here, and perhaps I can be of some help to you. In any case, hold June third open and let's get together.
'Regards to Miriam—all the best, Simcha.
'P.S. I'll call you from Gloucester to make specific arrangements.'

'Oh David, do you think he knows of a job for you?'
Her husband shook his head. 'It doesn't sound like it. I think he would have said so if

he had anything definite. He's probably got the names of a few colleges that have Judaica departments, and perhaps some rumors of some people in those departments who might be leaving or retiring.'

'But suppose he did have a job for you, wouldn't it be apt to be somewhere in the Midwest? Would you want to leave New England?'

'Well, I'd have to think hard about it, and it would have to be a pretty good job. But it makes no difference; I'd like to see Simcha anyway. I don't like the idea of driving all the way up to Gloucester—'

'It's only about thirty miles, less than an hour, and on a Sunday morning there's not likely to be much traffic.'

'Unless it's a sunny day. Tell you what, Miriam, why don't you inquire around and find out about train or bus service. Maybe there's a bus that runs between Gloucester and Barnard's Crossing, or a train from Gloucester that stops at the Swampscott station. Then when he calls, I can suggest that he take one or the other here instead of my going up there to pick him up.'

CHAPTER SIXTEEN

From the time of his appointment, Mark Levine had been conscientious in attending the meetings of the Board of Trustees of Windermere College. Not that he was particularly interested in the college, but because it gave him an excuse to escape the boisterous optimism of his associates in Texas for the quieter charms of Boston. He would arrive on Saturday and spend the day in the company of his friend, Don Macomber, and sometimes Macomber's daughter, who lived in Rockport and would come down to see 'Uncle Mark.' They would have dinner at the Ritz Carleton, where Mark stayed, and then go on to the theatre or a concert. Macomber's daughter would stay over at the president's house in the college, and then on Sunday they might all drive to her home in Rockport and spend the day there going through the various art galleries in which the town abounded. Monday, he would take care of any business he might have, or if the weather were fine, just walk the streets of the city. Tuesday morning he attended the board meeting. He could easily have come to Boston any time the spirit moved him, but he felt it was frivolous to leave his business without a specific reason, and the board meeting provided that.

But now he was in Boston on his own. He had come up in the middle of the week, and he had to fly back the next morning. He was taking dinner at the president's house, and it was a plainer meal than the Ritz dining room afforded because it had been prepared by the housekeeper, who also did the cooking for Macomber. They had just finished, and Levine lit a cigar. 'How are things going at the school?' he asked.

'All right so far, but applications for admission are down. Oh, there are a lot more applications than we can accommodate. I mean, even of those who are acceptable, but the trend is down.'

'Young people getting disenchanted with the idea of coming to Windermere?'

'Oh, it's national. It's not just us. Tuition is up everywhere, student loans harder to get because of government cutbacks, and there's a decline in the number of young people of college age in the population as a whole.'

'You mean you're worried about next year and the year after?'

'And the year after that and maybe for the next few years. A number of colleges have already closed down. The well-known schools, the prestige universities, won't feel it for a while, maybe never, but my guess is that they'll be taking in more and more students that they wouldn't have considered a few years ago. You might say that the bloom appears to be off. It's like any other business: in boom times it expands, and when there is a downturn, the weaker ones are driven to the wall.'

'But education is not a business,' Levine objected. 'I know what you mean, of course. Down in Dallas, when oil was selling at thirty dollars a barrel and higher, people began building like crazy, and now when it's selling at about half that, we have any number of real estate firms filing for bankruptcy and dragging the banks that gave them construction loans with them. But colleges . . .'

'Well, colleges are in the real estate business, too. They got up a bunch of new buildings, too, dormitories, laboratories, classrooms. We didn't because we had no land to expand on, but we took over all the old brownstones on Clark Street and converted them into dormitories, mostly. You see, as a fall-back school, we get a lot of out-of-towners. We're no longer a local college where the students live at home.'

'Are we in trouble?'

'Not yet, but looking ahead . . .'

There was a silence for a little while as Macomber sipped his coffee and Levine blew smoke up at the ceiling. Then Levine asked, 'So what do you plan to do?'

'I'm hoping to change the nature of the school. Make it a school of first choice rather than a fall-back school. Actually, it's what I've always wanted to do. It's my reason for coming here in the first place.'

'I've always wondered why you did,' said Levine, and then with a chuckle, 'I'm sure it wasn't for the money.'

Macomber smiled. 'No, it wasn't for the money. Fortunately, I don't depend on my salary.'

'And you certainly didn't take it for the prestige.'

'Hardly. Or you might say I took it because there was so little prestige attached to Windermere Christian.'

'I don't get it.'

'Do you remember Professor Cotton, Mark?'

'Of course, your guru,' he jeered. 'What did they call you guys who were his disciples? Oh yeah, Cottontails.'

Macomber chuckled. 'That's right, Cottontails. You never took a course with him, did you?'

'No, but at your urging I audited his course in Anthro 4 a couple of times when you were taking it.' He blew a smoke ring at the ceiling. 'I remember in one of those lectures, he spent the whole hour talking about the modern college, how it was becoming a kind of factory for the manufacture of knowledge rather than a means for passing on knowledge from one generation to the next; and that it was encouraging competition rather than cooperation. It was interesting, but what it had to do with anthropology, I don't know.'

'He was demonstrating how an institution, the college, that we were all familiar with, could change under our very eyes, and no one would notice it. And that was twenty-five years ago, Mark. It's a lot worse today. It now characterizes all education in this country. Education used to be the way we discovered ourselves, our humanness, our relation to society and the world. Now it's just a contest to get ahead of one's fellows to the next plateau, from where you go on to the next escalation. It starts back in the grade school where the kids are separated according to perceived capacity, the track system. Those on the highest track are eligible to take the college prep course when they get into high school, and there the competition is for admission to the better colleges where the competition is for admission to the graduate and professional schools, and there they compete for jobs in the more prestigious law firms, or internships in the best-known hospitals. It just goes on and on. It's a rat race.'

'It's the character of the times, Don.'

'No, it isn't. It's a confusion between training and education that developed as a result of a sudden increase in technology.'

'All right,' said Levine good-naturedly. 'So

114

what can you do about it?'

'I can try to make Windermere an institution for education.'

'How?'

'By gradually changing the attitude of the faculty so that they focus on the student rather than on research. I'd get away from the "publish or perish" idea. The way things are now, the emphasis is all on research. The professor gets advancement by publishing in the learned journals, and the better he is at it, the fewer courses he's required to teach. It hasn't happened to us as yet. But in some of our better-known colleges, the most prestigious professors, whose reputations attracted students to their school, never see a student. Even if they are listed in the school catalogue as giving a course or two, the lectures are apt to be given by a graduate assistant. Well, I'm going to try to attract teachers; men and women who know their subjects and whose primary interest is in transmitting their knowledge to their students, to exciting their interest and curiosity. And if they find something of particular interest that they feel the world should know about and want to publish their findings, they'll do it on their own time. And I could try to stop some of the competitive spirit that has changed the student's desire to learn into the desire to beat his classmates.'

'And how would you do that?'

'By changing the marking system,' said Macomber promptly. 'I'd have just two grades. Pass or Fail, or maybe Pass, Fail, and Honors. And I'd abolish so-called objective tests. Check one of five possible answers. That sort of thing. All testing in the humanities at least would be of the essay type.'

Levine nodded appreciatively. 'It might work. At least, it might teach them how to write English. So why haven't you done it up till now? You say it's what you've wanted since you came here, that it's why you came here in the first place.'

'I didn't have the backing of the board. I knew I didn't when I came here, but I thought I'd be able to win them over; change some, replace some over the years.'

'And now, you feel you've got the board behind you?'

'Well, I've got the votes for certain things, but not for others. You know, in nominating members for the board, I didn't grill them on their attitudes any more than I did you when I asked you to join. I chose people whom I thought would agree with me. Sometimes I made mistakes. Cyrus Merton, for example. He is against changing the name, and not merely against it, but in active opposition. He knows that the school is not and never was Christian in anything but name. Nevertheless—'

'He doesn't want to change it.'

'That's right. It's a kind of superstition with him. He's fighting a kind of religious war, and he thinks to change the name would be a victory for secularism.'

'And why are you so anxious to change the name? I mean, how does the change affect your plans for the school?'

'As long as we were a fall-back school, it didn't make too much difference. It may even have helped. You see, a youngster applies to Harvard, say, and then to Tufts or B.U. in case he doesn't make it. But Tufts and B.U. have raised their standards, so there's a good chance that he won't get into any of the three. So they'd also apply to Windermere Christian because it is thought that faith, perhaps, as attested by a letter from their priest or minister, maybe will take the place of good grades. As you know, I tried to offset the effect of the name by instituting a course in Judaica and having it taught by a rabbi. I imagine your name on the Board of Trustees also helped,' he added with a smile.

Levine laughed. 'I get two or three letters every year from coreligionists excoriating me for having converted.'

'Is that so? I'm sorry.'

'Oh, it doesn't bother me,' Levine assured him. 'But what makes you think you'll be successful this year? Has Cyrus changed his mind?'

'Oh, I'm sure he hasn't. But this time I might be able to offer him a quid pro quo that improves my bargaining position. His niece who is like his daughter, since he has no children of his own—is married to one of the young men on the faculty who hopes to get tenure. Well, I have the final say on who gets tenure.'

CHAPTER SEVENTEEN

Included in Cyrus Merton's notice of the date for the June meeting of the Board of Trustees of Windermere Christian College of Liberal Arts was the usual agenda of topics to be discussed and voted on. The items, he noted, were much the same as those that had appeared on previous agendas. In part this was due to continuous situations and problems that called for discussion meeting after meeting. Sometimes, even after they had seemingly been resolved, and been voted on, they recurred in slightly different form, and would again be discussed in a succession of meetings. In large part, however, the same subjects appeared on agenda after agenda because the board never really got a chance to deal with them. The meetings started at ten in the morning and ended at noon, when the members were served an elaborate catered

118

lunch.

Cyrus had inquired about it toward the end of the first year of his incumbency. 'Seems to me,' he said to the member who sat beside him at the luncheon table, 'that we have the same subjects on the agenda for each meeting, and most of them we don't ever get around to discussing.'

The other winked. 'We're not really expected to, you know. None of us have the knowledge of what's involved. How could we, when we come down for a couple of hours four times a year? Take this Black Studies thing, for instance. We don't know what's involved in getting teachers, or students, for that matter. We have no idea of what money is involved and whether we can afford it or not. See, we don't set policy because we can't. That's what Prex is for.'

'You mean this is all a charade? We don't make policy? We just come and sit around for a couple of hours, are given lunch, and then go home so we can tell our friends we're involved in running an educational institution?'

'Is it any different in a large business corporation? Doesn't the chairman usually decide what he wants to do, and then doesn't the board go along with it? We don't make policy, but we do have a function. We act as a kind of brake.'

'A brake?'

'That's right. If Prex goes off his chump and gets some crazy notion in his head, we're here to tell him he can't do it. See, we don't tell him what to do; we just tell him what he can't do. Take last year when Prex wanted to change the name. Now that called for a two-thirds majority, so there was no trouble voting it down. Most things call for a plain majority, though, and it's not so easy vetoing them because this Macomber is a wily bird, and he's usually pretty sure he's got a majority before he brings it up for a vote.'

And now, several years later, the question of changing the name of the school was again on the agenda. And this time it was the first item listed. He wondered if that meant that Macomber thought he had a chance of getting it passed. Or was it his last desperate effort to get the matter settled one way or the other? He decided to see President Macomber.

The next day he made a point of driving into Boston. After lunch he drove to the college. Instead of waiting in the anteroom as he usually did, he asked the secretary to tell the president that he wanted to see him, and a few minutes later he was ushered into the office.

'I got the agenda for the Board of Trustees meeting yesterday, and I thought I'd drop by and see if I could be of any help to you on any of the items you're particularly interested in and want to be sure of passing.'

120

'Well, that's very kind of you, Cyrus. I can't think of anything at the moment. Over the last few months I've heard from various members of the board, and there seems to be pretty general agreement.'

'I notice the first item, the change of name, that calls for a two-thirds majority. Is there, er—general agreement on that?'

'Anything that calls for a two-thirds majority is an iffy thing. I put it in because one of the board members suggested we vote on it again.'

'That was Levine, I suppose, who made the suggestion, I mean.'

'No ... I haven't spoken to Mark in some time. I think it was Raymond Oliver who suggested it. He came to see me because he was concerned about the course in Medieval History and the man who's giving it, a George Spenser, friend of his, I think, or a relative. The History Department put up his name for tenure. Know anything about it?'

'Spenser? No, Professor Sherwood hasn't given me the names of the History candidates yet. Actually, the names go to the dean and he passes them on to me as soon as he gets them.'

'How about the other departments?' Macomber said. 'How about the English Department?'

'No, I haven't heard from Sugrue yet. Is there any urgency?'

'Not really. I won't be announcing the appointments until after the board meeting. Because sometimes the board approves an item that involves a sizable increase in our expenditure, and as a result the money involved in the salary increases that go with tenure just aren't there.'

As he left the president's office, Cyrus Merton tried to assess what he had learned, if anything, from the meeting. Macomber had said nothing about the name change, except that the chances were iffy. Did that mean that he thought he had the necessary votes, but wasn't sure? And then he had shifted the conversation to the matter of tenure. And he had asked specifically about the English Department. Why not the Math or the Physics or the Sociology departments? Was he, perhaps, hinting that if Merton wanted tenure for Victor Joyce, he'd better vote the right way on the change of name?

He would have liked to consult with other members of the board, but he had never become friendly with any of them. They were polite to him when they met at the quarterly meetings, but that was all. Most were from old New England families, and their money was old money. Their values were different, and so were their interests. And they were all college men, graduates of New England colleges, for the most part.

Then he thought of Charles Dobson who

was the only other Catholic on the board. Dobson was a large friendly man who had played football for Dartmouth. Occasionally he would make some remark about nuns or the Pope, and then turn to him as another Catholic and wink. He felt he could talk to Dobson, and he remembered that he was another who had voted against the change of name the last time it had come up. He owned a large Cadillac agency in Boston. Well, although his car was barely two years old, there was no harm in checking out the Cadillac line. If Dobson had a really good deal . . .

To the salesman who came forward, he said, 'I'm just kind of looking around. Er, Mr. Dobson around?'

The salesman pointed. 'He's in his office there.'

The door of the office was open and Merton walked in. Instantly, Dobson's broad face broke into a smile. 'Merton, isn't it?'

'That's right, Cyrus Merton.'

'Sit down, Cy. Trade-in time? The old bus acting up? I got something out in the yard.'

'Oh, I was just driving by and I remembered that you had this place, so I thought I'd stop and say hello.'

'Well, that was mighty thoughtful of you, Cy. But now that you're here—'

'I've just been to see President Macomber,' Merton went on hastily. 'See, I got a copy of the agenda yesterday. Did you get one, Mr. Dobson?'

'Charlie. Call me Charlie. Everybody does. Yeah, I got one. It's around here someplace. What about it?'

'Did you notice that the first item was on the proposal to change the name of the college?'

'So?'

'So I wondered if he had the votes for the change. It takes a two-thirds majority, you know.'

'I know. And what did Prex say?'

'He didn't say anything. He said it was iffy. Now, you voted against it the last time it came up.'

'And you wonder if I will again? Probably. But it's a damn silly business. The school was never Christian and was never endowed by any church of any denomination whatsoever. The net effect of calling it Windermere Christian is to establish it as parochial.'

'Then why do you vote against changing the name?'

'Because our fellow trustee, George Farquahr Ridgeway the Third asked me to. And George Farquahr Ridgeway the Third comes all the way down from Augusta, Maine, to trade in his Cadillac every three years no matter how well it's running. He's against changing the name because his great-grandfather, or maybe it was his

124

great-great-grandfather, who was a Congregational minister, was on the first board, and that gives him a sense of continuity. And the others, why do they vote against the change? Well, there's Billy Chamberlain, who is against change in general. He'd be using a horse and buggy if he could get a stable boy to harness it up for him. And Burton Stover who opposes Prex and the majority in everything to show that he's an independent spirit. The others are in opposition for equally petty or frivolous reasons, although I guess with you, Cy, it's because you feel you're defending the faith.'

'Well, I think it's important. And I don't understand why the rest of the board, and President Macomber, are so anxious to change it.'

'You don't, huh? Have you ever wondered why they want to serve on the board at all?'

'I—I suppose they're that is, we're all interested in education.'

'You really think so? And those who are on twenty other boards, ranging from the Seaman's Retirement Home to the local hospital and the town library, are interested in all those things? No, Cy, it's because it's considered a kind of honor. Now if you're interested in honor, which would you rather be, a trustee of say, Holy Cross, which is unknown outside of New England, or of Harvard, which is known throughout the

125

world? Even if you were a bishop, I'll bet you'd choose Harvard. Of course, those who come from the wilds of northern Maine and New Hampshire and Vermont might serve because it gives them a chance to visit the big city a few times a year. And some, like my friend Ridgeway, have a family tradition of public service which they want to retain. They're too delicate to soil their hands by running for public office, so they go in for this kind of thing instead.' His face relaxed in a broad grin.

'And you think that's why Macomber is so anxious to change the name, so he won't be president of a parochial institution?'

'I'm sure of it.' He studied Merton's glum face. 'Something bothering you?'

'I've been sort of wondering. I went in to see him about the agenda, and he immediately switched the conversation to the subject of tenure. Now, Victor Joyce, who is married to my niece, is up for tenure in the English Department, and I'm wondering if—'

'If he offered you a *quid pro quo?* Tenure for your niece's husband in exchange for your vote on the name change? Oh, very possible. He's a cunning, artful rascal, our Prex.'

'He said he wouldn't announce the list for tenure until after the board meeting,' said Merton gloomily.

'Then you can be sure that's it.' He shook his head in admiration of Macomber's craftiness.

'So what can I do? I can't, I just can't vote against my conscience.'

'It's a tough one,' Dobson admitted judiciously. Then his face relaxed in a smile. 'Tell you what. When next you see him, don't get involved in any conversation about the name change. If he should ask you outright how you are going to vote, tell him you haven't decided yet. Then at the board meeting, when the matter comes up, you ask for a secret ballot. Or if you think that's obvious, then I will.'

'You will?' Merton considered, then he, too, smiled. 'Yes, that should do it. Thank you.'

With a deprecatory shrug, Dobson said, 'Don't mention it. But when you get around to trading in your car, give me a crack at it, will you?'

'Oh, I will, I will.'

CHAPTER EIGHTEEN

On the one or two nights a week that Alice Saxon and Victor Joyce saw each other, she was careful to shoo him out by nine o'clock. When he protested that he had hoped to stay the night, she said, 'Look, use a little common sense. If word got out that we were having an affair, you might just as well forget about tenure.'

'How would word get out?'

'In this section of town, I'm surrounded by college students, and faculty, too. There are two students from B.U. living right in this building.'

'But you say they're from B.U.'

'And you're certain they don't know or date any students from Windermere? Look, Victor, we've got to be circumspect. Where did you park your car?'

'Around the corner. It was the only place I could find.'

'Well, you plan on parking it there, or some distance away every time you come. We can't be too careful.'

'But when I get tenure?'

'We'll still have to be circumspect.'

'Why, if we both have tenure—'

'Windermere is a pretty conservative school. The Board of Trustees certainly is, and a good portion of the faculty, too. I'm an associate professor. I'd like a full professorship someday. If there were any question about my lifestyle, it would probably be withheld. When you get tenure, *and* a Church-approved separation, *and* a civil divorce, then maybe we can relax a little because it would be considered legitimate courting.'

'But when we get here around four or five

o'clock, and I stay till nine, don't you think it would occur to anyone who might be interested that part of that time is spent in bed?'

'Sure, to people whose minds run that way. But we are both legitimate scholars, and most people would assume that we're working on a paper together, or that you're editing my manuscript of a book.'

And to give verisimilitude to the idea, when he was leaving, she would make a point of calling out to him as he started downstairs, 'You won't forget about those notes, will you? And be sure and check that quotation.'

Occasionally, she did let him stay over on a Friday night. 'Because all the kids go away for the weekend, and we don't have to go in to school the next day, and because every now and then I like to wake up in the morning and feel a man in my bed.'

She was convincing, and yet there was always in back of his mind a tiny shred of doubt. When she sent him away in what was still the early part of the evening, was it because she was worried about him, or was it possible that she was expecting another visitor? And what of those nights when she refused to see him? He recalled that once or twice when he had arranged to spend the evening with her and she had canceled the appointment, he had seen her earlier lunching with Mordecai Jacobs and seemingly enjoying it.

★   ★   ★

The faculty dinner was held at the end of the week of final exams. On Friday, Alice cooked dinner for him and he stayed the night, but the next day she insisted that he leave early, shortly after noon. 'You're going to the dinner tonight, aren't you? Well, you'll have to change and—'

'But that won't take any time at all,' Victor objected.

'And I've got a bunch of blue books to grade so that I can get my marks in.'

'You've got all week for that.'

'You have because you've got only freshmen and sophomores, but I've got seniors, and their grades have to be in by Monday.'

'So you've got all day Sunday.'

'I've got other plans for Sunday.'

He knew better than to ask what they were. She had made it very plain, early on, that their relationship did not give him the right to intrude on her private life. 'So how are you getting to the dinner?' he asked.

'I've made arrangements. Arlene Winsor, French Department, is picking me up.'

He finally left, but he was reluctant to leave the city and go back to Barnard's Crossing, if only because Margaret did not work

Saturdays and might be around the house all afternoon. It was a warm, sunny day and he found it pleasant to just stroll along the streets. When he got hungry, he stopped in at a fast food restaurant and had a hamburger and coffee while he stared out of the window at people passing by. It was only when he thought of going back to the counter for dessert and another cup of coffee that it occurred to him that he did not have enough money to pay for them. He had planned to cash a check and forgotten. And now the banks were closed.

He was not too concerned, however. He had no plans for the evening except to go to the faculty dinner, and he had a ticket for that, and he thought there was some money in the top drawer of his bureau. He stayed in the city until late in the afternoon, reluctant to go home before he actually had to.

★   ★   ★

It was also late in the afternoon when Professor Mordecai Jacobs called Alice Saxon. 'Hey Alice, my girl just called. She's really insistent about my coming to her kid brother's Bar Mitzvah party tonight. Do you really think I have to go to the faculty dinner?'

'Your department head is on the committee.'

'But I bought a ticket.'

'Not good enough, Mord. You want him to see you. And Victor Joyce is going to be there. Keep that in mind. I don't know how things work in the English Department on the business of tenure, but I'm sure that Professor Sugrue has a lot to say about it. All right, you and Joyce are competing for the one tenured position. Suppose that in Sugrue's view of things you're all even, you and Joyce. But Joyce shows the old team spirit, whereas Jacobs doesn't appear to give a damn. Get it?'

'All right, all right, I'll go. Clara said Breverton was not far from Barnard's Crossing. I suppose I could go to the Bar Mitzvah party after I get out of the dinner.'

'That's the spirit, Mord. If I get there before you, I'll save a seat for you, and you do the same for me if you get there first. Otherwise I'll have to sit with Arlene Winsor, and she'll be with members of her department and they'll talk French all evening.'

'Okay. See you.'

CHAPTER NINETEEN

Except for Sundays, when they went to church together and to the Mertons for dinner, Victor and Margaret tended to avoid each other. They were indeed like a couple of strangers living in the same rooming house. They were polite to each other when they happened to meet, but nothing more. He ate all his meals out, and when he was home for an evening, he stayed either in his study or in his bedroom. She usually sat in the living room and read or watched TV, or went up to her bedroom, in which case she always locked the door with the bolt lest he misinterpret her retirement and try to follow. On the rare occasions when he, too, wanted to watch the TV program that she was watching, he came into the living room and took a seat at the back of the room, at some distance from her. Because he still felt guilty, he was never comfortable in her presence.

On the evening of the faculty dinner, Victor dawdled in the city and contrived to get home shortly after six o'clock, which gave him just enough time to shave, shower, and change. He transferred the contents of the pockets of his slacks, including his wallet, to the trousers of his dark gray suit. His wallet was empty of money and he'd found none in the bureau, but it held his driver's license and his ticket to the dinner. For a moment, it occurred to him that he might ask Margaret to lend him some money, but he immediately dismissed the idea; he did not expect to need money for the evening, and he disliked the idea of asking her.

She was in the living room reading a book when he came downstairs. He was a little surprised when she lowered her book and said, 'My aunt was here this afternoon.'

'Have a nice visit?' he asked politely, puzzled that she should bother to tell him.

'She had occasion to use the bathroom. She went to the one in the hallway, but the light didn't work.'

'Yeah, sometimes you've got to flip the switch a couple of times—a faulty connection.'

'So she went to the one in my room, and I'm sure she saw the bolt on the door.'

'What did she say when she came down?'

Margaret shook her head. 'She didn't say anything, just that she had to run along, and she left.'

'Wanted to discuss it with your uncle first, I suppose.'

'That's what I think.'

'I'll know soon enough. He's coming to the dinner.'

*   *   *

As he drove to Breverton, he considered the situation. There was no doubt in his mind that Agnes would tell Cyrus. Well, let her. He had made a bargain with Cyrus: he would marry his niece and in exchange he would get tenure. He had kept his part of the bargain.

134

That it had not turned out as expected was not his fault. He had done only what was natural. He would insist that Cyrus keep his part of the bargain. And he could, he told himself. She wanted a separation and a civil divorce. He was not sure what was required for the Church-approved separation, but he was certain that his cooperation would be necessary for the civil divorce. He would demand tenure as the price of his cooperation.

When he arrived at the parking lot of the Breverton Country Club, he noticed that the needle of his gas gauge was on Empty. It was obviously not his day; first Alice pushing him out of her apartment so early, then finding that he had no money in his wallet, then Margaret telling him about the visit of her aunt, and now an empty gas tank. He tried to remember what the car manual had said about the number of gallons of gas remaining when the needle touched Empty. He was sure there was enough to get home on, especially if he went by way of Pine Grove Road. But how long had it been on Empty?

$$\star \qquad \star \qquad \star$$

Back in the house on the Point, Agnes was telling her brother of her visit to their niece. 'I know things weren't going well almost from the beginning. When they'd come here, she'd always call him Victor.'

'Well, that's his name, isn't it?'

'A young bride, you'd think she'd call him 'dear' or some pet name. Not even Vic, but always Victor, as though she had just met him.'

'It's probably just a temporary falling out,' he urged.

'With a bolt on the bedroom door that she must have hired a carpenter to put on? And all his things in the guest room?'

She went on and on, blaming Cyrus for having pushed for the marriage before they had really got to know each other. Finally, he said, 'Look, I'll drive up to Breverton with him and find out what it's all about.'

But when he phoned, Margaret told him that Victor had already left.

'Okay,' he said to his sister, 'so I'll see him at the dinner and I'll get it straightened out. Maybe I'll drive home with him, and that will give me a chance to talk to both of them.'

'But you were planning to just have a drink and then leave.'

'So I'll stay for the dinner and leave when it's over. I'll have him drive back in my car, and then he can run up there tomorrow with Peg and retrieve his.'

*   *   *

Miriam had persuaded the rabbi to go to the

late movie. They were already out the door when the phone rang. As the rabbi turned to go back, she said, 'Let it ring. They can leave a message on the answering machine.'

'And I'll be wondering all through the movie who it was,' said the rabbi as he hurried back indoors. He talked for a few minutes and then rejoined Miriam, waiting impatiently at the door.

'It was Simcha,' he announced.

'He called from Chicago?'

'No, from Gloucester. He'd been to the wedding.'

'Oh. I thought he had decided not to go, since we hadn't heard from him.'

'Well, he didn't want to call on the Sabbath. He'd thought to call us early Sunday morning. But one of the guests is driving down to Boston tonight right after the wedding feast, and he told Simcha that he goes right by Barnard's Crossing. So Simcha thought maybe his friend could drop him off here, that is, if he could stay over. Of course, I told him he could. He can use Jonathon's room.'

'What time is he coming? Does that mean we can't go to the movie?'

'He figures, or his friend figures, he can come by around half past ten. That's about the time we get out of the movie. So I suggested he have his friend drop him off at the Donut Shop in the Mall, and we'll pick

137

him up. If we get there before him, we'll wait. And if he gets there before us, he'll wait and we'll be sure to be along shortly.'

'But doesn't the Donut Shop close—'

'Not until midnight on Saturdays. He can have a cup of coffee, and we'll be along, probably before he finishes.'

CHAPTER TWENTY

From the number of cars in the parking lot, Victor judged that he was among the later arrivals. He parked his car and hastened across the lawn to the steps that led up to the wide veranda that surrounded the clubhouse. The evening was warm, and a few of the guests were standing around leaning against the railing, drinks in hand. As he mounted the stairs, one or two nodded to him, but he had no inclination to stop and talk. All the way to Breverton he had been thinking of what he might say to Cyrus Merton. If Merton were to ask him outright about the bolt on the door, he might laugh it off and explain that such was his ardor that he and Peg felt it was the only safe way to curb it during the period when she was vulnerable, and that he would be sharing the bedroom with her once her infertile period began. Or should he tell him straight out that the marriage was a failure and that Margaret was planning to get a civil divorce? Or would Merton pretend not to know? Or would he wait until after church tomorrow, perhaps when they were both there for dinner? Or would...

A large double door, now standing open, led to a comfortable lounge with overstuffed leather chairs, and just beyond was the main dining room. On one side of the lounge was a small anteroom which served as the coatroom, and opposite was a small alcove where the bar had been set up. Although some were sitting about in the lounge, and a group was clustered around the bar, Victor could see that the majority were already seated at the tables in the dining room, or wandering around looking for a place to their liking. At a table in the middle of the room, he saw Alice Saxon, and beside her was his colleague and rival, Mordecai Jacobs. Victor Joyce felt that he badly needed a drink.

His ticket had a section at one end that could be torn off along a perforated line and exchanged for one free drink at the bar. He proceeded to make the exchange without delay.

'Whiskey. Scotch,' he ordered.

'Right. Water? Soda? Ice cube?'

'Nothing. Straight.' The depression caused by the sequence of the day's events required the treatment of whiskey undiluted. He tossed off his drink in a couple of swallows and felt a little better. He would have liked another drink, to sip at slowly, but his wallet was empty. He wandered about the room for a few minutes in the hope of seeing someone he knew well enough to ask for a loan, but the one or two possible were engaged in conversation and it would have been awkward. Noticing that the bar was at the moment free of customers, he strolled over. To the barman, who was idle, he said, 'Look, I forgot my wallet, but I'd like another drink. I'll—'

'You know I can't, Professor,' said the barman reproachfully. 'I'm not allowed to cuff drinks, the same rules as the taverns.'

'Oh sure, I understand.'

He noticed Alice Saxon was seemingly alone; at least, Jacobs was not in evidence. He hurried over to her table, and when she looked up at him, he asked jokingly, 'Where's your boyfriend?'

'The men's room, I suppose. Why? Do you want to see him?'

'Why didn't you tell me you were driving up with him?'

'Because I wasn't. I came up with Arlene Winsor. And I'm going back with her. I didn't want to sit with her because she is sitting with a couple of people from her department, and they talk French half the time. Oh, there's Cyrus Merton just come in.'

He turned around and saw that Cyrus had spotted him. He waved, and Cyrus smiled and beckoned to him. 'Look, I'd better go and talk to him. How about tomorrow? If I come in town, can we have dinner together?'

'Give me a ring in the afternoon,' she said, 'and I'll see how I feel then.'

He hurried over to where Cyrus was standing, just inside the dining room. He felt much better, almost euphoric. His jealousy of Mordecai Jacobs appeared to be groundless, and he was sure Alice Saxon would meet him tomorrow for dinner, and what was more, Cyrus was smiling in a most friendly fashion as he approached.

'I thought we'd drive up together,' said the older man, 'but Peg said you'd already left.' No hint that he was aware of a rift or a disagreement between Victor and his niece.

'Yeah, well I always come up to Breverton by way of Pine Grove, but this time I decided to go by the state road. I knew it was quite a bit longer, so I started out earlier. Say, how are you fixed for money? I meant to cash a check this morning, but I forgot, and I don't have a dime on me. And I'm low on gas.'

'Sure.' The old man drew out his wallet and held it open to him. 'Take what you need.' There were two fifty-dollar bills, three tens, and in a separate compartment, several ones.

'All right if I take the tens?'

'Help yourself.'

'I'll pay you back—'

'Anytime, my boy, anytime. But look here, if you're low on gas, why not plan on leaving your car here, and I'll drive you home. Then tomorrow you can drive up with Peg in her car and retrieve yours.'

'Oh, I'm sure I've got enough gas to get home on, but all right.'

At this point Professor Gates, who was the chairman of the Dinner Committee, came hurrying up. 'Oh, there you are, Mr. Merton. We're about to begin, and you are sitting at the head table.'

'Oh, all right.' To Victor he said, 'I'll see you later. By the way, where are you sitting?'

Victor looked around, and said, 'Oh, I'll sit here,' and pulled out a chair from the table where they were standing, where the dining room adjoined the lounge. It was farthest from the head table and behind a pillar, and out of sight of the occupants of the head table, which was probably why it was still vacant.

'Okay, I'll see you after the dinner,' said Merton, and allowed himself to be led away by the chairman. No sooner had he gone than Victor made his way to the bar. He ordered a double whiskey, and slapped one of the bills Cyrus had given him on the counter.

'Wine is being served at the tables,' said the barman.

'I can't stand the stuff,' said Victor. 'Put an ice cube and a thimble of soda in it.'

When he returned to his seat, he found that soup had already been served to his table. He tried a spoonful and then pushed the plate away. 'Whew, that's hot,' he remarked.

'It is a little peppery,' said the occupant of the next seat.

'Well, I'll stick with something cool,' said Victor, and sipped at his drink. He sat back and looked about him. He knew none of the others at his table. He had seen them about in the corridors and in the faculty lounge, of course, but he knew none of them by name. They were all in mathematics or the sciences, and he could not understand what they were talking about most of the time. But he was content.

He toyed with his salad, and finding that the dressing was sharp, he alleviated it with sips from his drink. Before he had finished, he noticed that his glass was empty and went back to the bar for a refill. There was a good deal of wandering about during the salad course, and he, too, did not return immediately to his table. He circled the room, nodding to the occasional greetings of those who knew him, but glancing frequently at the table where Alice Saxon was seated with Jacobs. Once, he came near the head table, and spotting Cyrus, he raised his glass in greeting Cyrus smiled and waved to him.

By the time he was ready to return to his seat, he noticed that more than half of his drink was gone. He made his way to the bar.

He held out his glass and said, 'Top it off, will you, Jack?'

'I'll have to charge you for another drink, Professor.'

'Of course.' And he slapped another bill on the counter. And because the bartender had filled it close to the brim, Victor held it out in front of him like a lighted candle and set it down carefully when he reached his table before he sat down. It occurred to him that quite suddenly his luck had changed and Fate was moving things in his favor. How things had changed in a few short hours! He had thought he'd lost Alice to his rival, Jacobs, and now he had practically arranged to spend Sunday evening, and maybe the night, with her. He had thought that his arrangement with Cyrus Merton was all over. He had expected him to be angry, that he would demand an explanation. And here he was as friendly as could be, suggesting that they ride home together. Cyrus had even given him money.

In the glow of the whiskey, and the new situation in which he found himself, he toyed with various possibilities. Suppose he were to leave now and drive home. If Peg were immersed in TV, or were up in her room, he might be able to swap his car for hers, which

144

he was sure had plenty of gas, and then he could come back before the dinner was over. He was sure he would be able to persuade Alice to tell her friend Arlene that she had changed her plans, and then let him drive her home. In which case he would of course spend the night with her. Or he might drive to Lynn, to an all-night gas station—he was sure he had enough gas to reach it—fill up there and drive back to Breverton for Alice. He chuckled.

'Something funny?' asked his neighbor.

'I just thought of something.' What he had thought of was that it would be the cream of the jest to make use of Merton's money to take Alice Saxon to bed. Or for that matter, on the alternative plan, to use Peg's car for the same purpose.

The waitress brought the main course, roast beef, and asked if he wanted red wine or white.

He dismissed her with a wave of the hand. 'No wine,' he said. 'Can't stand the stuff.' Then noticing that his glass was empty, he made his way to the bar for a refill. He returned with his glass, set it beside his plate and began to eat.

'Meat's pretty tough,' he murmured as he sawed away.

'You're using the wrong side of the knife,' said his neighbor.

'Oh, yeah.' And to relieve his

embarrassment, he took a long swig of his whiskey. He cut off a large piece of meat and chewed away at it mechanically, stopping every now and then to take a sip of his drink to aid mastication. Then he spasmodically swallowed the portion, still unchewed, that was left in his mouth. He felt a lump in his gullet and took a long swallow of his drink to ease it down.

Finding his glass empty, he suspected the bartender had given him a short drink. He decided it was beneath his dignity to accuse the man, but that from now on he would watch him as he poured. He made his way to the bar. He did not weave, and his walk was not unsteady, but it was very careful as he planted one foot in front of the other with studied concentration.

To the bartender he said, 'L'me have another drink.'

'I'm sorry, Professor, I'm afraid I can't serve you.'

'Why not? I got money.'

'I'm sorry, but the same rules apply like in a tavern.'

'You saying I'm drunk?'

'We've got to think of our license, Professor.'

'Well, ya know what you can do with your goddamn license, and your goddamn drink, too. I'm getting out of the goddamn place.' Abruptly, he turned away and crossed the lounge to the coatroom. To the coatroom attendant he said, 'Getting out a here. Gimme m'coat.' He fished in his pocket for a coin to toss on the plate on the shelf of the coatroom door, and came up empty-handed.

'Yes sir, may I have the check?'

As he fished again, the attendant said, 'Leaving early?'

Victor raised his left hand clenched in a fist and squinted carefully at the watch on the inside of his wrist. 'Not so early,' he said. 'Almost ten, quarter of. Gotta get home. Can't find the check.'

'Well, can you describe the coat?'

'Yeah. S'light brown, you know, beige. Got a belt. Nev'mind. 'Member now, left it in the car.' He turned with almost military precision and marched purposefully to the door.

CHAPTER TWENTY-ONE

Once a year the AFLINLMS—which stood for Association of Former Local Interns from Non-Local Medical Schools; the name kept expanding to more and more ridiculous lengths over the years—met in the Blue Room ('suitable for small parties of thirty or less') of the Breverton Country Club for dinner and an evening of high jinks. It had started twenty years ago with a membership of eight who had come with their wives and girlfriends—the latter for the most part nurses at the hospitals where they were interning—and had increased to a maximum set at a dozen. Over the years some had dropped out or moved out of the area—one had died—and a few had been added. In the early days the talk at the dinner table had been largely of the politics in their respective hospitals, their working conditions, and the opportunities for advancement. Nowadays, all of them now successful, the talk was apt to be about their stock portfolios, their vacation homes in Vermont, and the high cost of insurance. The wives talked about their children, the difficulty of getting decent household help, and the clothes they had bought or were hunting for.

The evening always ended with a fun meeting with silly suggestions offered as formal motions to be debated at length mock seriously and finally voted on.

'Mr. Chairman, I wish to make an amendment to the amendment of Dr. Herman—'

'What was Dr. Herman's amendment?'

'I don't know, I wasn't listening, but any amendment that Dr. Herman makes I want to make an amendment to.'

The chairman, whose badge of office was a head mirror, called for order by tapping on a gong—kept by the club for their meetings—with a rubber patella hammer. 'We'll now have a discussion of Dr. Larson's amendment, unstated, to Dr. Herman's amendment, unknown.'

That was the way their meetings usually went, but occasionally some things were offered seriously, and seriously debated and voted on. One, passed a good ten years before, had been to hold their dinners on Saturday nights instead of on Fridays, and to adjourn no later than ten o'clock since several of the members had early morning hospital rounds the next day and a long way to travel home. Another, passed only a few years back, had been to make the occasion formal with the men in black tie and the women in long gowns. It added to the fun of the thing to dress up for an occasion of no significance whatsoever.

Now, at ten o'clock as they headed for their cars in the parking lot, Sam Johnson, who had been the chairman for that particular meeting—they changed for each meeting— called out, 'Hey, you guys who are heading south on the state highway, the waiter said the State Troopers have set up a trap just below here, and they're pulling cars over. The bastards do it every time there's a big bash in the main dining room. If they smell liquor on your breath, they'll make you walk a straight line to prove you're not drunk, or maybe even make you blow into a breathalyzer.'

'So we'll go by way of Pine Grove Road,' said Mimi Gorfinkle to her ophthalmologist husband, Abner. The Gorfinkles lived in Barnard's Crossing.

'Why should we go Pine Grove Road?'

'Because you smell like a brewery. That's all you need is to have the State Troopers arrest you for drunk driving'

'I only had one drink.'

'You had two. I was watching. And that glass of beer that you spilled on your shirt.'

'Only half a glass of beer. Half I spilled. Okay, we'll go Pine Grove.'

Dr. Gorfinkle, small, rabbit-faced, and bald, was a careful driver, and even on Pine Grove Road with no traffic in either direction, he drove at a very moderate rate of speed. Beside him, Mimi, tall, large-breasted, with carefully coiffed blond hair, had dozed off, replete with rich food and wine. Suddenly, Gorfinkle applied the brakes and she awoke with a start. 'Whatsamatter?'

'Look—on the right.'

It was a car whose crumpled hood was wrapped almost halfway around the trunk of a tree as though clutching it in powerful jaws. 'Let me have the flashlight in the glove compartment,' he said. 'You wait here.'

He got out and swept the roadway with the light of his flashlight. 'Must've skidded on that patch of mud,' he called out. By the light of his flashlight he saw that the driver behind the wheel had slid down so that his head rested on the back of the seat below the headrest. His right hand was flung back and lay on the passenger seat, the other hung limp, palm down, on the shattered glass of the side window. His mouth was open and the doctor saw that he was breathing. Gingerly, Gorfinkle reached in and turned off the ignition. The motor was dead, but he had heard it was a good idea. Before withdrawing his hand, he let his fingertips rest lightly on the pulse at the throat. It was rapid and thready, but not alarmingly so. He came back to the passenger side of his car and motioned to his wife to lower the window. 'Let me have the box of tissues, will you.'

There were numerous cuts on the victim's face, and he wanted to make sure that none were serious. He dabbed the man's face and satisfied himself that they were superficial.

'Don't you dare do anything, Abner,' his wife called out. 'Remember what happened to Bill Sawyer when he played Good Samaritan a couple of years ago. He was sued for malpractice.'

He got back into his car and told his wife, 'He's unconscious, concussion.'

'So what are you going to do?'

'I'll notify the police, of course, What else can I do? What does the trip gauge say?'

'Five and seven-tenth miles. Why?'

151

'I'm wondering if it's worth going back. I'm not sure, but I think we are about as near to Barnard's Crossing as we are to Breverton.'

'You'll leave him just like that?'

'Well, do you want to get out and wait here while I go for the police?'

'Couldn't we wait and flag down a car?'

'On this road, this time of night? It could be an hour or more before another car came along.'

'But to just leave him . . .'

'Look, there's nothing I can do for the guy.'

He drove even slower the rest of the way, his speedometer rarely registering above thirty-five miles an hour. Shortly after they finally left Pine Grove Road, they came to an outdoor pay phone and he stopped the car.

'Why are we stopping?' she asked.

'So I can phone the police, of course.'

'That's silly. We're almost home. You can call them from there.'

But when they got home and he reached for the phone, she said, 'You get out of those clothes first.'

He looked at her in amazement. 'Why do I have to get undressed to phone the police?'

'Because they might send someone down to question you about it, and if he smells the beer on your shirt and cummerbund, he might think you had something to do with the accident.'

He knew better than to argue with her, so he undressed and put on a robe. Then he called the police.

'Barnard's Crossing Police Department. Sergeant Pierce speaking.'

'This is Dr. Gorfinkle, 23 Laurel Road.'

'Yes, Doctor. What can I do for you?'

'Well, I was just coming home from Breverton on the Pine Grove Road, and there was an accident. I don't mean that I was in it, but I saw this car. It had slammed into a tree. The driver was unconscious behind the wheel.'

'Passengers?'

'I didn't see any. I mean there were none in the car. Of course, there might have been and they could have gone off for help.'

'Just where on Pine Grove Road was this, Doctor?'

'Where? Just off the road.'

'I mean, was it before or after the boundary marker coming from Breverton?'

'Boundary marker?'

'Yeah, you know, the sign that says You Are Now Entering Barnard's Crossing'

'I didn't notice any sign. I mean it would be on the side of the road, wouldn't it? And I was keeping my eyes straight ahead of me on the road. Is it important?'

'Well, sure, if it's on the Breverton side of the line, they've got to handle it and—'

'Well, I can tell you how far it is from the

Breverton Country Club. It was five and seven-tenths miles.'

'How do you know that?'

'I've got one of those trip things on my odometer. You just press a button and these three numbers all go back to zero. I got into the habit of pressing the button every time I get into the car. That way, I always know just how far I've driven. So I looked at the trip gauge when I stopped and it was five-point-seven miles.'

'Five point seven. Just a minute.'

The doctor waited, his fingers drumming nervously on the telephone table. Finally, the sergeant came back on the line, 'Hello, Doctor? By our measurements on the map, I think the accident occurred in Breverton.'

'You mean, I've got to call them?'

'No, we'll call them. Now, can you give me an idea of how seriously he was hurt.'

'I didn't examine him. I'm an ophthalmologist, an eye doctor. I didn't want to touch anything. There might be broken bones or—you know, it's dangerous to move a man in that condition unless you know exactly what you're doing. I didn't touch anything except that I took his pulse and that seemed all right, a little thready perhaps. I reached in and turned off the ignition. The motor was dead but I read somewhere that it's a good idea to turn off the ignition.'

'I see. All right, we'll take care of it.'

Professor Mordecai Jacobs shook his head at the waitress who had stopped to refill coffee cups, and said to Alice Saxon, a hint of irritation in his voice, 'How long do these things last anyway? Do you have any idea?'

'Oh, there are always speeches,' she said, 'and usually resolutions are offered which are discussed and voted on. An hour or more, I'd say. But you can go now, if you like. Victor Joyce left some time ago.'

'Are you sure?'

'Well, I saw him go over to the coatroom and then go out the front door. That was a good fifteen minutes ago and he hasn't come back, so I guess he left for good.'

'Then I think I'll be going along.'

'To the Bar Mitzvah? Well, have fun.'

He nodded, and then he rose and sidled through the tables to the lounge. He looked back for a moment to see if perhaps Professor Sugrue was looking in his direction, and then strode purposefully to the front door. He paused momentarily on the veranda at the head of the stairs leading down to the parking lot. Hearing footsteps behind him, he turned. It was the young man who had been attending the coatroom.

'You leaving early, too, Professor?'

'Oh, hello—Aherne, isn't it?'

'That's right.'

'I have another engagement—in Barnard's Crossing. You taking a breather?'

'No, I'm through for the night. I work only until ten.'

'Then who's minding the store?'

'Oh, Mary Ellen, one of the regular waitresses.'

'Then she gets the tips?'

'No, the waitresses pool the tips, both what's left on the tables and what's left in the dish at the coatroom. I guess they figure a woman in the coatroom will draw more tips than a man. I just get paid by the hour.'

'That's very interesting. You live in Breverton?'

'No, in Swampscott, just beyond Barnard's Crossing, the next town. Ah, there's my jalopy.' He got out his keys. As Jacobs was about to walk on, he said, 'Oh, Professor, I've been meaning to ask you. '

'Yes?'

'The Survey course. All sections cover the same ground and take the same final. Right?'

'That's right. Each instructor emphasizes those aspects that interest him, but we cover the same ground, and we get together and make up one exam for all sections.'

'Well, this girl I used to go with, she was in Professor Joyce's section. After the exam, she thought she'd flubbed it. Two questions she didn't answer at all, and then there were a couple she was sure she got wrong—'

'Ah, that was first semester. There were ten essay-type questions.'

'That's right, first semester. I thought I did pretty good. I answered all questions. And you gave me a B.'

'That's pretty good.'

'Yes, but Joyce gave her an A, and like I said, there were two questions she didn't answer at all.'

'Well, grading essay-type exams is a pretty subjective business. Sometimes a student will concentrate on one or two questions, and his essays on those are so good, you might overlook his failure to answer the other questions. But this semester we used an objective type exam. How did your marks compare for the second semester?'

'I don't know. We kind of stopped seeing each other.'

'But you did well, I recall.'

'I guess so. You gave me a B plus.'

'Well, I didn't give many of those. Believe me.' He waved in dismissal, called out, 'Have a good summer,' and headed for his car.

He got into his car, eased out of the parking lot, and headed for Barnard's Crossing.

It was only after he'd reached the Crossing and made the turn onto Abbot Road that he realized his mistake in not reviewing the directions Clara had given him before he started. She had advised him quite specifically which road to take from the country club to Barnard's Crossing, and it was obvious as he now looked at the directions and noted the cross streets that he should've taken the other. He was on Abbot Road, yes, but the directions she had given him to reach the Charleton section didn't match with what he was seeing, and he was utterly confused. He was on the point of turning back when the police cruiser came along Abbot Road. He honked, and the cruiser stopped.

'I'm looking for the Charleton section,' he said.

'Right. Take your third left and go all the way. Then take another left.'

The directions were clear enough, but when he came to the Charleton section, he found that it was a large development with roads that turned every which way and with street signs that were only dimly lit by fake antique lanterns which were more picturesque than functional. It occurred to him that since it was a party, there would be a number of cars parked outside the house. So he drove around for a while looking for a house where a party might be in progress, only to come out once again to the road he had taken to arrive at Charleton. He took it as an omen, and drove back to Abbot Road and then to the state road and headed for home.

By the time he arrived at his furnished

158

apartment in Brookline, it was almost midnight. Nevertheless, he decided to call, on the chance that Clara might answer. If the phone rang for a while, and was then answered by someone else, he would simply hang up rather than try to explain why he was calling so late. The phone was answered on the second ring, but it was a man who answered.

'Is Clara Levenson there?' he asked.

'Well, she must be around someplace,' came the reply. 'Hold on.'

He waited, and waited, and then hung up. He was bothered, however, and he tried again, shortly after midnight. He reasoned that if the party were still going on at eleven, then even if it was now over, the family would not all have gone to bed. If Clara answered, he was sure she would not object because of the lateness of the hour, and if someone else answered, he would simply hang up again. But this time he got a message from an answering machine, which under the circumstances was even better. When he heard the beep, he said quickly, 'Clara? Mord Jacobs. I tried to make the party, but I couldn't find the house. I drove around looking for a place that was all lit up and had a lot of cars parked nearby. No luck, so I went on home.'

CHAPTER TWENTY-TWO

For three years the Barnard's Crossing Symphonic Orchestra, which drew members from various North Shore towns, including a violinist from as far away as Gloucester, had met every Saturday night for rehearsal for a concert that was presumably to be given at some as yet unannounced date. At first they had met in Veteran's Hall in Barnard's Crossing, hence the symphony's name. But when the veteran's organization that had let them use the auditorium at no cost decided the facility could be used to better advantage for a Bingo game which could bring in revenue, the rehearsal was shifted to the faculty lounge of the Breverton Junior High School, through the good offices of the assistant principal, who played the trombone.

It was one of several such organizations scattered throughout the area. The one in Rockport met on Wednesdays, the Wenham orchestra met on Friday nights, and the Lynn orchestra, whose conductor was a member of the Boston Symphony and was paid for his services, met Sunday mornings. They varied widely in size and proficiency but they all afforded the participants the opportunity to play orchestral music; in the case of the Barnard's Crossing group, light classical music, like the Poet and Peasant and William Tell overtures. Many played in more than one orchestra, and one, a barber, in all of them.

Herbert Rosen had joined shortly after moving to Barnard's Crossing. Since he was far and away the best musician, he was immediately made concertmaster, and when the conductor who was head of the Music Department of the Barnard's Crossing High School took another job in the western part of the state, Rosen became the conductor.

The orchestra, which had anywhere from as few as twenty-five to as many as fifty musicians, depending largely on weather conditions, was open to anyone who could play an orchestral instrument. There were no tryouts for proficiency. Anyone who was interested and who could play an instrument could come and play. If the piece or any portion of it was beyond his capacity, he stopped playing, and those who could, carried on. As a result, andante passages were apt to be played by the full complement, and scherzo passages only by the leaders of the various sections.

While there were a few regulars who attended each rehearsal religiously, there were those who came only occasionally, some of them only once, never to return. There was no telling on any given rehearsal night what instruments would be played. There was usually a large number of violins, perhaps

161

because while a single violin poorly played was characterized by squeaks and scratches, several playing together produced a melodious sound. There were almost always two cellos because they were regulars. Once or twice a double bass player appeared. They could usually count on flutes, clarinets, and the trombone of the assistant principal. There was an English horn who showed up about once a month, and a bassoon came every other week because he and his brother owned a small restaurant in Lynn and they alternated supervision of it on Saturday nights.

Amy Lanigan, the wife of Hugh Lanigan, the Barnard's Crossing police chief, played the flute with great enthusiasm, but with no great proficiency. She had learned to play when she was a girl and was a member of the high school band. After high school she had dropped it, but then took it up again when the orchestra was organized. She was the most devoted supporter of the orchestra and never missed a session.

When rehearsals were held in Barnard's Crossing, she would drive there in her own car, but once rehearsals were transferred to Breverton, her husband always drove her there and picked her up when the session ended, because she was hesitant about driving to and from Breverton, especially in the winter.

Sometimes, Hugh Lanigan would stay and listen to the rehearsal, and sometimes he would spend the time gossiping with the senior officers at the Breverton police station until it was time to go back to the school to pick up his wife. Although he had no great interest in music, he found it not unpleasant to sit and listen as the orchestra went through one piece after another. They did not really rehearse in the sense of trying to perfect or even improve their rendition of the piece. They merely played it, deriving pleasure from making orchestral sound and arriving at the end together.

Not that Rosen did nothing but beat time. There was first of all the necessity of 'balancing' the orchestra since at each rehearsal the number and the kind of instruments as well as the capacity of the players varied widely. He might say to a couple of the weaker violinists, 'Kate and Tom, don't try to play this next passage. Just play the top note of the chord on each downbeat. Or better still, Kate, you play the top note, and Tom, you play the bottom note.'

Or he might rap on his music stand with his baton and say, 'I think you're flat, Bill. Let me hear your A. Yup, you're flat.'

'It was on pitch when we started, but the peg keeps slipping.'

'Well, rub a little rosin on it. That will hold

it. Okay, let's start again, and this time let's see if we can't make those staccatos a little sharper, and follow the stick.'

Tonight, because it was the first week in June, and warm, the windows of the rehearsal room were all open. While open windows improved the quality of the air, especially after the smoking many of them went in for during the ten-minute break, they affected the acoustics, so that the orchestral volume was reduced and they sounded somewhat tinny.

They usually played until ten o'clock, but at a quarter to ten Rosen said, 'I think we'll call it a night. I've got to get home a little earlier tonight. We're expecting our daughter to call from San Francisco.' As the players began to put away their instruments, Chief Lanigan wandered over to Rosen, who was gathering up the music folders, and nodding toward the country club just across the road, he said, 'There's evidently a big shindig at the club. Watch it when you start out. The State Troopers may have set up a trap on the state road.'

'You mean they set up a trap every time there's a do at the club?'

'Not every time, but often enough to make you wonder.' He chuckled. 'When I first joined the force in Barnard's Crossing as a patrolman years ago, the chief was Jim Duggan. The town used to pay him fifty cents for everyone he had in jail, for their supper, you understand. Duggan never paid the restaurant that supplied the meals more than thirty cents apiece, giving him a net profit of twenty cents each meal. So we patrolmen had a kind of quota. We were expected to make a certain number of arrests every Saturday night. If anyone so much as stumbled over a pebble as he walked along the street, he was apt to be pulled in as a drunk and disorderly.'

'And you think the State Troopers have a similar quota?'

'Well, it never hurts to improve your arrest record.'

Rosen grinned. 'Then I'll follow you until we pass them. They'd never stop you, certainly not while you're in uniform.'

'Good enough.'

CHAPTER TWENTY-THREE

For Cyrus Merton the dinner had not been particularly enjoyable. He had not expected it to be. He had come, and decided to remain, in part because it was a sort of refuge from his sister. He tried to tell himself that she was exaggerating, that young newlyweds frequently quarreled in the very circumstance of adjusting to each other, that it would blow over and they would make up. On the other

165

hand, he had to admit that Agnes was a shrewd, intelligent woman, not given to overstatement.

Nor did the conversation at his table do anything to distract him. It was entirely academic and over his head. So he concentrated on his food, chewing away without appetite or pleasure as he wondered when he might properly leave. As the dishes were being cleared by the waitresses for the dessert and coffee that were to follow, Professor Gates, a twinkle in his eye, said, 'Ah, now for the interesting part of the evening.'

'What comes now?' asked Merton innocently.

Gates hesitated, and then said, 'Well, there'll be speeches, and a resolution is to be discussed and voted on, and Dr. Carpenter has written a long poem, doggerel to be sure, but amusing.'

Speeches, a resolution, doggerel verse- since all present were teachers, their target was likely to be the administration, perhaps even the Board of Trustees. Merton felt it might be embarrassing to remain. 'It's getting late,' he said, 'I think I'll be running along.'

'I understand,' said Gates sympathetically.

He rose and nodded his good-byes to the rest of the table. He made his way to where Victor had been sitting. The place was empty. He motioned and looked his question.

166

'Joyce? Oh, he's gone. Left some time ago.'

He was disappointed. He had hoped to ride home with Victor so that he could talk to him about his marital problems. Then, at Shurtcliffe Circle, he'd have Peg there as well. Perhaps he'd be able to knock some sense into them. But Victor was gone.

It was still too early to go home; Agnes would not as yet have gone to sleep, but with a possible stop at Shurtcliffe Circle to visit with Peg and Victor ... He made his way to the coatroom, gladdened the heart of the young woman in charge by leaving a dollar bill in the dish as he retrieved his topcoat, and hastened out to the car. He had intended going to the men's room before setting out on the trip home, but he was worried about Victor and wanted to get on the way; he'd be at the Circle soon enough. He turned the key and left the club parking lot.

★   ★   ★

Lanigan veered to the left in order to make the turn into Abbot Road and Barnard's Crossing. The light turned to red and he brought his car to a halt. Instead of following into the left lane, Rosen drove up beside him. Amy lowered her window and called out, 'Thought you had to get right home.'

'Yeah, but I promised Helen I'd pick up some doughnuts.'

'How about us going in for a cup of coffee?' Amy suggested as she raised her window.

'Naw,' said Lanigan. 'Saturday nights the place is full of kids, and seeing me in uniform is apt to put a damper on their fun.'

The light changed and the Lanigans made the turn into Abbot Road while Rosen continued on into the mall parking lot just beyond. He stopped just short of the store, and without bothering to lock his car, he hastened to the door.

Merton, meanwhile, had pulled in from the other end of the lot at almost the exact same time as Rosen. The house on Shurtcliffe Circle had been dark, and he was desperate for the Donut Shop's rest room. The parking lot of the mall was dark except for the light on one pylon, and Merton parked there. He turned off the lights and the motor and slid out, automatically pressing the button on the car door so that it locked when he slammed it shut. No sooner was he out when he realized he had left his key in the ignition, as he had on several previous occasions. He was not unduly concerned, however, and hurried toward the Donut Shop.

Merton was just opening the door as Rosen came up, and Merton motioned him to enter. Rosen smiled his thanks but gestured for the other to precede him. 'After you,' he said politely.

While Merton hurried down the aisle to the

rest rooms, Rosen went directly to the doughnut counter and said, 'Let me have a couple of those plain ones and a couple of the honey-dipped.'

'Right,' said the girl behind the counter, 'two plain and two honey-dipped.' She put the doughnuts in a box and Rosen paid and hurried out.

When Merton came out of the rest room a few minutes later, he felt an urgent need for a cup of coffee, since he had left the faculty dinner before it was served. He was on the point of walking around the doughnut counter to the other side of the shop where there were tables, but noticing that one of the stools at the counter was free, he sat down and asked the girl for a cup of black coffee.

Cyrus Merton finished his coffee and got up from his stool at the counter. He fished in his pocket for a coin, which he left beside his empty cup. Then, with a nod, he left. He was back in a few minutes, however.

'My car is gone,' he said to the manager, who had just come out of his office. 'It's been stolen. I've got to notify the police.'

'Are you sure?'

'Of course I'm sure. I know where I parked it, and it's not there.'

The manager nodded in the direction of the public phone. 'There's the phone. Do you have change? Or you can use our phone if you like.'

When the cruising car drew up to the door of the Donut Shop, both officers came in. The elder, a sergeant, graying and beginning to show a paunch, knew Cyrus Merton. 'Where were you parked, Mr. Merton? Over by the pylon there? Let's see, that's about fifty feet from here. Was it one of the company cars? Did it have your logo on the side?'

'No, it was my personal car.'

'Too bad. It would be easier to spot if it had the logo on the side. Did you lock it?'

'Yes, the doors were locked.'

'Windows all the way up to the top? I mean, no crack at the top where you could poke a wire '

'No, the windows were closed.'

The sergeant shook his head. 'That means it could be a pro. Now I'd like you to give Officer Stokes a full description of your car, license number, color, make, and if there were any obvious dents or scratches, you tell him. Were you on your way home? Because if you were, we can give you a lift.'

CHAPTER TWENTY-FOUR

As they drove away from the Donut Shop, Miriam asked, 'Did you have to wait long? Were you bored?'

Simcha, sitting upright in the backseat, large hands resting on bony knees, laughed a single explosive 'Ha' from a cavernous mouth. A broad smile split his craggy face. 'Why should I be bored when I had a chance to observe our young at close quarters, relaxed and enjoying themselves, rather than the way I usually see them in the classroom or tense during an exam? I learned that one Chuck Goretski was 'simply awesome.' I suppose that when one is no longer in fear or awe of a deity, the need for the feeling doesn't go away; it's apt to be transferred to a human who is above average. One young man insisted, 'He couldn't miss,' and another agreed by offering the comparative, 'He *just* couldn't miss,' while a third capped it with the superlative, 'He just couldn't miss if he tried.' What interested me particularly was that the girls appeared to be as knowledgeable about the game as the boys. In fact, from what I've seen in Chicago, and elsewhere, the women seem to be more interested in sports and exercise than the men. I haven't made a statistical study, but it seems to me that I see more women than men jogging, and the advertisements for membership in health clubs and gymnasia where they have all those crazy machines seem to be slanted to the women rather than to the men.'

'It's probably that women are more concerned with keeping slim,' suggested the rabbi.

'Perhaps that's it,' Simcha agreed. 'It could be they're more concerned with how they look in bathing suits.'

'Don't you approve of sports and exercise?' asked Miriam.

'Of exercise, not at all. No other animal engages in it. Lions sleep twenty hours a day. As for sport, I don't mind it as long as it's not competitive. To practice hours every day in order to run a fraction of a second faster than someone else, or jump a little higher, or hit a ball a little more accurately, seems absurd. And to subject a child who has not yet reached puberty to such a regimen in order to produce a champion tennis player or gymnast is an obscenity.'

'What if it's for the purpose of producing a great violinist or pianist?' asked Miriam.

'Same objection. It's a form of slavery.'

'I seem to remember that you used to play a musical instrument,' said the rabbi.

'I studied the violin. When I was a youngster, I was given violin lessons, as were all middle-class Jewish boys. I was never very proficient.' He grinned broadly. 'You know what Aristotle said: 'A gentleman should know how to play the flute, but not too well.'

'You know, Simcha,' said Miriam, 'I think you're an Apicorus in all kinds of things; not just in religion.'

He laughed uproariously. 'Very good,

Miriam. Very good, my dear.'

★　　★　　★

Sunday morning was sunny and mild, and as they made ready, Simcha asked, 'Is the temple far from here? Can we walk? Will we have time?'

'Oh, plenty of time,' the rabbi assured him. 'On Sundays the *shachriss* morning service is at nine o'clock. It's about a fifteen minute walk. Do you feel up to it?'

'So let's figure on twenty, twenty-five minutes, and we can stroll.'

As they walked along, they were hailed and then joined by Al Bergson. The rabbi made the introductions. 'Al Bergson, the president of our temple. Al, this is my cousin Simcha, whom you've heard me mention.'

'The one you call Simcha the, er—'

'Apicorus,' the rabbi finished for him, a wide grin on his face. 'That's right, Simcha the Apicorus, Simcha the Atheist.'

'Your first visit to Barnard's Crossing?' Bergson asked. 'You taking an early morning stroll to see the town?'

'Why no,' said Simcha, 'I'm going with David to your temple to daven *shachriss*.'

'But—But you're an atheist, or an agnostic—'

'Sometimes one, sometimes the other, as I happen to be feeling at the moment.'

173

'Oh, I see. It's a sort of social matter for you rather than religious.'

'Not at all. When I attend a service, I daven.'

Bergson turned to the rabbi. 'But if he doesn't believe, how can he pray?'

'Well, you know, we don't really pray,' said the rabbi, 'at least not in the sense of asking or begging for something. We daven. The origin of the word is obscure, but it consists largely in giving praise and thanks for the good things we receive.'

'And what's wrong with an atheist being grateful?' Simcha added. 'It makes for a wholesome humility.'

'But if you're an atheist, whom are you grateful to?'

'Good question,' said Simcha. He considered for a moment. 'I suppose that when something good happens to me, I'm grateful, or perhaps a better word is, glad. That's it: I'm glad it happened.'

'So you daven, but how about the rest of it? Do you keep the Sabbath? The dietary laws?'

'Oh, I keep the dietary laws out of habit, I suppose, rather than out of conscious choice. It's not easy to change the food habits you've grown up with, you know. In general, I'm inclined to observe the Mosaic laws because they're sensible and modern.'

'Modern?' asked Bergson doubtfully.

'Sure,' said Simcha. 'Moses established

174

rules by which the individual could order his life and by which a humane society can be maintained, everything from rules of personal cleanliness to proper treatment of the lower animals. There were very modern rules for women; incompatibility was grounds for a divorce—'

'And the Ketubah,' the rabbi pointed out, 'was a prenuptial agreement.'

'Right.' Simcha went on. 'And he established a very modern system of labor relations which gave the laborer the right to organize, and fixed his rate of pay so that the employer could not take advantage of his temporary need. And don't forget that the Sabbath gave him a day of rest every week. There were laws that gave aid and succor to the poor, and even laws governing the treatment of the lower animals, because he was aware of the relationship of all living things. He even had a sense of ecology, of the needs of the land itself, and ordered that it should not be planted every seventh year, but be permitted to lie fallow to renew itself.

'Some of the laws indicate a fastidiousness of mind and spirit, like the law forbidding the cooking of the flesh of the calf in the milk of its mother, which has led to our elaborate separation of meat and dairy foods and dishes. When you stop to think of it, it's a horrible thing to do. I suppose our special attitude toward the pig is due to the same

175

fastidious sense, since the pig is the only domestic animal that serves no purpose except to be eaten. To raise an animal, to feed it so that it will grow big and fat just so you can eat it—ugh!' He gave a shudder of disgust.

'But doesn't that show that it must have been the work of God rather than the work of mere man?' Bergson protested.

'Ah, now that was where Moses showed his genius. He knew that even if he could maintain the observance of these laws during the period when he was all-powerful, they would tend to be disregarded when he became old and weak, and even more when he died. So, instead of offering them as his own, he invented God, and said they were ordained by God, and he insisted that his was the only God, so that there could be no rival God that could be appealed to for a different opinion. That was where he showed his true superiority to all other law-givers, like Hammurabi or Solon or Lycurgus.

'Of course, he could not run the show single-handed, even in his prime. So he took the advice of his father-in-law, Jethro, and appointed a number of judges who later were the rabbis to help him run things. It was necessary, of course, but also unfortunate.'

'Why unfortunate?'

'Because it created a bureaucracy. Bureaucrats always multiply rules and regulations. And what develops is a pedantic meticulousness. That's how the business of two sets of dishes, one dairy, one meat, came about. An effort to avoid the most remote possibility of mixing the milk of the cow with the meat of the calf. Then this was extended to two sinks to wash the two kinds of dishes in, and the two dishcloths to wipe them with. Some even have two refrigerators in which to store the two kinds of food, and I have even heard, although it's probably apocryphal, of someone who went in for two sets of false teeth. You see, it's usually the extremists who set the pattern.

'Or consider the Sabbath. We are told to rest on the Sabbath, and this means we may not work. So then the question arises, what constitutes work? And it was decided that the different kinds of work that were involved and described in the construction of the tabernacle were work and would be taboo on the Sabbath. Making a fire was obviously one of these. It was necessary for the smelting of ores for metal, and then for working the metal for the various vessels that were required. And I suppose that in those days building a fire was work, and even though today all that's required is to strike a match, lighting a cigarette is regarded as work, which is why Orthodox Jews can't smoke on the Sabbath.

'Well, fire is fire, and a little one is just as

much fire as a big one.' His shoulders went up in a resigned shrug. 'But with the advent of electricity, the bureaucracy decided that an electric spark was also fire, and what's more, that every time you turn on an electric appliance of any kind, you create a spark. So the poor devil who walks up ten flights of stairs to reach his apartment is not doing any work, but his nonobservant neighbor who uses the elevator is, because he had to push a button and thereby made an electric contact. And that first one sits in the darkness rather than push a button that will turn on the electric light. If his daughter, say, is in the hospital, he can't call her on the phone to ask how she is because it is electrical and presumably makes a spark. And of course he can't go to see her unless the hospital is within walking distance.' He shook his head in annoyance.

They arrived at the temple and stopped momentarily so that Simcha could look around at the fine lawn surrounded by hedge and shrubbery and divided by the broad walk that led to the large, ornate doors of the sanctuary. There was a narrower walk that led to the short flight of stairs beyond, which was the vestry at the end of a long corridor.

'This is where the minyan holds its services weekdays and Sundays,' said Bergson. 'On the Sabbath we use the sanctuary, of course.'

'I'd like to see it,' said Simcha, 'but I

suppose it's closed now.'

'It's closed from the outside, but you can go up those stairs.'

As Simcha started for the stairs, the rabbi called after him, 'We'll be starting in a few minutes.'

'Oh, I'll be right down,' said Simcha.

The rabbi pointed. 'It's the last door on the right.'

When he left them, Bergson said, 'He's a very interesting man. Is he staying with you for a while?'

'I'm putting him on the train for Boston right after lunch. He has a conference he has to attend for a couple of days. Then perhaps he'll come back and spend the rest of the week with us.'

'Then I don't suppose you'll be coming to the board meeting today. There's nothing important on the agenda today anyway. When he comes back from Boston, I'd like to meet him again.' He hesitated. 'You know, David, I'm observant because it's the way I've been brought up, but I'm not very knowledgeable. Do you think—is it proper for an atheist to join the minyan in prayer?'

The rabbi chuckled. 'We are not concerned with a man's thoughts; only with his actions. The mind has a will of its own. Even controlling it for five or ten minutes is not easy. It tends to wander—to something you see out of the corner of your eye, or to a sound you hear, or something you smell, or accidentally touch. We are governed by the Commandments. And what is a commandment? It is something imposed by a superior—in this case, God—to an inferior, Man. And it is usually an order to do something we would normally not do, or would rather not do. But it is always well within our capacity. We are not asked to pluck out our eye if it offends us, or to cut off our right hand if it has caused us to sin.'

'Yes, but—'

'Even the most devout of us have doubts. My cousin merely expresses them. I'm sure he has doubts about his atheism. He said that sometimes he was an agnostic rather than an atheist. And what is an agnostic? It is someone who is not certain; who thinks sometimes that there is a God, and at other times that there isn't.'

★   ★   ★

As Simcha and the rabbi strolled home from the minyan, several people whom they passed said hello or good morning or waved a greeting.

'You seem pretty popular,' Simcha remarked.

'I don't know how popular I am,' said the rabbi, 'but I've been here for twenty-five years, so a lot of people know me. And in a

180

small town like Barnard's Crossing, even people who don't know you are apt to say hello when you're strolling along like this.'

On reaching the local drugstore, they were hailed by Herb Rosen, the Sunday newspaper under his arm. 'Oh, Rabbi, I received a card from the temple saying I had *Yahrzeit* for my father Monday. But they got the date wrong; he passed away in the middle of May.'

'No, I'm sure the date is right,' said the rabbi. 'We record the date by the Hebrew calendar, and that differs from the regular calendar by a few days each year.'

'Oh, is that it? Well, I'll be there. Let's see, I go to the evening service and then to the morning service the following day. Right?'

'That's right.'

'And the evening service is what time? I noted the day on my calendar, but I didn't put down the time, and I must have mislaid the card.'

'The evening service starts at half past six, and we try to start promptly. So I'll see you tomorrow evening—'

'Oh, it's not for tomorrow; it's for next Monday, that is, a week from tomorrow.'

'Ah, then in that case, it will be at seven. We hold the evening service a little later starting in June.'

'Okay, I'll be there.'

Simcha had been staring at Rosen as he talked with the rabbi. Now, he said, 'Don't I know you? Did you ever take a course with me?'

'I don't think so,' said Rosen uncertainly.

'But you did sit in on one of my courses,' Simcha insisted.

'Not that I know of.'

'But you *did* go to the University of Chicago.'

'No, I went to Juilliard.'

As they walked on, Simcha said, 'I'm sure I know that young man, unless he has a double living in Chicago. I should have asked him if he has a brother.' He shook his head in bafflement. 'I've always prided myself on my being able to remember faces, even if I can't always associate names to go with them. Students come to see me, some who studied with me twenty years ago, and I remember them instantly. Sometimes I can even remember where they sat in my class.'

'He probably looks like someone you once knew. Sometimes if you think of something else, it will come to you. It's not particularly important, is it?'

Simcha halted in his stride. 'When you get to be my age, David, this kind of thing becomes very important. I suffer from SCS—'

'SCS?'

'That's right, Senior Citizen Syndrome. You wake up in the morning and you find that you have an arthritic pain in an arm or a leg. Or you turn suddenly and you get a stitch

182

in your side. Or it might be a touch of vertigo when you look up suddenly from a book you're reading. Or a cramp in the belly right after eating. It doesn't last long, maybe a few minutes, or at most a couple of days, but it's annoying. And mentally you find yourself forgetting things, mislaying your keys or your wallet, or unable to remember something you're supposed to do, or unable to follow the train of thought in something you're reading. I suppose it's an augury of the ultimate dissolution,' he said gloomily.

'You're a long way from that, Simcha. And remembering whom Herb Rosen reminds you of is certainly not very important. I'm sure it will come to you, probably quite suddenly when you're thinking of something entirely different.'

'I suppose,' the other admitted, 'but it's annoying just the same. The other day during a lecture I referred to *The Golden Bough* and I couldn't remember the name of the author.'

'Frazer?'

'Of course, but I just couldn't think of it. For me that's like not being able to remember the name of Isaiah the prophet would be for you.'

They spent the rest of the morning talking about the rabbi's plans for the future and his chances of getting a teaching job, while Miriam busied herself preparing lunch.

'It's not going to be easy, David,' said

183

Simcha. 'I made some inquiries, general inquiries, to get the feel of the problem. For one thing, your age is against you.'

'I realize that.'

'For another, there is the matter of publication. Getting papers published is all-important.'

'Well, I have published.'

Simcha shook his head. 'I've read all your papers, at least all you've sent me.'

'I sent you every one.'

'And very good papers they were, very thoughtful and very well-written. But they're not the kind that a modem Semitics or Judaic department would be interested in; what they want now is something like an analysis by computer of the J and E elements, something dull and scientific. But don't worry, I'll be meeting with people from all over the country in the next week or ten days and I should be able to get some leads.'

After lunch the rabbi took Simcha to the train. 'When will you be coming back, Simcha?'

'I've got appointments all this week. Then Monday of next week, the Anthropological Society meets, and I'll have to be there. And the next day, I am to read a paper, and oh yes, I am to be given an honor, so I suppose I have to be there. Let's say Wednesday, unless something comes up.'

'Well, you call us and tell us when you can

come out, and I'll meet your train.'

'Fine.' The train came down the track and a moment later stopped. As Simcha grasped the handrail to board, he stopped and said, 'Oh David, if you should happen to run into that fellow, would you ask him if he has a brother living in Chicago?'

'Sure, Simcha.'

CHAPTER TWENTY-FIVE

When he came in Monday morning, Lanigan gave his usual cursory inspection to the events listed on the blotter Saturday night and Sunday when he had been off duty. There were the usual list of drunk and disorderlies to be expected on a Saturday night, as well as the usual petty thefts of hubcaps, minor vandalism, reports on noisy parties continued late into the night, at least beyond the bedtimes of the complaining neighbors. And there was the story of the accident on Pine Grove Road. From his point of view, none of it was unusual. He did not expect to see anything unusual reported, if only because he knew that if anything of importance had happened, he would have been called. There was also the report of the theft of Merton's car. This was not in itself unusual, although he sensed that because it was Merton who was involved, it might be troublesome. Merton would expect immediate results. Then he got a cup of coffee from the urn in the wardroom and sat back to read the Barnard's Crossing *Reporter*.

The report of the accident appeared on page four. There was a picture of the car taken just before the tow truck had hauled it away, showing the front end against the trunk of a tree. Although the picture was two columns wide, the story was covered in a couple of short paragraphs which told little more than that the victim was a Victor Jones who was a teacher in a Boston school, and that he had been taken to the Salem Hospital, where he had been pronounced dead on arrival. Lanigan sipped at his coffee and made the mental note that the car must have been going at least sixty miles an hour to have got wrapped around the tree as shown, and that he must have been drunk to have driven that fast on Pine Grove Road at night. The name of the victim meant nothing to him. Then he turned to the sports section which devoted a full page with several action photos to the basketball game between Barnard's Crossing High School and their archrivals, Swampscott High.

When he got home that evening, his wife Amy thrust the newspaper at him. It was open at page four and folded over in such a way that little except the story of the accident was showing. 'Did you see this?' she asked in a tragic voice.

'The auto accident? Yeah.'

'It was Victor Joyce who was killed. They got the name wrong.'

'So? Who's Victor Joyce?'

'Don't you remember? He's that handsome young man who married Margaret Merton, Cyrus Merton's niece.'

'Oh yeah. Let's see, they took a house in Shurtcliffe Circle, next door to the Rosens, a couple of months ago.'

'And she's such a lovely girl. Not pretty, to be sure, but awfully kind and sincere. That auction I ran for the scholarship fund of St. Joseph's, she offered to help and, well, she was there every minute that I needed her. I don't know what I would have done without her.'

'Yeah, I remember her. Sad eyes and prominent teeth—'

'But awfully good-hearted, Hugh.'

'I guess she'd have to be, wouldn't she. Cyrus Merton—there was something on him on the blotter. He had his car stolen. That same night, come to think of it.'

'Well, wouldn't you know it. Troubles— they never come singly. Hugh, we've got to go over there tomorrow.'

'Tomorrow? Where?'

'We've got to go see Margaret Joyce and offer our condolences.'

'But gosh, tomorrow I've got a thousand things lined up.'

'It's only for a half hour or so. Just to show that we care.'

'Well, all right, but I won't have time to change. I'll just call you and then run home and pick you up and go over there.'

'Well, you could at least wear the uniform that just came back from the cleaners.'

'All right. I'll wear the uniform that just came back from the cleaners.'

★   ★   ★

As the Lanigans drew up in front of the Joyce house shortly before noon, a group of half a dozen women all dressed like Amy, in appropriately dark, sober suits, emerged. Amy knew all of them, and they stopped to talk with her before making for their cars. Lanigan, self-conscious in his uniform, stood a little apart, his uniform cap in hand, and waited. He caught snatches of conversation:

'Isn't it terrible? And she's so brave...'

'Bearing up wonderfully...'

'Such a fine couple and...'

'You know, Amy, I think perhaps she'd like to be alone.'

'Oh, we don't plan to stay long.' This last from Amy, much to her husband's satisfaction.

Finally, the women went off to their cars,

and the Lanigans mounted the steps to the front door, which had been left ajar so that they did not have to ring. They pushed it open and entered. Margaret Merton, wearing a black skirt and jacket and a white blouse with a black ribbon at the throat, came forward to greet them. Amy embraced and kissed her, and then her husband came over and said, 'I'm terribly sorry, Mrs. Joyce.'

She nodded and said, 'Would you like some tea? Or perhaps a glass of sherry, or—'

'Tea will be fine. Please don't bother to get up. I'll pour it myself.'

'And you, Mrs. Lanigan?'

'Amy.'

Margaret Merton smiled faintly. 'All right, Amy. Will you have something?'

'Don't trouble yourself, Peg. Actually, right now I'd like to freshen up.'

'It's upstairs. Down the hall.'

'I'll find it.'

As Amy Lanigan mounted the stairs, the widow said, 'I'd like to consult with you, Chief Lanigan. I was planning to call you, or come down to the police station, but—'

'How about right now?'

'All right.' She rose and went to a door at the side and motioned him to follow her. It was a small back parlor which had been converted to a study. There was a bookcase and a desk, and against the wall, a couch. From the top drawer of the desk she drew a

189

large manila envelope, which she opened, dumping the contents on the desk.

'This is what your police brought me,' she said.

There was a wallet and a handkerchief, some loose change, a key case, a ballpoint pen, a comb, a small notebook, and a wedding ring.

Lanigan nodded and looked at her questioningly.

'His watch is not here. My husband's wristwatch is missing. I think it's terrible to take someone's watch when they're—when they're dead.'

'You think one of my men took it?' He shook his head, 'Very unlikely, ma'am, very unlikely. Was it an expensive watch?'

'Not very. It was gold-filled, not solid gold. It was my father's watch, and I gave it to Victor when we got engaged. My mother bought it for my father when they went to Rome for their tenth anniversary. And she had a relic mounted on the dial, a relic of Saint Ulric.'

'What kind of relic? I mean, what did it look like?'

'Oh, I was told it was a little bone chip, but it was enclosed in a tiny silver tube. It was the tube that was mounted on the watch dial just above the twelve, where it wouldn't interfere with the minute hand. I think they had a watchmaker shorten the hand a little because it was a large watch and the hand seemed sort of small. My father used to wear it inside his wrist because that way it was closer to his heart, to the blood vessels in the wrist, you know. And there was also a Sacred Heart painted on the dial. When I told Victor how Dad wore it, he said he'd wear it that same way, too. Dad was not wearing it when he, you know, died. He'd gone in swimming and—'

Lanigan nodded. 'I understand. Tell me, what kind of strap did it have?'

'It was metal. Gold-colored. There was a kind of curved bar that folded over and snapped.'

'Ah, well, that might explain it,' he said. 'Your husband must have been driving very fast when he hit.'

She nodded.

'So the strap could have opened and been flung off his wrist. I'll make inquiries, and I'll send someone up to the scene of the accident and have them rake over the area.' Then he added, 'Are you sure he was wearing it that night?'

He could tell by her reaction that she had not considered the possibility, but was somehow pleased by his suggestion, for she smiled. But then she said, 'Yes, I'm quite sure. Otherwise it would be in his dresser drawer, and it isn't.'

'All right. We'll look for it. Oh, and it

would be a good idea not to mention it, not to anyone, because *they* might mention it to someone.'

'I understand.'

He hesitated, reluctant to obtrude on her grief with questions, but then he essayed, 'Had he gone any place special that evening, or—'

'Oh, he'd gone to the Windermere faculty dinner at the Breverton Country Club,' she answered, seemingly surprised that he did not know.

'And he went alone?'

'Well, Uncle Cyrus was planning to go up with him, but Victor had already left by the time Uncle Cyrus called. If he had waited a few minutes, they would have gone up together. And, of course, they would have driven home together, and this—this wouldn't have happened.'

'On the other hand, both of them might have been injured,' Lanigan offered.

'Oh no. Uncle Cyrus wouldn't have let him drive if he thought he wasn't, you know, up to it.'

'And you? You didn't care to go?'

'Oh, it was only for the faculty, teaching faculty. No spouses, no administrative people, not even deans. As I understand it, they have like a business meeting afterward and have a chance to air their complaints.'

'But Cyrus Merton—'

192

She giggled. 'They made him an honorary member of the faculty a couple of years ago. Very proud of it, Uncle Cyrus was. And they send him a ticket to the dinner each year. He's never gone, but this year he decided to. Because Victor was going, I suppose.'

They heard Amy coming down the stairs, and they reentered the living room.

*   *   *

By the way Amy hurried the visit, Lanigan suspected that she wanted to tell him something. She had poured herself only half a cup of tea, and as soon as she finished it, she looked at her watch and said, 'You said you had to get back, Hugh.'

He picked up the cue and said, 'Yeah, that damn conference.'

When they were in their car, he said, 'Well, what is it?'

'What is what?' she asked innocently.

'C'mon, you know you want to tell me something. What is it?'

'Oh, Hugh, I was upstairs, and as I passed by the bedroom door, there was a sliding bolt on it.'

'On the bedroom door? You're sure it was the bedroom door?'

'Oh, yes, I looked in.'

'You snooped,' he accused.

'Well, it wasn't closed. I mean it was open

193

a crack, and all I did was push it open a little more. You know what that means.'

'I can imagine,' he said dryly.

'It means they were sleeping apart. They weren't having, you know, relations.'

'How can you know that? Maybe she used it as a kind of double protection on those nights when he came home late.'

'That's silly,' she declared. 'And how would he get to bed when he got home? Anyway, I looked in the room across the hallway.'

'Good lord, Woman, don't tell me that door was ajar, too.'

'Well, it wasn't closed. And it was his room. All his things, his suits and things, were there.'

'You mean you went in and opened the closet?'

'It was open and I could see it from the doorway,' she said defiantly.

'The poor devil,' he murmured.

'The poor girl, you mean.'

'All right then, both of them.'

$$\star \qquad \star \qquad \star$$

Not for a moment did Lanigan believe that one of his men might have stolen the watch. But neither did he believe that the shock of the crash had sent it flying off the man's wrist. It was possible but not much more. He was more inclined to think that Joyce may not have been wearing the watch. If the man drove down Pine Grove Road at breakneck speed, then there was a good chance that he had been drinking, and heavily. Lanigan knew drunks; they misplaced things; they lost things; worse, when momentarily short of cash, they might offer a bartender a ring or a watch as a surety or pawn for another drink.

Nevertheless, when he returned to the station house, he told his lieutenant to send someone out to the scene of the accident and have him go over the ground carefully. He described the watch. 'And have him take a rake with him. Oh, and who was on duty Saturday night? Was it Bob Pierce? Is he around? Send him in.'

When Sergeant Pierce presented himself, Lanigan said, 'There wasn't much on the blotter on that business Saturday night, except the accident on Pine Grove. Dr. Gorfinkle called you. What did he say?'

'Well, he said he'd seen this accident and he told me it was on Pine Grove Road and how far it was from the Breverton Country Club. He'd been to a formal dinner there. So I checked the mileage on the map and—'

'Never mind that. Did he say anything about the victim? What he looked like? What shape he was in?'

'Oh, yeah. He said he was unconscious but he took his pulse and it was pretty normal.'

'He said he took his pulse? You're sure?'

'Oh, yeah. I'm sure of that because I remember wondering how the guy could be unconscious and still have a normal pulse.'

'He can.'

'Yeah, I guess he can, but I remember wondering about it at the time.'

'Okay. Well, get me the pictures that were taken, will you?'

The police photo showed the victim behind the wheel of the car, his head lolling back just below the headrest, his left hand on the rim of the side window, which still retained some jagged pieces of shattered glass. The blood-soaked sleeve of his jacket covered the wrist, so that even if he had been wearing a wristwatch, it would not have shown in the photo. It occurred to Lanigan that if the watch was a large one, and if it had been worn on the inside of the wrist as his wife had insisted, Dr. Gorfinkle might very well have removed it in order to take his pulse. Where would he have put it? Perhaps on the dashboard, perhaps on the victim's lap, or perhaps he had just dropped it into his pocket and then forgotten it.

Later, when the policeman returned and reported he had found nothing, Lanigan flipped the intercom on his desk and said, 'I saw Bill Dunstable pouring himself a coffee in the wardroom when I came in, so he's probably still there. Would you please ask

196

him to come in to see me?'

Detective Sergeant William Dunstable did not wear a uniform, which made him useful to Lanigan when he wanted to minimize police concern in an inquiry. When he entered the office, Lanigan said, 'Sit down, Sergeant. You know about the accident on Park Grove Road the other night?'

'Yes, sir.'

'It was reported by a Dr. Gorfinkle. You know him?'

'No, sir.'

'He's been living in town for some years. His office is in Salem. He's an eye doctor. Now, Bob Pierce was on the desk that night. He says the doctor told him he took the pulse of the victim and it was pretty normal for all that he was unconscious. I went over to see the widow today to pay my respects and offer my condolences. She was terribly upset that her husband's wristwatch was not among his effects. As she described it, it's largish for a wristwatch, and he always wore it inside the wrist.'

'The English did that, at least in World War Two. I saw a movie—'

'Yes, it's a little unusual, but not uncommon. The watch has no great monetary value, but it has great sentimental value for her. It was her father's watch, and it had the relic of a saint set into the dial.' He looked at the sergeant severely as though daring him to make a joke or even manifest incredulity.

But Dunstable kept a straight face and said, 'I see.'

'And it has the Sacred Heart painted on the dial. I thought the band might have snapped open from the impact, and I sent Phelps up to comb the area. Zilch. Then it occurred to me that the doctor might have taken it off in order to feel the pulse, and put it in his pocket and forgotten about it.'

'I can see where it might get in the way, especially if it were largish and he wore it on the inside.'

'Right. So what I'd like you to do is to go and see the good doctor and ask him for the watch.'

'Wouldn't he have come across it by this time if he had it in his pocket since Saturday night?'

'I understand he was coming home from some formal dinner at the Breverton Country Club. So it would be in the pocket of his tuxedo and he might not come across it until the next time he went to some formal function.'

'Yes, I see that. I'll get on it right away.'

'Oh, no need to see him tonight. In fact, I'd rather you didn't. Tomorrow will do.'

CHAPTER TWENTY-SIX

The Board of Directors of the Barnard's Crossing temple met regularly on Sunday shortly after the end of the *shachriss* service. Because there was nothing of importance on the agenda, there was little urgency to get the meeting started. Those who had children in the Sunday school had brought them to their nine o'clock class and then attended the morning selvice, perhaps the only time they ever did. Now they were standing around in groups of two or three talking about baseball, their golf scores, their children, the weather, about almost anything except matters relating to the temple.

'How about getting started?' asked Al Bergson, the president. 'If you guys want to shmoose, do it after the meeting.'

Reluctantly, they took their places around the large oblong board table. One said, 'The rabbi is not here yet. Wasn't he at the service this morning?'

'Sure he was. He led the prayers today. But I guess he's not coming to the meeting'

'He's got a guest from out of town,' another explained. 'A relative.'

'The tall old geezer who sat in the back row?'

'Yeah, that's the one.'

'All right, so let's get started already,' said Bergson. He rapped on the table. 'This meeting is now called to order.'

'Gee, if the rabbi was planning on not coming, I should think he would have told someone.'

'He told me,' said Bergson. 'C'mon, let's get started. Will the secretary please read the minutes of the previous meeting.'

'Hey, don't we vote on the rabbi's contract about now?' asked Dr. Halperin.

'No, Doc,' said the secretary. He leafed through his notebook to the calendar at the back. 'I got that marked for next week.'

'We could take it up today,' suggested the president. 'It would save me asking him not to come to that meeting.'

'Why do we have to vote on his contract?' asked Myron Levitt. He was a new member of the board who had moved to Barnard's Crossing only the year before.

The president explained. 'The rabbi has a one-year contract, so it has to be voted each year.'

'He doesn't have a lifetime contract?' Levitt's tone registered disbelief.

'Uh-uh. Just year to year.'

'Gee, that's funny. I've belonged to quite a few temples. Working for G.E., you get moved around a lot. Every place I've been, what they do, when they hire a new rabbi, they give him a one-year contract, like a trial period. If he's okay, they give him maybe a five-year contract. Then, if they want him to stay on, they give him a life contract. If something has come up, and they don't want him, they sometimes—at least one place I was at—give him another one-year contract so he can look around for another temple.'

'Our rabbi wants us to vote each year.' said Bergson. 'It's like a vote of confidence.'

'But hasn't he been here quite a while?'

'Almost from the beginning. I think he came here the year after the temple started, in 'sixty-two. That's—hey guys, want to know something? The rabbi's been here twenty-five years.'

'Hey, that's right. Twenty-five years! That calls for some kind of celebration, doesn't it?'

'Like what?'

'How about a dinner dance, a real fancy one, maybe at a hotel in Boston.'

'You know how many dinner dances the rabbi and his missus are invited to each year? Half the weddings, yes, and the Bar Mitzvahs, too, they hold in fancy hotels in Boston.'

'Yeah, I guess so, but this would be different. I mean, he'd be the guest of honor, and we'd give him like a gift.'

'What kind of a gift?'

'Well, say a gold watch. A really good one, I mean.'

'He might take that as a kind of hint that

maybe he ought to be more careful to be on time, like for meetings, if he doesn't forget altogether.'

'I tell you what. It's twenty-five years, right? So what's a twenty-fifth anniversary? It's the silver anniversary. So, how about we give him and the rebbitzin a set of sterling silver?'

'And when would they use it? How much entertaining do the Smalls do?'

The much-traveled Myron Levitt offered a suggestion. 'In this temple I belonged to out in California, there was some kind of celebration for the rabbi, and they gave him a car.' He smiled. 'Of course, the chairman of the committee being in the auto business may have had something to do with it.'

'What kind of a car?'

'A Buick.'

'Did they take the rabbi's old car in trade?'

'No ... I don't think so. They had a banquet and there were speeches. And then they gave him the keys to the car. It was like a surprise.'

'If we did that with our rabbi, he'd have two cars. What would he do with two cars?'

'The rebbitzin could have the old one.'

'She doesn't drive.'

'So his son Jonathon—'

'He's away at law school in Washington.'

'So he could come home by plane and then drive it back'

'You know what I think, guys? I think if we spring for a big-ticket item like a car or even a set of sterling, it ought to be only if the rabbi signs a lifetime contract. I mean, what if the very next year some temple comes along and offers him a big increase in salary?'

'You got a point there.'

'You bet. No sense in—'

'Damn right. No lifetime contract, no present.'

'And how would we work that?' asked the president.

'What do you mean?'

The president explained. 'The present is supposed to be a surprise, right? So we hold this banquet, and then what do we do? Do we hand him a contract and the keys to the car and say, 'You sign this, Rabbi, you get these. And if you don't, you get nothing.' Is that what you'd like us to do?'

'Well...'

'Look, Al, you and the rabbi are pretty friendly. I mean you people see the rabbi socially. They've had dinner at your house.'

'Yeah, now and then.'

'They've never accepted an invitation to dinner at our house,' Dr. Halperin remarked. 'Whenever Rachel has invited them, they always had some prior engagement. How come they dine at your house?'

'Because we keep kosher, I suppose.'

'I suppose that's it. So why don't you invite

203

them over some evening, and while you're shmoosing over your roast chicken or whatever, you could ask them what they'd like for a gift.'

'Then they'd think that was why we invited them,' said Bergson.

Myron Levitt spoke up. 'Look, I'm not one for pussyfooting. What's involved is a big-ticket item, and that means it's serious business. And serious business should be conducted in a serious, businesslike way. So I suggest, and I'll make it a motion if you like, that the chairman appoint a committee to go and see the rabbi and put it to him straight.'

'Yeah, that's the ticket.'

'That's what we ought to do.'

'Right on.'

'All right,' said Bergson, 'who'd like to serve on this committee?'

No one raised his hand.

'How about you, Ed?'

'Aw, I couldn't. Me and the rabbi are like this and that. We say hello when we see each other, but we aren't what you could call friendly.'

'Ben?'

Ben shook his head. 'The guy taught me my Bar Mitzvah. He did that kind of thing back then. So I always feel a little like I'm just a kid when I'm with him.'

'I don't mind going to see him,' said Myron Levitt. But this was received with little enthusiasm. Not only was Levitt a new man, but he was also inclined to be outspoken. On the other hand, no one else appeared to be willing to serve.

Then someone suggested a possible solution. 'Look, if Al goes with him...'

'Yeah. How about it, Al?'

The president shrugged. 'Okay by me.' And to Levitt, 'How about sometime today?'

'But he's got a guest from out of town.'

'That's right. Maybe—how about next week, say, after the board meeting?'

'You mean while he's having his dinner?'

'No, of course not. I was figuring on around two o'clock.'

'Okay with me,' said Levitt. 'Matter of fact, there was something I wanted to do this afternoon.'

'Look,' said Ben Halperin, 'if Al and Myron are going, I don't mind going along.'

'Fine,' said the president. 'So we'll be a committee of three.'

CHAPTER TWENTY-SEVEN

As soon as her husband came in the door, Mimi Gorfinkle could see that something was amiss. He seemed worried and ill at ease. She always felt a little guilty on the rare Wednesday afternoons when she left him to his own devices, and always tried to make amends by preparing one of his favorite dishes for supper.

'Guess what I prepared for supper,' she said with forced gaiety.

'Gee, Mimi, I'm not very hungry,' he said.

'You had a hamburger before coming home,' she accused.

'No, it's just that I'm not particularly interested in food.'

'Something happened,' she stated positively. 'You operated and it didn't go well.'

'No. I didn't operate today. Nothing like that.'

'Then what?'

He knew she would keep after him until he told her, so he said, 'A guy came into the office this afternoon—'

'In the afternoon? Without an appointment? An emergency?'

'No, not a patient. He said he was a detective from the Barnard's Crossing Police Department. He was wearing an ordinary suit, but he showed me a badge in like a little leather case. He said he was investigating that car crash on Pine Grove Road Saturday night.'

'What was there to investigate?'

'He said where it's not a natural death, they got to investigate it.'

'So?'

'So he starts asking me a whole bunch of dumb questions. Did I know the man? Had he ever been a patient of mine? How fast was I driving? Had I been drinking? How far behind him was I? And every time I answer, he writes it down in his notebook. So I began to get a little nervous. From the questions I began to get the idea that maybe he thinks I drove him off the road. So I told him I had an important meeting at the hospital, and he says he'll come back tomorrow and he'll have my answers all typed out for me to sign.'

'So then what did you do?'

'I called Ira Lemer. He told me not to sign anything and not to answer any more questions. When he comes back tomorrow, I'm to tell him he should see my lawyer first.'

'So Lemer will see him and ask him what he wants. And if he's trying to make trouble, Lemer will know what to do.'

'Yeah, to him it's just another case,' Gorfinkle scoffed. 'And suppose it gets in the newspapers—"Doctor Questioned in Pine Grove Death"? And then goes on to say I refused to cooperate, will Lemer sue the police department? Or the newspaper?'

'So what else can you do?'

'I could go see the rabbi.'

'So he can offer a prayer or ask a blessing?' she asked scornfully.

'No, but he and the police chief are

207

buddy-buddy. Maybe he could ask him what gives.'

★   ★   ★

When Rabbi Small saw Dr. Gorfinkle among the fifteen or so congregants present at the evening minyan, he assumed that he had come to recite the Mourner's Kaddish on the anniversary of the death of a member of his family. Very few came to the daily services who were not mourners, and Dr. Gorfinkle was certainly not one of them. He did appear occasionally at the Sunday morning service, but that was because he had arrived early for the Board of Directors meeting that immediately followed, and attending the service was preferable to waiting in the corridor.

But Gorfinkle remained seated when the mourners rose to recite the Kaddish, which led the rabbi to suspect that he wanted to confer with him. The ruse was not infrequently employed by those who were unable to see him in his study during the day and were hesitant about obtruding on his privacy when he was home in the evening. Sometimes, he admitted ruefully, it was the only way they were able to make up the necessary ten for a minyan.

Sure enough, no sooner was the service over, when Gorfinkle said, 'Oh, I say, Rabbi, got a minute?'

'Sure.'

'Well ...' Gorfinkle hesitated, not out of uncertainty, but obviously because he did not want to be overheard by the other members of the minyan, who were now leaving. When the door swung behind the last of them, he said, 'You know the police chief, don't you? I mean you and he are pretty friendly from what I've heard.'

'Yes, we're friendly,' said the rabbi cautiously. 'Is there something...'

'I'm not sure. Today is Wednesday, and I take Wednesday afternoons off. Usually, the wife and I do something together, go into Boston maybe, have an early dinner and catch a movie. But today she had a luncheon to go to. So I thought I'd hang around the office and read some of the medical journals. It's not easy keeping up, you know. So there's a knock on the door, and when I open it, there's a man in an ordinary business suit who says he's from the police and he shows me a badge, and he says he's working on the Victor Joyce case. At first I didn't get it, and then it came to me: Victor Joyce was the guy who was in that accident on Pine Grove Road Saturday night. Did you see the item in the paper? They gave the name as Victor Jones, but it's the same guy.'

'Yes, I saw it.'

'Well, I was the one who reported it to the police. I was coming home from this formal dinner we hold once a month, and I see this car that's plowed into a tree. So naturally I stop. The side window is shattered with some jagged fragments along the bottom of the frame, and this guy's hand is sticking out. There was nothing I could do, but I reached in and turned off the ignition. I read somewhere that the car could explode if the ignition is on even if the motor has conked out. Then I took his pulse, and it was fairly normal even though he was unconscious.

'Well, I was halfway home, and what was the sense in turning around and going back to Breverton, so I went on home and called the police from there and reported it. If it had been on a regular street, I might have stayed there and stopped some car to report it while I waited. But Pine Grove Road and late at night, and misty at that, I could have been there for hours and no other car would come along.

'So he comes in—the guy in the business suit, I mean—and he sits down and takes out a notebook. I didn't know we had any plainclothesmen on the Barnard's Crossing police.'

'Well, Lieutenant Jennings doesn't always wear a uniform, and Chief Lanigan—'

'No, I know Eban Jennings.'

'I guess they have one on the force every now and then.'

'Well, anyway, he starts asking questions

and writing down what I say. Every now and then he looks at what he's written and kind of frowns like there's something he doesn't understand. Where was I coming from? What was I doing in Breverton? What time did I start out for Barnard's Crossing? Is there someone who can vouch for the time I left the club? Did I recognize Joyce? Was he maybe a patient of mine at one time? When did I first see his car? How far back was I? How fast was I driving? To tell the truth, Rabbi, I began to get a little nervous. It was like he was trying to make out that I hit the guy, or forced him off the road. So finally I say, "I'm sorry, but I've got to be at the hospital for an important consultation." I figured maybe I ought to see my lawyer, see. So he says, "All right, I'll get this typed out and bring it in sometime tomorrow for you to sign." He closes his notebook and gets up like he's ready to leave. Then he says, "By the way, was he wearing gloves?" and I tell him no. "And how about a wristwatch?" Well, I'm being careful now, you understand, so I say, "I didn't see a watch, but I saw a watchband. Maybe it got turned on his hand from the impact of the crash, or maybe he wears it with the watch on the inside." Then he opens the door and says, "I'll be back tomorrow with your statement, and if you'll bring the watch, I'll take it with me." And he's out of the door. Gone, just like that.

'What watch was he talking about, Rabbi? So I go to the door, and he's standing in front of the elevator. He's got the door open and is ready to go into the elevator, so I ask him what watch he's talking about. And he says, "I figure you took his watch off to take his pulse and you put it in your pocket and forgot about it." And he steps into the elevator and the door closes. But I didn't touch his wrist or his hand, Rabbi. I wouldn't because it might be broken and I could make it worse. It was when I reached in to turn off the ignition. I put my fingertips at his throat—his head was kind of lolling back against the headrest. That's when I took his pulse.'

'I see. And what do you want me to do?'

'Well, I figured where you and the chief are kind of friendly, if you were downtown and dropped into the station, like to say hello—'

'The Lanigans are coming over tonight for a bit of supper,' said the rabbi.

'Well gee, that's swell. If you could kind of bring it up. Don't tell him I came to you special, but you could say you bumped into me and—'

'I understand.'

'See, I was wondering was this official, or was this guy, the plainclothesman, I mean, just kind of fishing, you know, working on his own.'

CHAPTER TWENTY-EIGHT

Amy Lanigan was in the kitchen helping Miriam with the dishes. On the basis of previous experience, they were apt to remain there for some time after they finished, so the police chief and the rabbi repaired to the living room.

'You want another cup of coffee?' Miriam called out from the kitchen. Having received a nod of assent from Lanigan to his questioning look, the rabbi hurried out to the kitchen and returned a moment later with two steaming cups. Then he told his guest of his conversation with Gorfinkle, and explained just how the doctor had taken the victim's pulse after turning off the ignition.

Lanigan nodded and was silent for a moment. Then he said, 'I went to see the widow yesterday to offer my condolences.'

'Oh, you know her? Or is that your normal practice?'

'She's the niece of Cyrus Merton—'

'The big realtor?'

'Uh-huh. He makes a sizable contribution to the Policeman's Retirement Fund each year and buys I don't know how many tickets to the Policeman's Ball. You know how it is. She was more of a daughter than a niece; she was brought up in his house and he has no children of his own. I have seen her in church occasionally on a Sunday. But Amy knew her. She had worked with Amy on some church project Amy was interested in. She's a very devout girl, according to Amy. Brought up in convent schools, and then went to Saint Madelaine's, which is a very strict college run by the Sisters of the Sacred Heart. Amy says, from what she let drop from time to time, that she thought she had a vocation—'

'You mean to go into a convent?'

'Uh-huh. But then she met Victor Joyce and decided to get married. Happens a lot, I guess. Anyway, shortly after we arrived, she led me into what I guess was her husband's study. She shows me the stuff that had been turned over to her, her husband's effects: wedding ring, billfold, handkerchief—the usual stuff that a man has in his pockets. And then she tells me his watch is missing. She was terribly upset about it.'

'Was it a valuable watch?'

'Not particularly, from what I could gather. But it had been her father's. Her mother had bought it for him in Rome, where her parents had gone to celebrate their tenth wedding anniversary. She had had a relic mounted on the dial—'

'A relic?'

'That's right, a relic of a saint. A Saint Ulric, she said, whoever he was. A fragment of bone, in a tiny silver tube which her

mother had had mounted on the dial by a
watchmaker. Her father had always worn it
on the inside of his wrist so that it was closer
to his heart, nearer to the arteries and veins,
you know. She had given it to her husband
when they got engaged, and he had also worn
it inside his wrist. I told her that it was
unthinkable that one of my men would have
taken it, but I said I would check into it. I
thought maybe when he crashed, the impact
might have released the catch on the band
and that it had been flung off his wrist. So
when I got back to the station, I sent a man
up to the scene of the accident to comb the
area.'

'And?'

'Nothing. But I also had another idea. I
remembered that Dr. Gorfinkle had told
Sergeant Pierce, who was on the desk at the
time, that he had taken the victim's pulse. It
occurred to me that if Joyce was wearing a
wristwatch, especially if he was wearing it
inside his wrist, the doctor may have taken it
off in order to feel the pulse, that he had put
it in his pocket and forgotten about it. So I
sent Detective Sergeant Dunstable to ask him
about it. I sent Dunstable rather than a
uniformed man because I didn't want it to
appear to be an official inquiry, if you know
what I mean. If the neighbors see a policeman
in uniform ringing your doorbell, they may
think you're in some sort of trouble. So I

215

wanted him just to ask, not institute an official inquiry.'

'It evidently didn't work out that way,' observed the rabbi.

'I guess not. I try to impress on my men that we are a smalltown police force and that the people we have to deal with are our friends and neighbors, and what's more, that each year they vote our salaries at the town meeting. But they watch TV and sometimes they tend to model their behavior on what they see in the crime shows, and besides, it's hard to resist the lure of authority.

'I'm sorry that Gorfinkle was upset, and you can tell him that I'll see to it that Dunstable doesn't bother him again. I guess what happened is that someone came along after Gorfinkle left, and seeing the watch and that the owner was unconscious, simply took it.'

'But wouldn't he have called the police to notify them of the accident? He wouldn't have had to leave his name.'

'You'd think so, wouldn't you? But the autopsy report said he had died as a result of hemorrhage from a ruptured artery in the left wrist. I guess that in trying to get the watch off, he cut the artery along the jagged row of glass and the blood began to spurt.'

'Or possibly the other way around,' said the rabbi.

'What do you mean the other way around?'

'Well, you think he may have cut the artery in order to remove the watch. It's also possible that he removed the watch in order to cut the artery.'

'But that's murder. Why would anyone kill—'

'I didn't mean to suggest that anyone did,' the rabbi said hastily. 'Merely that it is just as logical to assume that the watch was taken to expose the blood vessels in the wrist as it is to assume that they were accidentally severed in removing the watch.'

'But the watch is gone,' Lanigan insisted.

'And the man is dead,' said the rabbi.

'But it doesn't take any animus to steal a man's watch. All that's required is opportunity. But to kill someone calls for a powerful motive.'

'A powerful motive is needed to plot a murder,' the rabbi said slowly, 'but suppose there is an opportunity to get rid of someone who is a nuisance, an inconvenience. You don't hate him or fear him. He's just troublesome, and you can get rid of him with no effort on your part, as here, where all that was required was to press down on the man's wrist.'

'I suppose so,' Lanigan admitted. 'And it could be that all that was involved was the taking of a watch, but the thief was nervous or clumsy and pressed down too hard. A little thing can make all the difference. The widow said that if Victor Joyce had only waited a few minutes before setting off for this dinner he was going to, it wouldn't have happened. See, Cyrus Merton was going to that same dinner and he came by to pick up Joyce so they could drive up together. Then they would have come home together.'

'Then both might have been injured,' said the rabbi.

'Exactly what I said. But she said Cyrus would not have let him drive if he were drunk. It's all a matter of luck, I suppose, and for the Mertons it was all bad. That same night Cyrus had his car stolen.'

'While he was at dinner in Breverton?'

'No, right here in Barnard's Crossing, at the mall, while he was at the Donut Shop.'

'What was he doing there?'

'Having a cup of coffee, I understand.'

The entrance of the wives from the kitchen halted further discussion, but later as they were driving home, Lanigan thought about it. His policeman's instincts were aroused. Even if the blood vessels had been cut as a result of removing the watch, it would still be murder, felony murder. In any case, it was far more important than the theft of a watch.

*   *   *

Early the next morning he called in Sergeant Dunstable. 'What are you working on,

Sergeant?' he asked.

'Well, I was just going to type out that statement of Gorfinkle's so I could—'

'Don't bother, Sergeant. I inquired into it myself and it seems that he took the pulse by placing his fingertips at the man's throat. He didn't touch the man's wrist at all. Which means that someone came along afterward, and if he cut the man's wrist in trying to take his watch, that's felony murder.'

'But that could have been Gorfinkle.'

Lanigan shook his head vigorously. 'Would a successful doctor—and believe me, Gorfinkle is a successful doctor—steal a man's watch? With his wife right there looking on? What's more, if he had started to bleed profusely, he would have told us the man was critical. So we could get out there in a hurry. He wouldn't have suggested the guy was stable by saying his pulse was normal. So what I want you to do is run up to Breverton and make inquiries around the club. Maybe you can find out if he was wearing a watch in the first place.'

'But you said his wife told you—'

'Yeah, but if he was driving at the speed he must have been driving to wrap himself around a tree, on Pine Grove Road at night, he must have been drunk. And drunks are always misplacing things. He may have even given the watch to someone for money for a drink So you go up there and see what you

219

can find out. Who left when? Was there any sort of row before he left? Did anything unusual at all happen that night? Got it?'

'Got it.'

CHAPTER TWENTY-NINE

It was four o'clock when Dunstable returned to Barnard's Crossing. He went straight to Lanigan's office. 'I was lucky, Chief,' he said, 'real lucky. I see the manager'—a glance at his notebook—'Gerald Foster, and he tells me it was a banquet of the faculty of the Windermere Christian College of Liberal Arts. Just the faculty; no wives, no husbands, no secretaries, just the teachers. Now you've got to know the layout in order to get the picture. There's this lounge with a coatroom on one side and a kind of alcove on the other side, which is the bar. And beyond is the dining room.'

Lanigan nodded. 'I know the layout. I've had dinner there several times.'

'Oh yeah? Well, the point is that the bartender and the coatroom attendant can see the whole scene. I mean, if there was anything going on, like a fight or a big argument, they'd see it. So I see the bartender'—another glance at the notebook—'Jack Bohrman.' Dunstable chuckled. 'He says, 'I'm Bohrman the barman.' A regular card, that one. And he knows Victor Joyce. Ask me how he knows Victor Joyce.'

'All right, how does Bohrman know Joyce?'

'On account he played golf there a few times. And he tells me Joyce was a champion on the nineteenth hole. See, there are eighteen holes in a golf course, and—'

'I know what the nineteenth hole is, Sergeant. You mean Joyce was a boozer.'

'Yeah, according to Bohrman, he'd lap it up. Well, for the banquet they had what they call a cash bar. The first drink was free, but after that you had to pay. See, there was like a stub on their tickets, that they tore off and gave the bartender for their first drink. So Joyce hands in his stub, gets his drink, tosses it off, and wants another. But he doesn't have any money on him, and Bohrman tells him he's not allowed to cuff drinks. But later he comes back, and he's got plenty of money now. Bohrman figures he must have had about four drinks altogether. Scotch. Doubles.'

'That's a lot of scotch,' Lanigan remarked. 'Where'd he get the money?'

'Aha, I had the same idea. Did he sell the watch to one of the other guests? So I ask Bohrman was Joyce wearing a watch, but he couldn't remember. I didn't really expect him to. Just thought I'd chance it. Anyway, Joyce comes up to the bar for another double scotch, and Bohrman refuses to serve him. Claims he was like weaving. So he refuses him, says he's got his license to think of. So Joyce tells him to shove it, and walks across the lounge to get his coat.'

'Typical,' said Lanigan.

'Typical of Joyce?'

'Typical of drunks.'

'Yeah, there's where I get lucky, real lucky. I'm lucky that the coatroom guy is there. See, they don't operate the coatroom fulltime. I mean, you go there for lunch or dinner, you hang your coat up yourself in the coatroom. They don't have an attendant. Only when they have one of these big affairs. What's more, this kid, the coatroom attendant, Charlie Aherne, he's there only part-time, doing all kinds of odd jobs, whatever they ask him. The rest of the time he goes to school, in Boston, and get this: to Windermere, where he's going into his junior year, so he knows all the guests at the dinner.

'Does he know Victor Joyce: sure he knows Professor Joyce. And what time did he leave? He knows exactly on account he says to him, "Leaving early, Professor?" because the clock on the wall said quarter to ten. And Joyce raises his fist like he's just won some victory—that's what the kid said—see, Joyce wears his watch on the inside of his wrist, and he closes one eye and kind of squints, and says, "Almost ten. Late enough." So we

222

know the time he left. And we know he was wearing his watch.'

'And by the way he looked at his watch, that he was probably squiffed,' murmured Lanigan.

Dunstable was ecstatic. 'That's just what I figured. Fact, I said to the kid, "You mean he was drunk?" And he says, "Well, he was feeling no pain." And if you need more proof, the kid tells me he asks for his raincoat, but he can't find his check. So the kid asks him to describe the coat, and then he remembers he left it in the car, and turns and goes for the door.'

'Very good, Sergeant. Very good indeed. Now, did anyone else leave early?'

'Yeah. Fifteen minutes later another guy left.' Again he referred to his notebook. 'A Professor Jacobs. Mordecai Jacobs. I'm not sure I'm pronouncing that right. The kid spelled it out for me. Mordecai—I never heard the name before. He hadn't checked anything, at least not anything of his own, so—'

'What do you mean he didn't check anything of his own? Did he check somebody else's coat?'

'That's right. He was with a lady professor, a Professor Saxon, so he checked her wrap for her, but it was after they were seated. This weather, not too many of the men wore coats, although some had raincoats just in case. But, of course, almost all the women wore coats.'

'I see. So did he claim the woman's coat?'

'No, he just walked out the door. This kid, Aherne, he'd had him in an English course, and I guess he liked him, so he followed him out. He was just going down the stairs when he said to him something like, "You leaving early, too, Professor?" And the professor told him he had another party to go to.'

'You mean he left the coatroom unattended?'

'Oh no. He called over one of the two regular waitresses, a Mary Ellen Brown. The other waitresses are all temporaries. See, Aherne works only until ten. Then either Mary Ellen or the other regular takes over, and Aherne goes home.'

'And the tips? Who gets those?'

'All tips, the ones the guests leave on the tables and those they leave at the coatroom, are pooled and the girls divide them up. Aherne doesn't share; he's on a straight hourly basis.'

'I see. So this Jacobs left at ten.'

'That's right.'

'Anybody else leave early?'

'Nope. Just those two all the time Aherne was there.'

'Yes, but how about right afterward? Did you question this Mary Ellen?'

'I did, but she tells me she didn't take over the coatroom in person until sometime later, maybe around half past on account they were busy serving second cups of coffee and clearing away dishes. See, what they do, they put up a little sign which says 'Ring for service', with an arrow pointing to a button you press. Then any one of the waitresses who happens to be nearby goes over and gets your coat.'

'I see. And the party broke up when?'

'Around eleven, eleven-fifteen. Then they all went for their coats, those that had checked them. From what this Mary Ellen said, some of them just folded them up and put them under their chairs. She thought it was a cheap crowd, and the tips weren't all that much either.'

'Good work, Sergeant. Now, I'd like you to get in touch with this Professor Jacobs and—'

'See what he knows?'

'Right.'

CHAPTER THIRTY

On leaving Lanigan's office, Sergeant Dunstable telephoned Professor Jacobs to set up an appointment. The telephone rang several times and then a voice said, 'I cannot speak on the telephone at this time, but I will get back to you. At the sound of the beep, please leave your name and telephone number. Thank you.'

The sergeant waited a moment, and then when he heard the beep he said, 'Sergeant Dunstable, Barnard's Crossing Police Department,' but since he was on his way home he gave his home telephone number. He waited all evening, but his call was not returned. Before going to bed he called again, but heard only the recorded message.

The next day, Friday, he tried again, but again heard only the recorded message. It occurred to him that Professor Jacobs had probably received his message but had not bothered to call back because he did not want to be bothered or did not want to get involved. Dunstable decided to drive to Boston.

It was a large apartment house near Coolidge Corner in Brookline. While not run down, it showed signs of neglect. There was a hedge in front and it was untrimmed and broken in a couple of places, and the glass in the front door had a small crack in one corner. In the lobby there were three rows of names, each with a push button beside it. Mordecai Jacobs, Apartment 61, was the first name on the third row. Dunstable pushed the button but no voice responded through the phone and there was no answering buzz that would release the catch on the door. He waited. The guy might be in the toilet. Then he tried again. A middle-aged woman, her hair in curlers under a scarf, carrying a mesh bag with groceries, came in and watched as he pressed the button.

'He's not in,' she said.

'Who's not in?'

'The one you're ringing, sixty-one. I'm across the hall from him. He left.'

'What do you mean he left? You mean he's gone for good?'

She shrugged. 'Well, he was carrying a suitcase.'

'But the furniture, he's moved it out?'

'What furniture? It's a furnished flat.'

'When did he leave?'

'Yesterday. I was just coming home, so it was around seven.' Back in his car, Dunstable reflected his trip to the city had not been a total failure. He had learned that Jacobs had left, which might be of significance, or it might not. Still, it was slim pickings. He knew Lanigan would not criticize him for his initiative when he reported to him, but he might appear amused.

He wondered uneasily if he hadn't made a mistake in giving his connection with the police department when he telephoned. His reason for wanting to see Jacobs had been merely to round out his inquiry. But now it occurred to him that Jacobs might have a closer connection to the case. He had left the dinner before it was over, he had left the woman he had brought, and presumably she

227

would have to find someone else to drive her back to Boston; he had left shortly after Joyce, and could be said to have followed him out of the club; and now, after learning that the police wanted to speak with him, he had left—moved out?—of his apartment. Dunstable decided to see the woman Jacobs had brought to the dinner—a Professor Saxon, according to his notes—who might tell him what excuse Jacobs had given her for leaving her.

He called the college, and when he asked for Professor Saxon, was connected with the Psychology Department. The one who answered there, said, 'Alice Saxon? She came in, but she's not here at the moment. I guess she'll be in and out all morning, at least.'

He drove to the college and was directed to the Psychology Department on the third floor. A young man there said, 'Professor Saxon? Her office is down the corridor, last door on the left.'

The door was open, but the office was empty. Although there was a visitor's chair in front of the desk, he decided to wait in the corridor. After five or ten minutes he was about to go in and sit down, when he heard the click of high heels on the uncarpeted floor. She looked at him questioningly, and he said, 'Professor Saxon?'

She nodded.

'Detective Sergeant Dunstable, BCPD.'

'B.C.? Before Christ?'

'Barnard's Crossing Police Department,' he said stiffly.

She smiled. 'Oh, sorry. Stupid of me. And what can I do for you, Sergeant?'

'I'm investigating the cause of the accident on Pine Grove Road last Saturday night.'

'Well, come in. It was a terrible thing,' she said, 'but is there any mystery about it? From what people said around school, Mr. Joyce had been drinking rather heavily and he ran his car off the road.'

Dunstable nodded. 'That's probably what happened. But there was some talk among the help at the club the next day, and that started some rumors that we felt we had to check out.'

'Rumors? What sort of—'

'Well, someone left a little after Joyce, followed him, you might say. And that was before the dinner was over, at least before the dessert and coffee, which is kind of strange. So if he followed Joyce, that suggested the possibility that he might have forced him off the road. What makes it kind of funny is that he not only left before he finished his dinner, but that he also left the woman he'd brought to the dinner, you, and you had to get someone else to drive you back to Boston.'

'You're talking about Professor Jacobs?'

'Yeah, Mordecai Jacobs.'

'And what did he have to say?'

229

'I haven't spoken with him. I called him yesterday and left my name and number with his answering machine. He didn't call back. So I went to see him. He wasn't in, and a neighbor said that she had seen him leave his apartment, carrying a suitcase.'

'Oh, he probably went home. The school year is over, you know.'

'And where is home for him? Do you know?'

She laughed. 'I certainly do because it's my hometown too. Higginstown. It's a small town in Pennsylvania. That's how I know Mordecai Jacobs. I got him the job here. I mean, I told him there was a vacancy and he applied and got it.'

'Oh.'

'And he didn't leave me in the lurch. He wasn't planning to drive back to Boston after the dinner. In fact, he was going to leave at the earliest opportunity because he had another party to go to. He didn't want to go to the dinner at all. I persuaded him that it would be a good idea if he did.'

'Why didn't he want to go?' asked Dunstable seriously.

'Lot of faculty don't. Only about a third actually attended.'

'But why don't they want to go? It's their organization, isn't it? Their school?'

'Because the school year has finished, and they want to go off to their summer places.

230

Because they don't want to spend twenty-five dollars for a ticket. Because their wives don't like to be left at home while their husbands, they think, are having a good time. Because it means driving out of the city for an hour or more. And I suppose because in the last analysis, it's a drag.'

'So why did you persuade him to go?'

'Because he's up for tenure, and I thought it might do him some good.'

'Tenure? That means they can't fire him?'

'Oh, they can, but it has to be for something Godawful and even then not without a hearing.'

'You mean that makes it a lifetime job.'

'Pretty much.'

'And is it such a wonderful job?'

'Sergeant, it's the best job in the world, especially nowadays when salary schedules are pretty reasonable.'

'And you get tenure by—by showing you're one of the gang? By participating in—in whatever is going on?'

She shook her head. 'I don't know how you get tenure. It differs from one department to another. In some departments it's the chairman who decides, sometimes with the advice of the senior members, sometimes alone. One thing I was sure of was that it wouldn't do any harm, and it might do some good. I thought he ought to go. But, he had this other party to go to and it was a lot more important to him.'

'Oh, yeah? What was so important about the other party?'

'There's a girl who works in Boston that he is serious about. Her family lives in Barnard's Crossing and her kid brother was having a Bar Mitzvah party to which she had invited him. My guess is, to show him off to her folks. So naturally...'

'Naturally,' Dunstable agreed. 'And what is her name?'

Alice Saxon shook her head. 'I don't know. I never met her.'

★   ★   ★

He was methodical. He outlined the next steps he would take. He would return to Barnard's Crossing and go to see Rabbi Small who would surely know who had a Bar Mitzvah last Saturday. Then he would go to see the family of the Bar Mitzvah and find out from them just when Jacobs had arrived. Was he nervous? Was he shaken up? Then he would lay it all before Lanigan: motive Joyce was his rival for what the lady professor had called the best job in the world; opportunity—he had actually followed Joyce out of the club; weapon—it was right there, the shattered window. He would get permission from Lanigan—how could he refuse to go to Higginstown where he would question, maybe arrest, Jacobs. He might find a dent in the fender of his car. He might—

And then it occurred to him that Rabbi Small was a friend of Lanigan's. Lanigan might not take kindly to his interrogating the rabbi. Maybe it would be better to see Lanigan first.

CHAPTER THIRTY-ONE

Thursday night was Amy Lanigan's night out with 'the girls.' Why Thursday? 'Because Thursday is maid's night off.' They might go to a movie, or to dinner at a restaurant and then to one of the large shopping malls to wander around the stores, or they might meet at the house of one of them to play bridge and gossip. Because Chief Lanigan knew that what awaited him at home was perhaps cold meat and a bottle of beer, he tended to work late Thursday nights.

It was after seven when he decided to call it a day and left the station house. But when he got into his car, it occurred to him that he might call on Cyrus Merton. So instead of driving home, he drove to the Point. It was the housekeeper who answered when he pushed the doorbell.

He looked at her wonderingly. 'Nellie?' he

hazarded. She smiled as she saw him struggling to recall her surname. 'Nellie, Nellie'—then triumphantly, 'Nellie Heath.'

'That's right, but it's Nellie Marston now.'

'I didn't know you worked here. I didn't know you were back in town.'

'I've been back five or six years now. When Bill died, I came back here because my daughter was living in Swampscott, and then I got this job as housekeeper and stayed on after she moved down to Florida. And you're the big chief here, eh?'

'I'm chief of police, but I don't know that it makes me the big chief.'

'And you married Amy Harper.'

'That's right.'

'She wasn't in our class, seems to me.'

'Oh no. She was a freshman when we were seniors.'

'Yeah, I remember some of the girls saying you're robbing the cradle when you took her to the senior prom. Well, well. You want to see Mr. Merton? He's not in. If it's urgent, you can find them, him and his sister, at their niece's in Shurtcliffe Circle. They've been going over there for supper since the accident. They wanted her to move back here, at least for a while, but she wouldn't. So they go there and Mrs. Burke makes the supper so Margaret won't be eating alone. Or you can come in and wait here. They're usually back by eight.'

'I think I'll wait here,' said Lanigan.

She ushered him into a small room with leather chairs, which he assumed was Cyrus Merton's study. 'You'll be more comfortable here than in the living room. Would you care for a cup of coffee?'

'I'll have a cup if you'll join me,' he said.

She hesitated. 'Well, all right.'

She left and returned in a little while with a pot of coffee, a plate of cookies, and two cups and saucers on a tray. 'What a terrible thing to happen,' she said as she poured the coffee.

'The Mertons took it hard, I suppose,' he suggested.

'Oh yes, especially him.' She dropped her voice as if to tell a secret. 'You know, I think they cared more about him than they did about her.'

'Didn't they like her?'

'Well, of course they did. I mean, she was their niece, actually their only living relative. But there wasn't much affection. Not them to her, nor she to them.' Once again she dropped her voice. 'You understand, they didn't talk in front of me, but me in the house with them, just the three of us most of the time, except when Margaret was here, or the cleaning woman who came in a couple of times a week, and me serving them, and going back and forth from my kitchen to the dining room, I couldn't help overhearing.'

He nodded understanding.

Her voice still low, she went on, 'I got the impression they'd had nothing to do with Margaret's father, their brother, when he married her mother, on account she was Puerto Rican. 'That spic,' the missus called her. When she was left an orphan, they had to take her in. That was before my time, but since I've been here I never once saw them put an arm around her, or give her anything but a kind of polite peck when she came home from school.'

'And she to them?'

'Pretty much. Of course, she was grateful when they'd buy her things, like when they bought her the car, but that's about it. I mean she was grateful and that's all. And for all they were so religious, they were real upset when she told them she was planning to go into a convent, especially His Nibs. See, that would be the end of the family. Once I heard the missus say she didn't seem to be interested in men, and he said it was just what he called a defense mechanism. She didn't think she could get a man, so she told herself she didn't want one. Then he said, 'But if I arrange for a real nice-looking guy to go after her, that'll start her juices flowing.' And I guess that's how it worked out. They hurried it right along, too, I suppose because one or the other of them might back out.'

They heard a car turn into the driveway. She rose hastily. 'I better go and tell them

236

you're here,' she said, and gathering up her cup and saucer, she left the room.

★   ★   ★

Cyrus Merton came into the room with hand extended. 'Ah, Lanigan, I see Mrs. Marston has given you coffee. Good, good. You've come with good news. You've found my car.'

'I'm afraid not,' said Lanigan. 'You know how it is. If it's kids, they might ride around for a while, and then leave it. Sometimes, they'll ride it until they run out of gas, and then abandon it. And sometimes they vandalize it before they abandon it, out of sheer nastiness. If they had left it somewhere in the area, we would have had it by now. But if we haven't found it by now, there's a good chance they sold it. So if we don't find it in a day or two, you'd better claim on your insurance. No, I came about the accident on Pine Grove Road.'

Merton shook his head. 'A terrible business, Chief. Such a fine young man, so full of life. And Margaret, my poor niece, is all broken up about it. We wanted her to come back here, but she won't leave the house, as though she's still hoping that he'll come back. So we've been going over there every night to sit with her. Agnes, my sister, you know, makes her some supper and we have our evening meal with her so she won't have to eat alone. What is it you . . .'

'Want to know? Well, we're required to investigate any death that is not due to natural causes. You know, who or what caused it.'

'Ah, I see, I see.' He nodded reflectively and then asked, 'Have you seen my niece about this?'

'No . . . we just went over to pay our respects, my wife and I, and offer our condolences. Amy, my wife, worked with her on some church matter.'

'Well, I wish you wouldn't, unless you absolutely have to, of course. It would just cause the poor girl more grief. She is bearing up but—' He stopped abruptly, too moved to continue. He was silent for a moment and then his manner changed. He straightened up in his chair and said in a voice calm and controlled, 'I have a confession to make. I was the cause of the poor fellow's death.'

'You?'

'Yes, I haven't seen the autopsy report, but I'm sure, from all I've heard, that the poor fellow was drunk. And I was the cause of his drunkenness. You see, he'd forgotten to cash a check, and he'd arrived at the dinner with no money to speak of, and he wanted to buy a drink. So he asked me to lend him some. I simply held out my wallet to him, and as near as I can make out, he took thirty dollars. Which he proceeded to drink up. Not that he was an alcoholic, you understand. Just that he liked a drink on a festive occasion. Well, I feel that I was responsible for his getting drunk and so was responsible for his death. And that's why I'd rather you didn't talk to my niece about it. You know, that it should be someone in the family that was the cause of her misfortune.'

'I understand,' said Lanigan sympathetically. He rose, and so did Merton. 'I don't see any reason for telling the widow about it, and I promise I won't.'

'That's very decent of you, Chief. Can I offer you a drink before you leave?'

Lanigan smiled faintly. 'I don't think I'd better.'

CHAPTER THIRTY-TWO

Back in Barnard's Crossing it occurred to Sergeant Dunstable that he did not have to ask Rabbi Small, or get Lanigan to ask him, which family had had a Bar Mitzvah party. It was almost sure to have been mentioned in the social notes of the local newspaper. So he repaired to the library and secured a copy of the previous week's *Reporter*. And there it was: Bernard Lerner will celebrate his Bar Mitzvah at the temple, Rabbi David Small officiating. It went on to say that after the service there would be a collation in the vestry and a party at the Lerner home in Charleton Park in the evening.

Charleton Park was a real estate development covering a large tract of land. The road wound and twisted, sometimes all but encircling individual houses. The developer had built only two or three houses and had then decided it was more profitable, and quicker, to sell house lots. And these ranged in size from ten thousand square feet, the town minimum, to twenty-five thousand square feet. The houses were large and varied in style, in accordance with the owner's taste. There were ultramodern houses that looked like small factories, constructed of cement blocks and glass, and there were modernized Victorian houses with cornices and gables. There were colonial houses with verandas and a row of pillars in front, and there were low Spanish houses with a surrounding wall and a patio. To Sergeant Dunstable, they all smelled of money, and he realized he would have to tread cautiously.

When he rang the bell, he heard a young woman's voice beyond the door calling out, 'I'll get it, Maud.' A moment later the door was opened by a young woman he judged to be in her early twenties, who was wearing slacks and a sweater. She looked at him inquiringly.

'Sergeant Dunstable of the Barnard's

Crossing Police Department,' he announced, and showed his badge.

'Oh, you want my father. He's not in. He's in his office in Lynn, unless he's at the courthouse or the Registry.'

'And why would I want your father, miss?'

'Because you said you were from the police department, I suppose it has to do with one of his cases. If it's just to leave something, you can leave it with me and I'll see that he gets it.'

'No, it's not concerned with—I'm making inquiries—look, can I come in?'

'Sure,' and she stepped aside so that he could enter.

'You had a party here last Saturday night, didn't you?'

'Oh, so that's it? Some of the neighbors complain of the noise?'

'No, at least not that I know of. Were you expecting a visitor?'

'Well, of course. It was my kid brother's Bar Mitzvah party. We expected and received a whole bunch of visitors, only we call them guests. It was a party, wasn't it? And we had a mob.'

He tried again. 'I mean were you expecting a particular visitor to arrive quite late?'

'Who did you have in mind, Sergeant?'

'A Professor Jacobs.'

'Oh, Mord Jacobs. Yeah, he said he'd try to make it. See, there was another party, up in Breverton, that he had to go to. But he said he might be able to break away early and come down. I gave him explicit directions. I told him to go Pine Grove Road and that would enable him to get to Barnard's Crossing a lot quicker than if he went by way of the state road. And he didn't show. I thought he hadn't been able to break away, but he called me, quite late, and said he was back home in Brookline, that he'd tried to make it but had got lost. He finally got into Charleton Park and couldn't find the house. He said he'd driven around looking for a house all lit up with a lot of cars parked in front. Imagine! But typical. But why are you interested in Mord, in Professor Jacobs?'

'Well, there was an accident on Pine Grove Road last night—'

'Oh, yes. Wasn't it terrible? And he was a colleague of Mord's at Windermere. Both in the same department. What's Mord got to do with it?'

She was pert and self-assured, and Dunstable was annoyed that he could not seem to control the conversation. She was evidently not in the slightest awe of the police department or of him, a sergeant. 'Well, see, we have to investigate every death that was not due to natural causes.'

'But the story around town is that the man was drunk, so he slammed into a tree. He was probably going a hundred miles an hour.

Maybe he just blacked out. That's not a natural way of dying, but I'd say the reason is clear enough. So what's to investigate?'

'Well, we've got to,' he said doggedly.

'And what's it got to do with Mord?'

'Well, see, he left a little after Joyce, so we thought he might have seen him and maybe spoken to him just before. We'd like to talk to Professor Jacobs to clear things up, you know. But he's not at his apartment, and he's left town.'

'Yes, he went home. His mother isn't well, and he goes back every chance he gets. But he'll be back in town in a couple of days, I guess. He's doing some research, and also preparing for his summer classes.'

'Then I guess we'll just have to wait,' he said philosophically. 'Sorry to have troubled you.'

★   ★   ★

While the Lerners were not particularly observant, Mrs. Lerner kept a kosher house, and they attended the Friday evening services with some regularity. Usually, only Mr. and Mrs. Lerner went, but tonight Mr. Lerner insisted that his son go, too.

'Oh Dad, none of the guys go.'

'You were Bar Mitzvahed just last week. The least you can do is show up for the first Sabbath. And you ought to go, too, Clara. I

243

mean we ought to go as a family.'

But she said she had 'things to do,' and they did not press her. They suspected she was expecting a phone call from her friend, the professor.

No sooner had they left than she went to the telephone and called the Jacobses' number in Higginstown.

'Clara? I was going to call you.'

'Yeah, sure.'

'No, really. See, there's a departmental meeting Monday for those who'll be teaching in the summer session, so I'll be back no later than Sunday. And from something Sugrue said before I left, I got the feeling that he was planning to submit my name for tenure, so—'

'What did he say?'

'He said he thought he might have something to tell me when I came back for the meeting.'

'You think that means tenure?'

'I'm hoping. I was going to call you to keep Monday night free so we can celebrate if it is.'

'You mean dinner at a fancy restaurant?'

'That's right. Anyplace you say. And the theatre afterward, and—'

'Then how about dinner here at my house?'

'We-el, if that's what you want. Sure. All right, sure. But you'll have to give me better directions than you did last time. I wouldn't want to get lost again.'

'Oh, I'll see to that. I'll have you come in

by train and I'll meet you at the station. Just how long did you drive around looking for the house?'

'It seemed like hours, but it was probably only about twenty minutes after I got to Charleton Park. Why?'

'What time did you leave Breverton?'

'Around ten.'

'Did you see anything unusual on your way to Barnard's Crossing?'

'Unusual? No-o. Why all these questions, Clara?'

'Somebody from the police department came to see me this morning, a Sergeant Dunstable—'

'Oh, yeah. He called me and left his name and phone number on my answering machine. What did he want?'

'He said he was investigating the death of Victor Joyce. He said he thought you might have seen him when he left, that perhaps you knew something—'

'I left about a quarter of an hour after he did, and I took the state road, whereas—'

'Oh, Mord, can you prove it?'

'Prove what? That I went by way of the state road? Well, when I got off the state road to take the road that takes you into Barnard's Crossing—'

'Abbot Road.'

'Yes, Abbot Road, I stopped a police cruiser to ask directions to your place. So that

245

shows that I was on the state road, doesn't it?'

'And what did they tell you?'

'They said to take the third road to the left, and go straight to the end. That's right, isn't it?'

'Yes, that's right,' she said, but she could not help but reflect that it proved nothing since the point where Pine Grove Road met Abbot Road was a hundred yards behind him when he had stopped the police car, and as far as they could tell, he might have entered Abbot Road from Pine Grove. 'You call me, when you get in, and I'll tell you what train to take.'

★   ★   ★

The Friday evening service was more of a social occasion than a prayer service. Unlike the evening service on the rest of the days of the week, it was held after dinner, at half past eight instead of at sunset, and attracted about a hundred members of the congregation, men and women, instead of the twelve or fifteen men who came during the week. It was held in the sanctuary instead of in the vestry in the basement, and the prayers were led by the cantor in full regalia—high betasseled yarmulke, black gown, and long silken prayer shawl—instead of by one of the members of the minyan. The Sisterhood prepared an arrangement of flowers on the bema in front of the Ark, and the atmosphere was festive. The service itself lasted about a half hour, with the prayer portion kept to a minimum and with most of the time taken up by a sermon by the rabbi. After the service the congregation repaired to the vestry, where a long table had been laid out with a coffee urn at one end and a large teapot at the other, along with large trays of cups and saucers. There were several vases with flowers in the center and numerous plates with cakes and cookies, all provided by the Sisterhood, two of whose members sat at either end of the table and dispensed the tea and coffee.

Ira Lerner was a fairly regular attendant at the Friday evening service. It was pleasant socializing in the vestry over coffee and cake. While most remained standing or wandering about greeting first one group and then another, there were a few small tables at the side at which one could sit and have one's coffee and cake in comparative comfort. Occasionally, he even picked up some business as a result of his being there. Someone would come over to him and say, 'Hey, Ira, a funny thing happened the other day. Maybe you can suggest what I might do.' He would listen for a moment and then explain that he did not feel right about talking business on the Sabbath. 'Especially in the temple. Why don't you ring me at the office Monday morning?'

247

But this Friday evening it was he who had the problem and hoped to get some information or advice. As soon as the service was over, he approached the rabbi and stuck close to him when he went to the table for refreshment. He pulled back a chair from one of the tables and said, 'Why don't we sit down to drink our coffee? Standing, with a plate of cake in one hand and coffee in the other, is not the way to enjoy your coffee.'

When they were seated, he said, 'A client of mine, Doc Gorfinkle, tells me you were able to use your friendship with the chief of police on his behalf.'

'The Lanigans were having a bite of supper at our house, and I asked him about it. The widow of the man who was killed in the Pine Grove accident was upset because her husband's watch was not included in the effects which were turned over to her by the police. When Dr. Gorfinkle reported the accident, he told the desk sergeant that he had taken the man's pulse. So Lanigan thought perhaps the doctor had removed it so that he could take his pulse. He thought that perhaps he had absentmindedly put it in his jacket pocket and then forgotten about it. He sent a plainclothesman, rather than a uniformed policeman, to ask for it because he didn't want it to appear that the good doctor was having some business with the police.'

'And this detective fellow tried to make a

big thing out of it, eh?'

'That's about it. I don't think Dr. Gorfinkle will be troubled again.'

'No, I don't think he will, but that same detective fellow came to my house to question us about one of the guests we expected at the Bar Mitzvah, a Mordecai Jacobs who teaches at Windermere Christian. It was my Clara he spoke to. She doesn't get upset easily, and she didn't. But I'm bothered. Is that guy—the detective, I mean—trying to pin something on us?'

'Us?'

'Yeah, Jews. First he sees Gorfinkle, and then when he's warned off by Lanigan, he comes to my house and questions my daughter.'

'I'm sure there's nothing of that involved. Lanigan wouldn't stand it for a moment,' said the rabbi.

'All right. So that brings up another question. Is this guy Jacobs involved in some police matter? It's important. The reason it's important is that my Clara wants—no, intends to marry this Jacobs. And I don't want to be in the position of announcing my daughter's engagement and then have the prospective groom arrested.'

'I see.' The rabbi drummed the table for a moment, and then said, 'All right, I'll talk to Lanigan, maybe over the weekend. He may not want to tell me what's involved, but I'll do what I can.'

CHAPTER THIRTY-THREE

Saturday morning gave promise of a warm, sunny day. Chief Lanigan had chosen to wear a light tropical suit instead of his uniform. It was a lovely day to be outdoors, and only his conscience kept him at his desk.

As he had so many times since he had gone with Amy to pay his respects to Victor Joyce's widow, he went over the file on the case. Once again it struck him, in reading the notes he had made on Dunstable's oral report of his activities the previous day, that the sergeant was not at his best interrogating women. He normally tried to establish his ascendancy over the subject, and it usually worked. But a daughter of two prominent lawyers, like Clara Lerner, was not easily intimidated, and Alice Saxon, professor of Psychology, wasn't likely to be either. Nevertheless, he had probably got what information the Lerner girl could give, although Lanigan suspected her relations to Professor Jacobs were probably closer than she had indicated. But it seemed to him that Professor Saxon had a good deal more to tell than Dunstable had been able to glean. He thought she could be induced to tell more if she were properly approached. He was also mildly curious about Dunstable's referring to her as 'quite a dish.' And perhaps because he wanted an excuse to leave the office, he reached for the Boston telephone directory and dialed her number.

When she answered, he said, 'This is Chief Lanigan of the Barnard's Crossing police. I'm calling because I think you can help us on an inquiry we're making.'

'About Victor Joyce? I've already spoken to someone from your department.'

'Yes, Sergeant Dunstable. I've been going over his report and there are a couple of points I'd like to get cleared up.'

'I'm sorry, but I can't talk to you now. I was just on my way out when the phone rang. But, look here, I'll be at the college most of the day and—'

'I could come there.'

'Well, all right. I'll be in and out of my office all day. If I'm not in my office when you get there, you can wait. I'm sure to be along in five or ten minutes. I'm just clearing up some last minute things.'

She was there when he arrived shortly before noon. She had her handbag over her shoulder and was evidently on her way out. He looked at her appreciatively and said, 'I'm Chief Lanigan.'

'I was just going out for a bite,' she said.

'Can I take you to lunch?'

She looked him over, a small smile on her

lips. 'Why not? Best offer I've had today. In fact, it's the only offer.' The smile broadened. 'Do you want to grill me? That's the term, isn't it?'

He grinned at her. 'I'm afraid I forgot to bring my rubber blackjack with me, so suppose we just talk.'

'Suits me. Do you have a restaurant in mind?'

'I don't know the city very well, so you pick the place.'

'There's a place around the corner where you can get soup and a sandwich, which is all I usually have for lunch. With classes over, it will be practically empty. All right?'

'Fine.'

They found a table in a corner, and when they had given their orders, she said, 'All right, what do you want to know? It seems you people are going to an awful lot of trouble investigating a drunk driver accident. I suspect—'

'What do you suspect?'

'I suspect it's because of Cyrus Merton. He's the big noise in your town, I suppose—'

'Because he's rich? We have quite a few rich people in our town.'

'Yes, but I imagine he throws his weight around more than the others. His son-in-law, or his nephew-in-law, or whatever you call him, gets drunk and wraps his car around a tree. That bothers him, so he's trying to find

252

someone to blame it on so he can tell himself it wasn't Victor's fault, or not all his fault. And you people—the police, I mean—have to go along. I suppose that's the way small towns are. I come from one, so I know.'

'And what town was that?'

'Higginstown, Pennsylvania.'

'The same town that—'

'Mord Jacobs comes from. That's right. I knew him from there. As a matter of fact, I put him on to this job. I heard there was an opening and told him to apply. He did, and got the job.'

'Because of your influence?'

'Oh no. I'm in psychology. What influence would I have with the English Department? No, he got it on his own. They were glad to get him. He's a real scholar.'

'You meant that if he hadn't got this job—'

'He would have got another,' she said promptly, 'but he might have had to go way out west, or down south. See, he's young—twenty-seven—and he's already published half a dozen papers. And he's an Old English man. That seems to mean a lot in English departments. I suppose because it's all dull stuff. You take someone in modern or contemporary literature, the stuff he has to read he'd be apt to read even if he weren't in the field. He'd read it for pleasure, if you see what I mean. But the Old English stuff, Anglo-Saxon, no one would read that unless

253

he were involved in it. So the Old English people are apt to get preference because it's presumed that they must be scholars.'

'Then he wasn't anxious for tenure?'

'Of course he wanted it. Not only would it give him security here, but it would give him a leg up in applying for another job.'

'How about Victor Joyce?' he asked.

'Well, Victor was in a different situation entirely. He was older, in his thirties, and he hadn't done much, very little publishing, if any. His only chance against Mord Jacobs was that Merton was behind him.'

'I don't understand. What does Cyrus Merton have to do with it?'

She shrugged. 'He was on the Faculty Committee of the Board of Trustees, chairman, I think. I guess they pass on faculty budgets and that sort of thing. I suppose the heads of departments naturally tend to keep on the good side of him.'

'How about the other members of the committee?'

'They could be important, too, but Merton is active. When there was a faculty raise a few years back, everyone thought it was he who pushed it through. They made him an honorary member of the faculty for it, a kind of joke, but they always invited him to the faculty dinner after that.'

'So that's how he happened to be there.'

'Uh-huh. Usually he'd just put in an

254

appearance for a couple of minutes, but that night he decided to stay. Maybe he hadn't eaten yet and was hungry.'

'Maybe he came because Joyce was going to be there,' Lanigan suggested.

'Possible. He may have wanted to keep tabs on him. Victor was a chaser, you know.'

'A chaser?'

'That's right. The gossip around school was that any coed who sat in the front row and crossed her legs in one of his classes was sure of a good grade.'

'You mean he was apt to make a pass at one of the female guests?'

'There were a few that he might be interested in, and it could be one of the waitresses, or—'

He smiled. 'Did he ever make a pass at you?'

'Oh yes.'

'And?'

'Oh, there were several times when he spent the night at my place. Shocked?'

'I've been a policeman all my adult life, Miss Saxon. It's not easy to shock me. But I wonder—you knew he was married.'

'Oh yes, and that his marriage was all washed up; that his wife was getting a separation and a civil divorce.'

'He told you that?'

'You're thinking it was a variation of the 'my wife doesn't understand me' ploy.' She shook her head. 'No. Helen Rosen, who lives next door to the Joyces, is a very good friend of mine, and we talk on the phone two or three times a week. She told me. Maybe if you ask the widow, she might be willing to confirm it.'

'Maybe I'll do that. And do you have a—a romantic interest in Jacobs?'

She laughed. 'Hardly. I babysat with him when he was a youngster.'

'Yet he was with you all through the dinner.'

'Sure, we're good friends, very good friends. He didn't want to go to the dinner at all, but I persuaded him, so the least I could do was sit with him.'

'Why didn't he want to go and why did you persuade him?'

'He didn't want to go because he thought it would be a drag. He didn't go last year, either. But Professor Sugrue, the head of his department, was on the banquet committee, and I thought Mord could score more points with him if he went. He'd been invited to a Bar Mitzvah for that same night, but I persuaded him to go to the faculty dinner instead. He left early because he saw that Victor had already left. So he felt that since his rival had gone, there was no reason why he should remain.'

'But he did set out for the Bar Mitzvah.'

'Oh yes.'

'And he didn't get there because he got lost. At least, that's what he told the Lerner girl.'

'Yes ... Knowing Mord, it's not hard to imagine his getting lost. But I'm inclined to think he didn't spend too much time trying to find the place.'

'Why not?'

She thought for a moment and then said, 'You've got to know Mord Jacobs to understand. He's old-fashioned, and small-town, and—and very young. In his mind, to come to dinner and meet a girl's parents is tantamount to announcing that you're planning to marry her.'

'And he isn't?'

'Oh, I expect he is—when he feels he can support her and ensure her of financial stability.'

'You mean when he got tenure?'

'Yes, I think that would do it.'

'But he was planning to go to the Bar Mitzvah,' Lanigan insisted.

'Ah, but that was different. It was a big party and there'd be all sorts of people there. So he agreed to go, and then I persuaded him to go to the faculty dinner instead.'

'And he left the dinner early.'

'Yes, and my guess is that it occurred to him that he'd be arriving late and alone, and that that would be interpreted as having the same significance as going to her house for

257

dinner.'

'Then why did he bother? Why didn't he just stay on at the dinner, or go directly back to Boston?'

'Because he'd promised the girl, so he had to make the attempt.' She glanced at her watch. 'Goodness, I've got to be getting back. Did you get all you need? Investigation narrowing down?'

'Investigations tend to expand,' he said. 'It's only at the end, when they're almost over, that they narrow down.'

They walked back to the school together, and as she was about to turn away to enter the building, he said, 'You know, you don't seem particularly upset over the death of—of—'

'Of someone I've slept with?' she finished for him. She smiled faintly as she considered. Then she said, 'If the sexes were reversed, if I were the man and he a woman I had slept with, would you be surprised if I weren't terribly upset a week after he'd been in a fatal accident?'

Lanigan smiled. 'I see. He was just a—a pretty face you picked up.'

'That's about it.' She smiled and waved and then turned to enter the building.

* * *

In his chair, tilted back and a foot braced against a protruding lower drawer, President

258

Macomber leafed through the morning paper. Then an item in the back pages caught his attention and he straightened up and drew a line around it. He rang for his secretary and showed her the penciled item. 'We must have got some notice of this, Janet,' he said.

She glanced over the item and said, 'Oh, I'm sure they sent us a notice, but it would probably have gone to the Anthropology Department, or if it came to the university, it would have been sent over there for posting.'

'I don't suppose anyone is in the office now, but if they posted it on the bulletin board, it's probably still there. Look, would you run down and see if it's there? Oh, and bring it back with you if it is.

She was back in a few minutes to report that the bulletin board of the Anthropology Department had been cleared. 'Should I check the one in the Faculty Room?'

'No, don't bother. This calls for a little detective work. It says here that Professor-Emeritus Cotton of the University of Chicago is to be awarded the Dreyfus Medal. Now it's important that I get in touch with him. So call the Anthropology Society and find out where he's staying, and call him.'

In fifteen minutes she was back to tell him. 'He's being put up at the Harvard Club. I then called there and they said he hadn't checked in yet, that they weren't expecting

259

him until Sunday. I left a message for him to call you.'

'Well, that's fine, but he may not ask if there are any messages for him, and they may fail to tell him. So if he doesn't call back by Monday morning, you try them again. It's important.'

CHAPTER THIRTY-FOUR

Back in his office, Lanigan sat at his desk with the file on the case spread out before him. He went over everything in the file, from the notes he had had the desk sergeant make of his recollection of what Dr. Gorfinkle said when he called in to inform the police of the accident on Pine Grove Road, through Dunstable's reports of conversations he had had with Gorfinkle, Professor Saxon, Clara Lerner, and the various people he had interviewed at the club. There were his own notes on his first meeting with Margaret Joyce, of his talks with Nellie Marston and Cyrus Merton, and the hurriedly penciled memorandum of his conversation with Professor Saxon, made as soon as he got back to his office. He also had the file on the theft of Merton's car, if only because Cyrus Merton was involved in both, and they both had occurred on the same night.

He was looking for possible leads. His eyes narrowed at the desk sergeant's note that there was no answer when he had called the Joyce residence the first time they learned the name of the injured man. He made a note to question Margaret Joyce about it. Again, in going over Dunstable's report on the people he had interviewed at the club, he noted that the checkroom boy had gone off shortly after Joyce had left. The young man was a student at Windermere, and Miss Saxon had said Joyce was a chaser. What was it she had said about the school gossip to the effect that a coed who sat in front and crossed her legs in his class was sure of a good mark? Was there some connection between Joyce and the young man of the coatroom? Was there perhaps a coed he was sweet on that Joyce might have made advances to, which he might have resented? He made a note to have Dunstable go up to Breverton and interview the young man again.

He sat back and tried to think of what other lines he might follow. It occurred to him that it might be helpful to talk to Jacobs in Higginstown, and he reached for the phone. He had no trouble getting the number from Information, and when he dialed, it was Professor Jacobs himself who answered.

When Lanigan identified himself, Jacobs asked, 'Is it about Victor Joyce?'

'And why do you think that, Professor?'

261

'Well, there was someone, a sergeant, who came to my friend Clara Lerner with questions about him.'

'I see. Well, we are making a few inquiries about Joyce,' Lanigan admitted.

'And how can I help you?'

'Well, you see, you left right after him, the faculty dinner, I mean. Did he say anything to you? Did you agree to leave early? Did you two talk about leaving early?'

'We didn't talk at all. I may have said hello, but that's about it. We were friendly enough, but hardly pals. The story around school was that he left because the barman refused to serve him. And I left because I had another party to go to. And it wasn't right after him. It was some little time after.'

'Just what time was it, Professor?'

'It was pretty close to ten. Not that I looked at my watch and decided it was time to leave, but as I was standing on the porch about to go down the steps to the parking lot, a former student of mine, who had been running the coatroom, joined me. He said he got through at ten and that one of the waitresses was taking over. So, if he left at ten, then I must have. We talked for a few minutes and then went to our cars.'

'Oh yeah, what did you talk about?'

'School stuff. Primarily, he was concerned about the mark I had given him.'

'Thought he should have got a higher

mark?'

'Well, his girlfriend had taken the same course, but in Joyce's section, and she had gotten a higher mark. And he thought *he* should have got the higher mark because he had answered all the questions and she hadn't.'

'So what did you tell him?' asked Lanigan.

'Oh, I explained that it was an essay-type test and the marking is pretty subjective. I have given A's on occasion—rare occasions, to be sure—to students who answered only one question of the half-dozen in the test. You see, they get so involved in the subject matter of that particular question that they spend the whole hour on it, and it's not bulling—you can always spot that. To me, that's apt to demonstrate a superior knowledge, and interest, I might add, of the subject matter of the course. So I give him an A.'

'You explained all that to him?'

'More or less.'

'And then you got in your car? It must have been quite a little while after ten that you started out.'

'I suppose it was. Maybe ten after or a quarter after.'

'So when did you get to Barnard's Crossing?'

'Around a quarter of eleven, I suppose.'

'Kind of late to go visiting, isn't it?'

263

'It was a party, and I wasn't expected until late.'

'Why didn't you go by way of Pine Grove Road? That would have got you to Barnard's Crossing a lot sooner.'

'I was planning to. Clara Lerner had suggested it, but I missed the turnoff, and I didn't want to tum around and go looking for it. To tell the truth, I wasn't terribly anxious to get to the party at all.'

'No? Why was that?'

'Well, coming in at that hour, it occurred to me I'd be rather conspicuous.'

'And you didn't want to be. Then why go at all?'

'I'd promised,' said Jacobs simply.

'I see. Look, I may have a lot more questions in the next day or two. I'll be able to reach you at this number, won't I?'

'No, I'm coming back to Boston. I've got a meeting Monday that I've got to go to.'

'You'll be able to drive up Monday morning and get here in time for your meeting?'

'Oh, I wasn't going to drive. I was planning on flying up.'

'But your car—'

'I'm leaving it here. It's an old car and I barely made it to Higginstown. And it's a nuisance in the city. It was useful when I was living in Cambridge, but after I moved to Beacon Street, I really had no need for it. So I plan to leave it here and sell it when I come home after summer session. Or maybe I'll trade it.'

'Then I'll be able to get hold of you in the city.'

'Oh yes. I'll be available all through the summer.'

Lanigan teetered back and forth in his chair as he thought about the conversation. It all seemed straightforward, and jibed with what he had heard from Professor Saxon and what Dunstable had reported of his interview with the Lerner girl. It occurred to him that perhaps it jibed too well. Had Professor Saxon called Jacobs as soon as she had returned to her office after lunching with him, to tell him what she had said and what he should say if he were interrogated? It might be worth checking phone records.

The guy had been smooth over the phone, but hell, why wouldn't he be? He was an English professor, wasn't he? And an interrogation on the telephone was hardly ideal. If there had been a sudden flick of the eyes or a blush at an embarrassing question, he could not see it. And the car, why was it being left in Higginstown? If it was an old jalopy, why had he undertaken to drive it to Higginstown? Was the reason for leaving it there as he had stated it, or was there perhaps a bloodstain on the upholstery that he had been unable to get out? Perhaps he could have the Higginstown police check it out for him. He admitted to himself that he had uncovered nothing startling as a result of his day's activity, but there were some possible leads. Maybe Dunstable would be able to get something out of Aherne when he questioned him again. Or perhaps he might see the young man himself; he had to make the trip to Breverton that evening for Amy's rehearsal. He reached for the phone and dialed the country club.

He asked for the manager, and when he was connected, he said, 'That young fellow, Aherne, the one who ran the checkroom the night of the Windermere dinner, is he around, or will he be around tonight?'

'No, he's got another job for the summer. He said he was available Sundays if we needed him.'

'I see. Are you going to be around this evening?'

'Oh, I'll be around. Why?'

'You wouldn't have a list of those who attended the doctor's dinner that same night, would you?'

'Why wouldn't I?'

'You mean you do?'

'Sure.'

'Okay, I'll see you.'

★   ★   ★

266

When they arrived at the rehearsal hall, and Lanigan parked his car, Amy said, 'Oh, you're going to stay for the rehearsal, aren't you? You'll like it. We're doing Strauss waltzes tonight.'

'No, I'm going to walk over to the country club and—'

'For a couple of beers, I suppose,' she said.

'No, Amy, it's business, but I won't be gone long.'

It was a short walk to the club, about five minutes, and he was able to see the manager immediately.

'I made a list for you, Chief. It's a list of the members. The ones with a star against their names didn't show up that night. Maybe they were involved with patients, or maybe they just decided not to come because of the weather. It was a misty night, if you remember.'

'Do you know where each one lives—the town, I mean?'

'Oh, yeah, sure. Let's see, Johnson lives in Eastham, Silsby comes all the way from Andover. Look, let me have that back and I'll write in the towns.'

'Maybe that won't be necessary,' said Lanigan. 'Just tell me, which of them was apt to use Pine Grove Road to go home.'

'Nobody,' said the manager promptly.

'Nobody?'

'Nobody in his right mind, when you

267

consider the weather conditions. And none of them live south of here, except Doc Leamis, who lives in Lynn. And oh yes, Doc Gorfinkle. He lives in Barnard's Crossing. He might use it if it was a clear night.'

'He did use it,' said Lanigan.

The manager laughed. 'Oh yes, I heard them talking about it. Seems he spilled some beer on his waistcoat. It was his wife's idea that they go by way of Pine Grove because there was some talk of a trap on the state road by the State Troopers, and if they were to stop him, they'd judge him to be driving under the influence just by the way he smelled.'

'Okay. You've been very helpful,' said Lanigan.'

'Can I offer you something, Chief?'

'No, I've got to go and listen to some Strauss waltzes.'

CHAPTER THIRTY-FIVE

Early afternoon on Sunday, the rabbi called Lanigan at home, only to learn that he had gone to the station house. He did not call the station house since it was a public building and so he felt he did not need permission to go there. And also because he thought Lanigan might put him off.

However, when the rabbi arrived at the station house shortly after noon, Lanigan appeared curiously happy to see him. 'Come in, David. Sit down.'

'I'm not interfering with something important?'

'Not at all. I'm free. I've got nothing to do except routine reports that I can do anytime. To tell the truth, I came here in order to get out of the house. Amy was playing the flute, practicing for the next meeting of her group, and I can't stand very much of it. And of course I can't use the TV because that would interfere with her. Now, I know you just didn't happen to be passing.'

'No, that's your ploy,' said the rabbi with a smile. 'No, I had a definite purpose in coming to see you,' and he recounted his conversation with Lerner.

Lanigan nodded. 'Yeah, I can see where Lerner might be concerned. But you opened that can of worms yourself, if you remember. It was you who pointed out that the watch might have been taken off Joyce's wrist not for the sake of the watch, but in order to expose the artery in the wrist to the jagged glass.'

'I was only making the point that—'

'Yes, yes, I know. But in either case it's murder. In one case it's premeditated murder, and in the other it's a felony murder. So what do we have? The weapon, the jagged

269

glass, is there for anyone to use.'

'Or for no one to use,' said the rabbi.

'How do you mean?'

'Even though Joyce was unconscious, he might have moved his hand spasmodically, perhaps, and cut his wrist that way.'

Lanigan nodded. 'It's possible, but we know someone was there after Gorfinkle examined him, because the watch is gone. So now we consider opportunity. This took place not in a house where only a few people might have access, but on an open road. But the road was one that few people would use at night, especially on a rainy, misty night, and then only to go to Barnard's Crossing from Breverton.'

'Or to go from Breverton to Barnard's Crossing.'

'All right.'

'And it might be used by a couple . . .' the rabbi added.

'You mean a lover's lane. Possible, but not likely. It's a narrow road, and there aren't many places where the shoulder is wide enough to turn and park. You'd be apt to go into the ditch that runs alongside. No, I think we can rule out a couple going there to park. So we think of opportunity. Who could have been on that road at the time? We know Joyce left the faculty dinner at quarter to ten, because the young man in charge of the checkroom asked him if he were leaving early

270

when he came to claim his coat, which he then remembered having left in his car. He held his hand up—remember, he wore his watch on the inside of his wrist—and said it was almost ten, which the coatroom guy, a fellow named Aherne, confirmed by glancing at the clock on the wall. Now we don't have the exact time when Gorfinkle left, but it must have been around ten because the doctor's party breaks up at that time. It's a sort of rule or a tradition with them. Some of them have early rounds at their hospitals the next day. It was even more important when they first started to meet and most of them were interns or residents. They start at half past six and go till half past nine, never later than ten. Three hours—it's enough. So figure another ten or fifteen minutes for them to get their things to say good-bye, to finish up what they happened to be saying when they adjourned. Let's say Gorfinkle started out at quarter to ten, and he was the only one who was apt to use Pine Grove Road because he was the only one who lived in Barnard's Crossing. Which brings us back to the faculty dinner. They finished serving around ten, and then there was going to be a lot of speechifying. One person, and only one other than Joyce, left even before dessert and coffee. It was this Jacobs that Lerner is concerned with. He left at ten. How do we know that? Because Aherne leaves at ten, and one of the regular waitresses takes over his station in the checkroom. See, he gets paid by the hour; the waitresses get a flat sum for the evening and they pool and share the tips. Aherne leaves at ten and goes out to his car. Jacobs was at the head of the stairs leading to the parking lot, and Aherne spoke to him. This Aherne knew him because he's a student at Windermere and had taken a course with him.'

Lanigan leaned back in his chair and smiled. 'All right. We have weapon and opportunity. So now let's consider motive. You yourself pointed out that in a murder of this kind, where all that is required is pushing an unconscious man's hand a couple of inches, no planning, no special arrangements, no violence, no great physical effort is required. His wife could have done it. She was out, or at least she didn't answer the phone when our desk sergeant called to give her the news, and the rumor is that the marriage was on the rocks. This Aherne fellow might have done it because of some fancied grievance against Joyce. Had Joyce given him a bad grade in some course? As far as motive goes, all possible. But—' He held up an admonishing forefinger. 'Jacobs had a very good motive. He and Joyce were rivals for tenure, which I gather is hot stuff. But it was even more important for Jacobs because it would mean that he'd be able to marry the

Lerner girl. Now that's a real motive.'

'And why would he take the watch?' asked the rabbi.

'To make it look like a robbery,' Lanigan replied promptly.

The rabbi was silent, and Lanigan went on. 'There are a couple of other points that should be considered. First, he starts out for the Lerner celebration, and please note that in giving him directions on how to get there, Clara Lerner told him to take Pine Grove Road to get there quicker. And he never showed. Was it, perhaps, because he noticed that he had blood on his shirt or on his jacket? Second, Dunstable called him in order to set up a meeting so he could ask him a few questions. His answering machine said he couldn't speak at the time, but that he would get back to him. That was around five o'clock in the afternoon just as the sergeant was going off duty. Although he identified himself as from the Barnard's Crossing police, he gave his home phone number. Jacobs did not return the call, and when Dunstable called again later in the evening, all he got was the same message from the answering machine. So the next morning, Dunstable goes calling on him. He has a flat on Beacon Street, near Coolidge Corner in Brookline. There a neighbor tells him that Jacobs left around seven the evening before-two hours after Dunstable's phone call, mind you—and that he was carrying a suitcase. Not going out for a bite, or to go to a movie, but going away, leaving town.'

'Is that all of it?' asked the rabbi.

'Isn't it enough to justify our making further inquiries about him?'

The telephone rang, and Lanigan scooped up the instrument and said, 'Lanigan here.' He listened for a few moments and said, 'Hold it.' To the rabbi he said, 'Look, David, something's come up and I'm going to be pretty busy for the next couple of hours.'

'I was just going.'

CHAPTER THIRTY-SIX

Ben Clayman was the first to arrive. Miriam, who opened the door in response to his ring, said, 'Come in, Mr. Clayman. Oh, will you excuse me, the coffee is perking.'

On the coffee table there was a tray with cups and saucers and a plate of cookies. He shook hands with the rabbi, and when they sat down, the rabbi asked, 'What's this all about?'

'Didn't Al Bergson tell you?'

'Only that a committee of three, I think he said, wanted to see me.'

'Yeah, that's right, there are three of us.' The doorbell rang and he said, 'That's either

274

Levitt or Bergson. I'll get it.'

It was Levitt, and almost immediately afterward Bergson. Miriam came in with the coffeepot. Clayman and Levitt both shook their heads as she was about to pour, but Bergson said, 'Yes, I'll have a cup, Miriam.'

She poured a cup for him and the rabbi. 'I'll leave the pot here in case you gentlemen change your mind.'

As she turned to go back to the kitchen, Levitt said, 'No, Mrs. Small, I think you ought to remain. This concerns you, too.'

She glanced uncertainly at the men, and then poured herself a cup of coffee and sat down.

Ben Clayman expected Al Bergson, as president of the congregation, to act as their spokesman, but it was Levitt who took the lead. 'I understand we vote on your contract next week, Rabbi. Now I'm kind of new in town. When you work for a big corporation like General Electric, you get moved around a lot. I've lived in a number of places, and I've been a member of a lot of temples and synagogues as a result. First thing I do when I move to a new town is join one of the local synagogues.'

'Very commendable,' the rabbi murmured.

'Eh? Yeah, well I don't just join. I get involved, so I'm apt to become a member of the Board of Directors. So I guess I know more than most of the other members of our

275

board here what the general practice is as far as their dealing with rabbis goes. And I tell you I was pretty shook up when I heard your contract was for only one year, especially when you've been here twenty-five years.'

'It's the way I wanted it,' said the rabbi.

Levitt looked his surprised belief, and Clayman stepped into the breach. 'It's like this, Rabbi, when we realized you'd been here twenty-five years, we thought we ought to do something to, you know, sort of celebrate the occasion.'

'You mean a party for the whole congregation?' asked the rabbi.

'Oh, we'd have a big party for sure, but we'd also want to give you a gift. Al Bergson was supposed to sound you out on what you and Mrs. Small might like. We had in mind something big, like a new car—'

'I have a car,' said the rabbi.

Clayman sniffed contemptuously. 'You mean that jalopy you come to the temple in?'

'It's only four years old and it's gone less than twenty thousand miles.'

'Four years, twenty thousand miles. You don't do much driving, do you?' said Levitt. 'Maybe with a big, comfortable car you'd ride more.'

'But then I'd have two cars. What would I do with two cars?'

'Mrs. Small could use the other,' said Clayman.

276

'I don't drive,' said Miriam.

'So you could trade it in and we'd get an even bigger one than the one we thought of.'

'I have enough trouble driving this one. Parking, you know. A bigger one would be even more trouble.'

'All right. How about something else, then? How about a complete service of sterling silver?'

'When would we use it?' asked Miriam.

'And wouldn't it be a temptation for someone to break in?' suggested the rabbi.

'Well, do you have any suggestions of your own? How about a fine watch, a solid gold Rolex?'

The rabbi smiled and held up his wrist. 'I paid fifteen dollars, I think, for this one. There was a warranty that came with it which said it was accurate to within one minute a month. Would the Rolex be any more accurate?'

A painting or a sculpture was suggested, or a trip around the world. As the rabbi turned down each of their suggestions in turn, it became apparent, at least to Clayman and Levitt that, for whatever reason, the rabbi did not care to discuss the matter. Finally, Clayman said, 'Look, Rabbi, will you think about it? Talk it over with Mrs. Small, and then you can let us know what you decide. Whatever it is, within reason, I'm sure the board will go along.'

'All right,' said the rabbi good-naturedly.

'Well, I've got to be running along,' Clayman went on. 'I promised the wife I'd be home early.'

'Yeah, me too,' said Levitt. He looked questioningly at Bergson. 'You coming, Al?'

'I'll just finish my coffee,' said Bergson.

So the two left him, and as they made their way to their cars, Clayman confided, 'Al will work something out with him. You'll see. The Smalls and the Bergsons are very close. They dine at each other's houses.'

'Doesn't the rabbi dine at other members' houses?'

'Very few. See, the Bergsons keep kosher. They wouldn't dine at my house, for example, because although we don't use pork or anything *trefe,* we don't keep two sets of dishes.'

'I guess that's the same with us,' said Levitt, 'although once in a while we have lobsters.'

When they were gone, Bergson said, 'All right, David, now what's it all about? Why don't you want to accept a gift from the congregation?'

'Because then I'd feel obligated. Could I accept a fine car, or some other valuable gift, and then resign?'

'But why would you want to resign?'

'Because I'm fifty-three. If I don't quit now, I'll be too old to get another job.'

'Were you thinking of getting another job? Have you had an offer from a bigger congregation, perhaps?'

'No, I want to get out of the rabbinate altogether. Maybe a teaching job, or editing, or just going to Israel without having to think about getting back by a particular date.'

'And when were you planning to resign?'

The rabbi smiled. 'I rather thought next week would be a good time. I complete my twenty-fifth year then, and I could go on pension.'

'But if you go on pension, you lose twenty-five percent of your income.'

'Well, I don't need as much now. Hepsibah is getting married in September, and Jonathon is getting a job with a good law firm. There'll be just the two of us.'

'You agree with David on all this, Miriam?'

'David is in charge of grand strategy; I take charge of logistics,' she answered.

'Well, David, I'll tell you what I'm going to do. If you submit your resignation, I'll refuse to accept it.'

'I don't see how you can stop it, Al.'

'I'll have the board vote an indefinite leave of absence for you, and anyone we hire to replace you will be told the job is temporary.'

The rabbi shrugged. 'You do whatever you think you have to do, Al.'

CHAPTER THIRTY-SEVEN

As soon as the door closed behind the rabbi, Lanigan said into the phone, 'Rabbi gone, Eban?'

'Just went out the door.'

'Good. Now what's this about Tim Phelps having something on the Joyce case?'

'He's in the cruising car. Why don't I let him tell it?'

'All right. Hook him up.' Then to the policeman in the cruising car, 'Chief Lanigan. What is it, Tim?'

'I just stopped a guy for speeding and passing a red light.'

'So?'

'And he don't have his registration.'

'So?'

'And he's wearing a watch just like the one you described when you sent me to take up along Pine Grove Road.'

'Is that so? Did you say anything about it to him?'

'No. I thought I'd talk to you first.'

'That's right. Don't show any interest in it. Who's with you on the cruiser?'

'Bill Stone.'

'Okay, have Bill get in the car with him and have him drive to the station house. You follow in the cruiser.'

His name was Malcolm Dorfbetter, and according to his driver's license, he was twenty-five years old. He said he lived on 30 Lowell Road, which was in a newly developed part of town, where many of the streets were not yet paved and some of the lawns, while rolled and seeded, had not yet produced grass.

His hair was long, coming to his coat collar in back, and he wore a gold earring. He was sure of himself, even brash.

He argued with Officer Phelps as he was brought into the station house.

'Look, I didn't realize I was speeding. My speedometer, I got to have it checked—'

'You also passed a red light.'

'Yeah, well, I was watching the guy in front of me and I didn't see the light. Besides, it just changed—'

'No, it changed when you were still seventy feet back of it.'

'Okay, so I figured I'd sneak through 'stead of jamming on my brakes and maybe going through the windshield. So I made a mistake, and it's a traffic violation. So why don't you just give me a ticket and I'll be on my way.'

'You don't have a registration.'

'Yeah, well, like I said, it's at home. I could drive there and get it and be back in ten, fifteen minutes.'

'It's as much as my job is worth to let you drive off without a registration.'

'So take me down there, and you can even come in the house with me.'

'Just relax, mister, and you can make your pitch to the chief.'

Officer Phelps looked at the desk sergeant questioningly, who nodded toward Lanigan's office. He marched the young man in and handed Lanigan the driver's license. Lanigan made quite a show of checking the license, peering first at the young man and then at the picture on the plastic card.

'This gives your address as St. Paul Street, Brookline.'

'Yeah, well, that is where I was living up to about a month ago.'

'Okay. Sit down. I'll be with you in a minute.' To Phelps he said, 'You can get back to the cruiser, Tim, and will you ask Sergeant Dunstable and Lieutenant Jennings to come in.' Officer Phelps left, and Dunstable entered almost immediately, as though he had been waiting at the door, as indeed he had. In a minute or two Eban Jennings came in. He put a slip of paper on Lanigan's desk and sat down.

Lanigan glanced at the paper and said, 'According to our records, Thirty Lowell Road is occupied by the Leaming family, Mary and Arthur Leaming, no Dorfbetter.'

'Yeah, well, she's my ma. After my old man died, she married this guy, Leaming.'

'And you live with them?'

'Well, I have been for about a month now.'

'They're new in town?'

'They came the first of the year.'

'They home now?'

'No, they're driving across country to L.A. I'm sort of looking after the place while they're gone. Look, I've got an appointment.' He glanced at his watch. 'And I'm kind of late for it right now.'

'That's quite a watch you have there,' said Lanigan. 'May I see it?'

'Sure.' Dorfbetter snapped the catch and handed it over. Lanigan noted that it was the sort of catch Margaret Joyce had described to him.

'You a Catholic?' asked Lanigan.

'Naw. We don't belong to anything. Why?'

'Because this is a Catholic watch.'

'You mean, I'm not allowed to wear it?'

'You can wear it, but you wouldn't buy it. Where did you get it?'

'I—I found it.'

'That so? Where did you find it?'

'I found it in Boston, or rather, in Brookline.'

Lanigan glanced at Dunstable. There was no doubt in his mind that this was Joyce's watch. It was just as Margaret Joyce had described it, with a little silver tube just

283

above the twelve.

'Just where in Brookline?' asked Dunstable.

'Near Coolidge Corner. I was walking along Beacon Street, and I saw a sort of, you know, like a glitter under the bushes in front of this apartment house, because of the way the sun hit it. So I picked it up and I see it's a watch. If it had been a one-family house, I might have knocked on the door and asked if someone there had lost a watch, but it was this big apartment house, so what was the use?'

'This watch has been reported stolen,' said Lanigan flatly.

Dorfbetter manifested polite interest and mild surprise. 'What do you know!'

'Take him into your office, Eban,' Lanigan said to his lieutenant, 'and fill out the necessary forms.'

He realized that he had not actually identified the watch as Joyce's. He had never been to Rome, but he recalled that someone who had just come back from a tour had described Rome, and more particularly Vatican City, as full of places selling 'all kinds of religious touristy knickknacks.' What if watches like Joyce's were a regular article of trade there? It was incumbent on him to get positive identification.

He reached for the phone and called the Joyce house. When Margaret answered, he said, 'Chief Lanigan. Look, I've got to see you for a minute. I'm coming right over.'

Without waiting for an answer, he went out to his car, calling back over his shoulder to the desk sergeant that he would be back.

When he arrived at the house in Shurtcliffe Circle, she greeted him with, 'You have good news for me. I just know you have.'

Smiling, he said, 'Well, maybe. First, could you identify the watch—'

'But I described it to you. It has the Sacred Heart on the dial and the little tube above the twelve.'

'Yes, but suppose there are others just like it? A friend of mine who just came from Rome said he saw others like it for sale.'

'Oh, that can't be,' she insisted. 'I know my mother had it painted on after she bought it.'

'But that was some years ago, wasn't it? Since then, some enterprising jeweler, maybe even the one who did it for your mother, got the idea that it made a fine souvenir of the city and would sell well and produced a whole slew of them. Now is there anything, a scratch of—'

'I see.' She closed her eyes as she tried to visualize the watch as she had last seen it. Then she said doubtfully, 'Not on the watch, that I remember, but on the bracelet there was like a dent in one of the links, in the first one, next to the watch.'

He drew the watch from his pocket, peered at the bracelet, and then held it out to her. 'Is this your husband's watch?'

She all but grabbed it from his hand and clutched it to her bosom. 'Oh, it is, it is. I'm sure. That little dent, I made it myself once when I was playing with it. I was going to get another bracelet for it before giving it to Victor, but I didn't have time, and I didn't think he'd notice it.'

'That's fine,' he said, 'but I'm afraid we'll have to keep it for a while. It's evidence, you see.' He held out his hand.

She yielded the watch with great reluctance. 'But I'll get it back.'

'Oh, certainly.' He hesitated and then said, 'You know, we made a number of inquiries at the college—'

'You mean you went into Boston about a lost watch? Oh, that was really very good of you. I had no idea the police were so thorough about something that isn't really very valuable.'

'Well, we knew it meant a lot to you, and then there were, well, other angles that had to be explored. There was a story around that you and your husband were planning to get a divorce.'

She was not embarrassed. 'Yes, that's true,' she said. 'I was planning to ask the Church to grant me a separation and then to get a civil divorce. I'm surprised that Victor let it be known around the school. I would have thought he'd be worried about my uncle hearing about it. We kept it from him because Victor thought it would affect his chances of getting tenure. You see, my uncle is a trustee of the college. So although we weren't living together as man and wife, we'd still go to church together and then to Sunday dinner at my uncle's house afterward.'

'And your uncle and aunt didn't know or suspect?'

'I'm sure my aunt knew. I think she suspected all along, but then on the afternoon of the dinner, she came here. She had occasion to go upstairs and—and I'm sure she saw that we were—were living apart. I don't think she told my uncle, though, because when he called to arrange to drive up with Victor, he didn't seem in the least upset.'

'And he would have been if he knew?'

'At least he would have talked to me about it.'

'Yes, I suppose he would,' said Lanigan. He rose to go. 'By the way,' he said, 'when the desk sergeant called to tell you Saturday night, there was no answer.'

'I was out. I'd gone to a movie.'

'To the Criterion in town?'

'No, I'd seen that picture before, so I went up to the Excelsior in Breverton. Then I met some people I know and joined them for coffee afterward. I didn't get home till almost midnight.'

He nodded, and she led him to the door. 'Where was it found?' she asked as she opened the door.

'In Brookline near Coolidge Corner.'

'You mean he may have dropped it while, er—visiting someone? Oh, but he couldn't have. He was wearing it that night. I'm—I'm almost sure of it.'

'But you're not absolutely sure, are you?'

'Well, I think—no, I can't be absolutely sure.'

*　　*　　*

Although Dorfbetter's saying that he had found the watch on Beacon Street near Coolidge Corner tended to confirm his suspicions of Jacob, it occurred to Dunstable that he might have lied, and that he had actually taken the watch from the wrist of the unfortunate Joyce. Suppose he had got blood on his shirt cuff in the process. What would he do with a bloody shirt? He might try to wash it off, of course. Or he might bury it, or burn it. Or he might just take it off, perhaps leave it on the floor of his bedroom with the rest of his dirty laundry until he got a big enough pile to take down to the Laundromat.

To the desk sergeant he said, 'Let me see that key ring we took off the young fellow, will you.'

The sergeant tossed the ring onto the counter. To be sure, there were house keys on the ring. 'I'll borrow this for a while,' Dunstable said. 'I just want to see if one of those actually fits the front door of Thirty Lowell.'

'Well, you be sure and bring them back.'

Key ring in hand, Dunstable loafed into the wardroom and saw that Patrolman Sterling had just changed into civilian clothes preparatory to going off duty. 'You in a hurry, Bob?' he asked.

'Not particularly, Sarge. What's up?'

'I want to take a look at Thirty Lowell Road. All right if we use your car?'

'Sure.'

They drove to Lowell Road, and when they reached the number 30, Dunstable said, 'Go up about fifty feet and park there.'

'There's a car under a tarpaulin in the driveway,' Sterling pointed out.

'Probably his stepfather's.'

'But isn't he supposed to be driving across the country?'

'So? If you were going to drive cross-country, would you try to do it in this heap? You'd leave it and rent a car.'

'So why didn't he park it in his garage?'

'Because I suppose the garage is full of summer furniture and a lawn mower and snow tires. Look, just wait here while I go up to the house.'

Dunstable went up the walk and mounted the stairs. He looked along the street and was annoyed to see that Sterling had left his post and was loafing up the driveway to the car under the tarpaulin. He was on the point of inserting a key in the lock when Sterling called out, 'Hey Sarge, c'mere.'

He crossed the lawn. 'What is it?'

Sterling lifted the tarpaulin and was pointing 'Isn't that the license of the car that was reported missing: 111 123. It's an easy number to remember.'

'Son of a gun!'

'What do we do now, Sarge?'

For a moment Dunstable was tempted to enter the house and use the telephone, but then he thought better of it. 'Look, you stay here and keep an eye out just in case. I'll drive back to the station house and see the chief.'

'He went out. I saw him drive off.'

'So he may be back by now. Or I can talk to the lieutenant. Give me your keys.'

★   ★   ★

But Lanigan was already back at his desk when Dunstable arrived. He told of his discovery and then added, 'For all I know, the keys might even be in the ignition. I'd have no trouble starting it by crossing the wires—'

'No,' said Lanigan decisively. 'I'll send the tow truck down and bring it back here, tarpaulin and all.' He got up and circled his desk, and then pointed. 'I want it parked right there where it can be seen by someone sitting in that chair. Got it?'

'Right.'

'How did you happen to go out there, Sergeant?'

'Just to see if one of the keys on the ring would fit the door.'

'All right. You go out with the tow truck. And mind where I said I wanted it parked.'

Later, when Lanigan heard the thump of the car as its rear wheels hit the ground, he had Dorfbetter brought to his office. He motioned to the chair near the window and said, 'I want to know—'

But the young man had caught sight of the tarpaulin. 'Jeesus!' he cried, and buried his face in his hands. But only for a moment. Then he looked up and began to babble. 'I saw the keys in the car and the door was locked, so I knew the guy had locked himself out of his car. My old man used to do that—lock himself out of his car, I mean. My real father, I mean, not my stepfather; *he* never makes mistakes. Once, he spent over an hour trying to work a wire coat hanger through a crack at the top of the window to hook onto the handle inside. Another time, he had to break the glass. Then he got wise and bought himself one of those little bumper magnetic boxes that you put a duplicate key in and hide it under the bumper. So I felt along the rear bumper and there it was in the same place my father used to keep his. I mean, it was like Fate. I was only going to take a little ride and then bring it back. But when I came back, I saw the police cruiser there, so I drove on home, thinking to take it back later.'

'I'm charging you with the larceny of an automobile,' said Lanigan, and picking up a card from his desk, he proceeded to read him his rights. Then he said, 'Now, suppose you tell me just which route you took.'

'I'm not saying another word, and you can't make me,' said the young man, 'not until I see a lawyer.'

$$\star \qquad \star \qquad \star$$

Luigi Tomasello was the senior Assistant District Attorney, and since Lanigan had established a good working relationship with him over the years, he felt no hesitancy in calling him at his home.

'See, Luigi, I didn't push him on the watch, because where he said he found it kind of tied in with another line we were pursuing and seemed to confirm it. But then we found Merton's car in his driveway and he tried to tell us that he'd just wanted to take a little ride and was going to bring it back to where he got it, but he saw the police cruiser there, so he didn't stop. So then I charged him with grand larceny and read him his rights.'

'*Then* you read him his rights.'

'Yeah, but I hadn't questioned him or anything. I didn't even what you might call confront him with it. I just had it parked where it could be seen from my office and I had him come in to the office. I didn't say a word. He did all the talking.'

'All right, so did he still claim he found the watch?'

'He didn't say anything. When I read him his rights, he clammed up and said he wouldn't say another word until he had a chance to see a lawyer, so I didn't press him.'

'You should have charged him and read him his rights as soon as you found the car in his driveway. A smart lawyer could make it look as though you forced a confession out of him one way or another. And don't kid yourself, Hugh. If this should turn out to be murder, it won't be one of the kids just out of law school in the Public Defender's office who will be acting for him. John Stewart himself will take over. So I tell you what you do. You process him, mug shots, fingerprints, the whole business, and send it on through. Then tomorrow we bring him up for arraignment for larceny of an automobile.'

'And the watch?'

'We don't mention it because he says he found it. We can always add it afterward.'

'But I want a warrant to search his house. There might be a shirt with a bloodstain, and—'

'We'll apply for the warrant after he's arraigned. The thing to remember, Hugh, is that you don't want your police work to get in the way of my getting a conviction. All right?'

'Okay, Luigi.'

★ ★ ★

His earlier elation at having found the watch and solved the mystery of Joyce's murder was somewhat tempered by his conversation with Tomasello. Had he been a little too cute in arranging for Dorfbetter to see the car under the tarpaulin in the police parking lot? Was there a chance that his lawyer could get him off on the grounds that the police had acted improperly? He reflected that perhaps Tomasello's reproof had been for the purpose of getting him to toe the line from here on rather than criticism of what he had done.

He felt quite sure that he knew what had actually happened. He was quite willing to believe that Dorfbetter had seen the keys in the ignition and had then found another key in a magnetic container behind the rear bumper. He could understand that it might seem like the hand of Fate to the young man.

But what was he doing wandering among the cars in the parking lot in the first place? Was it not with the thought of stealing a car? Quite possibly, all he wanted was to take a ride. So where would he go? It had a license number that was easily recognized—and remembered; 111 123. Wouldn't he try to avoid the main streets? And if he knew the area at all, what better road to take than Pine Grove?

So he leaves the parking lot and drives a short distance along Abbot Road and then enters Pine Grove. He drives along and sees the smashed car with what appeared to be a dead man, certainly an unconscious one, behind the wheel, and dangling out of the side of the car the man's hand with what looked like a gold bracelet. Again Fate appeared to be handing him something on a platter. Quite possibly, he didn't even leave his car. He may have edged close to the smashed car, rolled his window down, seized the wrist and pulled the watch off. Then he had flung down the arm, perhaps in violent disgust because it was bloody, and driven off.

He leaned back in his chair and stretched luxuriously, deciding that it had been a good day and perhaps he'd take Amy out to dinner to celebrate.

It was with great satisfaction that he started for home, but as he neared the street on which the rabbi lived, it occurred to him that he ought to tell him that perhaps Professor

Jacobs was now probably in the clear. After all, there was no sense in upsetting Lerner unnecessarily. He turned into the street and slowed down as he approached the rabbi's house. But there were a couple of cars in the driveway and one parked directly in front of the house. Must be a party, he thought, and drove on. He could make contact tomorrow.

CHAPTER THIRTY-EIGHT

It was afternoon when Lanigan finished with the arraignment of Dorfbetter and headed back to the station house. But it occurred to him that he ought to tell the rabbi that he now had another suspect so that he could pass the information on to Lerner. In all probability the rabbi was at the temple, but since he was at the moment near the rabbi's house, he drove up to it.

'David home?' he asked when Miriam opened the door in response to his ring.

'Come in and have a cup of tea. David is in his study, but he'll be out in a moment.'

'If he's busy—' Lanigan began.

'Oh no, he's napping. He likes to lie down after lunch for a short siesta. It's a habit he picked up in Israel. I suspect when he's at his study in the temple, he dozes off in his chair.'

When the rabbi appeared a moment later,

yawning and stretching, Lanigan asked in sarcastic politeness, 'You awake and ready to face the world?'

'Oh, hello, Chief. Very refreshing, a nap after lunch, but I heard you ring.'

'Nice business if you can get it. You spoken to Lerner yet?'

'No, not yet. I expect he's planning to come to the evening service. I'll speak to him then.'

'Well, maybe you can give him some good news when you see him. We've got another and more likely suspect.'

'More likely how?'

'With Jacobs we had motive and opportunity, but no hard evidence, but with this one we have positive evidence. He had the missing watch.'

'Is that so!'

'Yup, he was wearing it. Pure accident, to be sure, but if we didn't get the breaks occasionally, an awful lot of cases wouldn't get solved. You remember I sent a man up to the scene of the accident to rake over the area? Naturally, I described the watch to him so he'd know what he was looking for. Well, Officer Phelps, the raker, was on the cruising car yesterday. He stops a car for passing a red light, and he notices that the driver is wearing a watch just like the one I had described. So while his partner is checking for license and registration, Phelps calls me at the station house. Come to think of it, you were there when the call came in.'

'So that's why you hustled me out.'

'Uh-huh.' He went on to tell of his interviews with Dorfbetter. 'One of those hippy types with long hair, an earring, and wearing those baggy pants that narrow down and wrinkle at the ankle. When he said he'd found it under a hedge in front of an apartment house on Beacon Street near Coolidge Corner, Sergeant Dunstable gave me a sign, and I figured we had confirmatory evidence against Jacobs because it could be his house. So now I wanted to be very careful. I wanted positive identification that this was Joyce's watch.'

'But didn't it match the description that Mrs. Joyce gave you?'

'Sure, but what if it should turn out to be a regular trade item for tourists-to Rome? Besides, there were a couple of questions I wanted to ask her, like where she'd been the night of the accident. There was no answer when the desk sergeant called to notify her.'

'And?'

'She'd been to a movie in Breverton, then bumped into some people she knew, and they'd gone someplace for coffee, so she didn't get home until almost midnight.'

The rabbi raised his eyebrows. 'She'd gone alone?'

'Surprised? Me, too. But it tended to

confirm a rumor I had heard, that the marriage was on the rocks and she was planning to get a divorce.'

'A divorce? How could she? Didn't you tell me that she was very devout?'

'A civil divorce and a Church-sanctioned separation,' Lanigan explained. 'So I asked her and she admitted it. In fact, they had been living apart, although in the same house, for some time.'

'And her folks, her uncle and aunt, didn't know about it?'

'She said she thought her aunt did, but she didn't think her uncle did.'

'I would think that if the aunt knew about it, then the uncle did, too. He may have been better able to conceal his emotions, however,' said the rabbi dryly.

'You may be right. Anyway, the widow had identified the watch, which was what I came for, so I went back to the station house, and found that Dunstable had gone out to the Leaming house on Lowell Road, to see if Dorfbetter's key fit. That's what he said, but our Dunstable can be kind of devious at times, and I suspect he was planning to have a look around on the chance of finding a shirt with bloodstains, perhaps. He took Bob Sterling with him, and while he was trying the front door, Sterling went up the driveway where there was a car parked under a tarpaulin. Sterling lifted the edge of the tarp, and what do you know, it was Merton's car, which had been stolen from the mall parking lot that night.' He went on to tell, with great self-satisfaction, how he had had the car brought down to the station house and placed where Dorfbetter could see it. 'Well, that broke it. I read him his rights and then arrested him for the theft of a motor vehicle.'

'He confessed?'

'No, he clammed up and refused to say a word without his lawyer present. So we locked him up and brought him down to the court for arraignment. As far as I was concerned, I had my case. He took the car, maybe just for a joyride, drove up Pine Grove—'

'Why to Pine Grove?'

'Because it was a big, flashy car with a license number that was easily remembered. On Pine Grove he wasn't likely to be seen by a cop with an eye out for a stolen car. As he drives up he sees a wreck with a dead man or an unconscious man at the wheel, his hand sticking out the window with what looks like a gold bracelet on the wrist. My guess is that he didn't even get out. He probably just drove up, lowered his window and grabbed the watch, and scooted.'

'Why didn't he notify the police?' asked the rabbi. 'He wouldn't have had to identify himself.'

Lanigan shrugged. 'Oh, that type, they're

300

just interested in themselves.'

'Are you sure you're not convicting him in your mind because of his lifestyle?'

'How do you mean?'

'The long hair and the earring, the general appearance, isn't that affecting your judgment of his guilt?'

Lanigan considered. 'I suppose it does to some extent,' he admitted. 'It's normal. We all do it. Weren't you doing it when you came to see me about Jacobs, because he was one of your own?'

'I suppose I was. As you say, we all do it, but it can interfere with our thinking.'

'Yeah, but we've got good solid evidence on this one.'

'Well, I'll admit that it strains the bounds of credulity that he found the nephew's watch in Brookline and then took the uncle's car in Barnard's Crossing.'

Lanigan got up to leave. 'I drove by here yesterday to tell you the good news so you could pass it on to Lerner, but there were a bunch of cars in front of your house, so I thought maybe you were having some sort of party, and drove on.'

'Oh, that was very good of you. It wasn't a party, just a committee meeting. I will probably see Lerner at the evening service and—'

'Tell him? No need to,' said Lanigan,

grinning broadly. 'I saw him at the courthouse.'

CHAPTER THIRTY-NINE

The phone rang just as the rabbi was on his way to the evening service. Miriam answered as the rabbi waited at the door. It was Simcha. 'Miriam? Simcha. I've been so busy. It's the first chance I've had to call you. Look, something's come up and I won't be able to come out to Barnard's Crossing before Wednesday. A favorite pupil of mine lives in the city, and he insists I have dinner with him Tuesday night, so—'

'Wednesday will be fine, Simcha. You call us and let us know which train you're taking and David will meet you at the station.'

'Is David there?'

'Just a minute.' She handed the instrument to the rabbi.

'Yes, Simcha, we'll be seeing you Wednesday, I gather.'

'That's right. You didn't happen to see that fellow we met on our way back from the temple, did you?'

'Herb Rosen? No, but I expect to see him at the minyan tonight.'

'Well, if you do, and you happen to think of it—'

'You'd like me to ask him if he has a

302

brother who went to the University of Chicago. All right, I will. And if he doesn't happen to come to the minyan tonight, I'll see that you meet him when you come Wednesday.'

'It's a silly business, David, but you know how sometimes your mind gets fixed on something.'

'I understand. See you Wednesday.'

'What was all that about Herb Rosen?' asked Miriam curiously when he hung up.

'Oh, we bumped into him on our way back from the temple last Sunday. Simcha was sure he knew him, thought he might have taken a course with him, or at least had seen him around the university. When Rosen told him he'd never gone to the University of Chicago, Simcha thought maybe he has a brother who went there.'

'Why is Simcha so concerned?'

'I suppose because he's an old man. He finds himself forgetting things and misplacing things. He probably thinks it represents deterioration, so it bothers him.'

'He must have seen him at the Donut Shop.'

'Why at the Donut Shop?'

'Because it was the only place he could have seen him. He was dropped off there, and it was there that we picked him up. That was all he saw of Barnard's Crossing, so if he saw someone, it had to be there.'

'But what was Rosen doing there?'

'Buying doughnuts, or having a cup of coffee, or a sundae.'

The rabbi shook his head. 'No, according to Lanigan, he ended the rehearsal early because he was expecting a call from his daughter on the West Coast.'

'Well, you ask him, and you'll see.'

'All right, I will.'

When the rabbi arrived at the temple, he noted with satisfaction that Rosen was there, but since the service was on the point of beginning, he was unable to speak to him. As soon as it was over, however, he approached him and said, 'I see you made it, Mr. Rosen.'

'Oh, I make a point of saying Kaddish for my father. I haven't missed once since he died. I feel I owe it to him.'

'You're not saying it for him, you know,' the rabbi pointed out.

'How do you mean?'

'Well, if you read it over, you'll see that there is no mention of the departed.'

'I'm afraid my Hebrew is not up to it.'

'It's not in Hebrew; it's in Aramaic. But there's an English translation on the opposite page in your prayer book. You will find that it is a doxology, an elaborate praise of God. When you consider that the mourner's Kaddish is recited only in the course of a public service, never when praying alone, and that it is said aloud, unlike our normal way of praying, you'll realize that what you're saying in effect is that although you have lost someone who is dear to you, you reaffirm your faith in God.'

Rosen smiled. 'I suppose that's the rationale of the ritual, but I'm a musician, and it's feelings and emotion that are important. So I do it for my father.'

The rabbi smiled. 'You do it for whatever reason suits you, as long as you do it.' As the other was about to turn away, he said, 'Oh, Mr. Rosen, were you at the Donut Shop last Saturday night?'

'Yeah, I stopped off on my way home from rehearsal. How did you know?'

'I suspect my cousin saw you, and that's why he thought he knew you.'

'Oh, he was there, was he? At one of the tables, I suppose.'

'That's right. I wonder why he happened to notice you of all who were there?'

'Probably because I was the only adult present.'

'What do you mean?'

'The place was full of high school kids, celebrating after the big basketball game. I came in with Cyrus Merton, the real estate guy, but he scooted down the side aisle to the john in the back, so your cousin didn't see him. I went straight to the doughnut counter.'

'You mean you were with Merton?'

'No, we met at the door, got there at the same time. We did an Alphonse and Gaston act at the door for a few seconds. Then he entered and I followed, and went right to the doughnut counter.'

As the rabbi came out to the parking lot, he saw Ben Clayman sitting in his car. 'I thought I might just catch you,' said Clayman. 'Morris Fisher is back in the hospital. I thought you'd like to know.'

'Is it bad?'

Clayman shrugged. 'All I know is his doctor saw him this morning and ordered him to the hospital. You think you could go to see him?'

'He's at the Salem Hospital?'

'That's right.'

'Well, tomorrow is my day for going to the Salem Hospital. I'll look in on him.'

'Swell. I don't see your car in the parking lot, Rabbi. Can I give you a lift home?'

'No thanks. I think I'd like to walk.'

*   *   *

'Well, was he, or wasn't he?' Miriam asked as the rabbi closed the door behind him.

'Was he or wasn't he what? What are you talking about, Miriam?' the rabbi asked irritably.

'Was Herb Rosen at the Donut Shop, or wasn't he? You said you'd ask him. Did you forget, or didn't he come to the minyan?'

'Oh, I asked him. And you were right; he was there buying doughnuts.' He went to the telephone.

'Are you calling Simcha to set his poor mind at ease?'

He smiled grimly. 'No, I'm not setting any minds at ease. I'm calling Lanigan, and I expect it will upset him.'

He dialed, and when Lanigan answered, he said, 'David Small here, Chief. I think I know where Dorfbetter got the watch, and it wasn't from Joyce.'

'No? Then where—no, don't tell me. Hold it. I'm coming over.'

As soon as Miriam opened the door to him, and he caught sight of the rabbi in the living room, Lanigan demanded, 'All right, David, what've you got?'

'I saw Mr. Rosen at our evening service tonight.'

'Herb Rosen?'

'Yes, the one who conducts the orchestra Amy belongs to. He said he'd been in the Donut Shop last Saturday night.'

'So? I knew that. What about it? He left the rehearsal at the same time we did, and the two cars were within sight of each other until we reached Abbot Road, where we took the left lane to make the turn, but he drove up on the next lane beside us. He said he was going to stop off to get some doughnuts.'

'What time was that? Do you know?'

'I didn't look at my watch, but let's see, we left the junior high where he holds the rehearsals a little before ten. He stopped a little earlier than usual because he said he had to get home for a phone call from his daughter. So, it was probably just about half past ten when we got to the lights and I turned off.'

'He said he got to the door of the Donut Shop and was heading out just as Cyrus Merton was coming in. In fact, as he put it, they did an Alphonse and Gaston act at the door.'

'So?'

'So how did he get there?'

'I told you how, he came down the state road—'

'Not Rosen, Merton. How did Merton get there at half past ten?'

'I don't—what are you driving at, David?'

'The country club and the junior high school are about the same distance from the state road. One is on the right-hand side of the road and the other on the left, but they're about the same distance away. Rosen leaves a little before ten, but Merton leaves sometime after ten. You were very definite about that: only two men, Joyce and Jacobs, left the country club dinner before ten. So if Merton left after ten, how did he get to the Donut Shop at the same time that Rosen did? The

308

only way he could was to use the Pine Grove Road. And I think, under the circumstances, it would be the road he'd be likely to take, because he knew Joyce had been drinking. If Joyce got into some trouble, an accident of some sort on the state road, someone would be sure to come along in a minute or two. But if he got into an accident on Pine Grove, on a foggy, misty night at that, it might be an hour or more before another car came along. So Merton chose the Pine Grove Road. And in that case, he must have seen the wreck with Joyce's hand sticking out of the broken window. Maybe his first thought was to remove the watch lest someone come along and take it. But then why didn't he report the accident to the police? Which suggests the alternative I pointed out to you when you first told me about the accident.'

'That he killed him? Why would he want to kill Joyce?'

The rabbi shook his head. 'I don't know any of these people, neither Joyce nor his wife, nor Jacobs, nor Merton. I can only guess. Mrs. Joyce was sure her aunt knew that she was planning to get a Church-approved separation and a civil divorce. She thought her uncle did not know. But I'm inclined to believe that if her aunt knew, then her uncle knew. Well, where would that leave her? She'd be in the anomalous position of a grass widow, without

309

a husband and unable to remarry. You want to know where Dorfbetter found the watch? He found it in the glove compartment of Merton's car.'

'But why—I mean, how—'

'The watch contained a saint's relic, so Merton wouldn't throw it away. To a man like Merton, that would be sacrilegious. And if it had blood on it, he wouldn't put it in his pocket, or even on the seat of the car, where it would stain the upholstery. But the glove compartment is where you keep your registration and garage bills, almost anything except gloves, which you keep in your pocket. You might even find a bloodstain on one of those papers that could be identified.'

Lanigan sat in silence for a minute. Then he rose abruptly and said, 'I've got to get back to the station house. I've got to think this through.'

*   *   *

The first thing Lanigan did when he reached the station house was to call the Assistant District Attorney. 'I've got to see you. Something has come up on the Joyce case.'

'All right, drop in tomorrow morning and—'

'No, Lou, it's urgent. I've got to see you now.'

'Well, all right. It won't be the first time

310

Angela has had to wait supper.'

When he heard Lanigan out, he said, 'It's weak, Hugh, but it's good enough to proceed on. I think it's enough to charge the sonofabitch. I want you to go through the regular procedure, mug shots, prints, the works, and then lock him up. He'll spend the night in jail, and then tomorrow morning we'll bring him up for arraignment.'

'What have you got against him, Lou?' asked Lanigan curiously.

'I'll tell you what I've got against the sanctimonious bastard. When we first moved into the area, we bought a house from him—on the recommendation of Father Joe, by the way. What did we know about houses? We assumed that someone recommended by the local priest would treat us right. Well, when we moved in we found the place was infested with termites. And he knew about it because the expert we got to get rid of them said there'd been a half-assed attempt at it earlier. So if he spends a night in jail, it won't bother me one little bit.'

'He's been spending the evenings with his widowed niece at her house. I don't like to do it in front of her. Besides, I'd like to check and see if there's a bloodstain in the glove compartment.'

'All right. So first thing tomorrow morning, here's what you do...'

CHAPTER FORTY

Although the meeting of the Windermere Board of Trustees was scheduled for ten o'clock, the program of events started much earlier, with an informal breakfast served in the cafeteria from half past seven to nine, at which time there would be a tour of the buildings. Those who came early, the out-of-town people who had been put up at hotels mostly, had large breakfasts of eggs and bacon and sausages, but others who drifted in later and had already breakfasted at home, took only coffee, perhaps with a doughnut or a piece of toast. It was an opportunity to renew their acquaintance and to urge and argue over pet projects.

President Macomber was not present, but Mark Levine was very much in evidence. He made no effort to campaign for the name change, feeling it would be counterproductive. Instead, he made a point of circulating, greeting new arrivals, and manifesting general friendship and bonhomie.

Charles Dobson was also one of the early arrivals. Because he was in the automobile business, his opinion was sought on various makes of cars, their comfort, their sturdiness, their retail value. 'What do you think of this new Nissan that's just come out?' And his

312

answer always began, 'Well, it's no Cadillac.' He, in turn, inquired about Cyrus Merton. 'Have you seen Cy Merton around? You heard about his niece's husband getting killed?'

He wanted to see Cyrus, to ask if he had been approached by Macomber and whether the death of Joyce had affected his decision on the name change, and as the hour approached nine, he wondered at his continued absence. He asked several of the others if they had seen him, and when they said they had not, he thought of calling his house in Barnard's Crossing. He mentioned it to his friend Ridgeway, who reassured him. 'Oh, he'll be along for the meeting. Seems to me he didn't come to the breakfast last time, either. Have you ever driven with him? He's a very careful driver. He once gave me a lift to Cambridge. I thought we'd never get there. My guess is that he didn't come to the breakfast because he didn't want to buck the morning traffic. Or maybe he didn't want to see Macomber until he had to.'

At nine o'clock President Macomber arrived and announced, 'I'm having Mr. Perkins, our custodian, take us around. He'll tell you as we go along about a number of repairs and some remodeling we are contemplating. And we'll meet Professor Sykes, head of our Physics Department, who will show you around our new Physics

313

laboratory.'

Macomber set out and the rest straggled after him. The tour started at the corner house, and Ridgeway pointed and said, as he had on similar occasions, 'That's the Clark house. I've had dinner there. I was at school with Roger Clark.' And Dobson replied, as he had on similar occasions, 'What d'ya know!'

Levine came up beside Macomber and whispered, 'How is it going, Don?'

'No change,' said Macomber gloomily.

'But Merton isn't here. Maybe he won't come.'

'Oh, he'll come all right. He wouldn't miss the meeting.'

★   ★   ★

But early in the morning, Lieutenant Jennings and a uniformed policeman had driven up to Merton's house. Mrs. Marston opened the door in response to their ring, but Cyrus, who was about to set out for Boston and the meeting of the trustees, was right behind her.

'You've come about my car, haven't you?'

'That's right,' said Jennings. 'We've got it down at the station house. If you'll come with us, you can check it out, and then if it's okay, you can drive it off.'

'Splendid! Was it damaged? It wasn't vandalized, was it?'

314

'Well, that's why we want you to look it over.'

Merton glanced at his watch. He had plenty of time, even though he assumed there would be some delay, if only to sign some papers and fill out some forms. It was worth it to drive his own car rather than the car with the company logo.

All the way down to the station house he asked questions. Where was it found? Do they know who took it? Was it a professional car thief, or was it some kid who had taken it joyriding? To all of which Jennings was careful to be noncommittal. 'I don't rightly know.' 'The chief will explain all that.' 'Chief Lanigan will tell you all about it.'

Lanigan was waiting for them in the parking lot when they drove up. 'Is that the car?' he asked, smiling.

'It sure is.'

'Now will you look it over carefully and see if there was any damage done?'

Slowly, Merton walked around the vehicle.

'That scratch on the fender,' Lanigan suggested.

'No ... that was there. I did that backing out of the garage one day.'

Lanigan got in behind the wheel and released the catch that opened the trunk. 'Anything missing?' he called out.

'There doesn't seem to be.'

Lanigan then leaned over and opened the

passenger door. 'If you'll come in and look around,' he suggested. Merton slid in beside him, and then twisted around to look at the backseat. 'Looks okay,' he said.

'How about the glove compartment?'

Merton opened the lid, gave a quick glance, and closed it.

Lanigan leaned across him and lowered the glove compartment lid. 'There's a watch in there.' He drew it out. 'Isn't this Joyce's watch? It looks just like the one his wife described.'

Merton reddened. Then he essayed a smile. 'Yes, it's his watch. I'm afraid I was not entirely candid with you. It was rather embarrassing. You see, when Victor borrowed the money from me at the club, he insisted I take the watch as security. I didn't want to, but he insisted, and I'm a little ashamed to say I let myself be persuaded.'

'We have incontrovertible evidence that he was wearing it when he left the club,' said Lanigan evenly.

Merton remained silent, and then said, 'If—you'll have one of your men drive me home, I'd appreciate it. I think I should call my attorney.'

'You can call him from here,' said Lanigan. 'We have a pay station, or you can use the phone in my office.' The steely glint in Lanigan's blue eyes made it clear that he would not be allowed to leave.

* * *

The meeting of the Windermere Board of Trustees was held on the fourth floor of the Administration Building. It was a large room with half a dozen round tables, each covered with a snowy white tablecloth and the necessary china, silverware, and glasses for the elaborate lunch which a caterer would bring in and serve at the conclusion of the board meeting.

In back of the room, beyond the round tables, was a long oblong table at which the board transacted its business. There were twenty-two small metal chairs with padded leather seats arranged around the table, for the twenty members of the board plus the secretary and the president, each with a small pad of paper, a pencil, a ballpoint pen, and a printed copy of the agenda in front of it. The meeting was scheduled for ten o'clock. At ten, whilst half a dozen or so had already taken their places at one end of the table, the others were still standing around and talking.

Mark Levine approached his friend, the president. 'How does it look, Don?' he asked.

Macomber nodded at those already seated. 'There's six of them. If they hold firm with Merton, we're licked. I'm hoping we might be able to detach at least one of them. It's possible with a secret ballot, but I'm not too sanguine.'

'But Merton is not here yet,' said Levine. 'Maybe he won't show,' he added hopefully.

'Oh, he'll show up all right,' said Macomber bitterly. 'Believe me, this is one meeting he's not going to miss.'

'Look, Don, maybe he's been held up by traffic, or he could have had a flat tire or something. It's ten o'clock right now. Why not call the meeting. Maybe we can put it to a vote before he gets here.'

'It's tempting, Mark, but there'd be hell to pay if he showed up right after the vote was taken. We'll wait a little while longer.'

Mark Levine shrugged and turned away. But at half past ten he decided to take a hand in the matter. 'Hey, Don,' he called out, 'it's half past ten. When are we going to get started?'

'Cyrus Merton is not here yet,' someone said.

'So? We've got a quorum, haven't we?'

'Yeah, but—look, he's got to come all the way from Barnard's Crossing.'

'So what? I had to come all the way from Dallas, Texas.'

'Yes, and I came down from Bangor, Maine,' said another. 'Let's get the show on the road, Prex.'

'Very well,' said Macomber. 'Will you all please take seats.' And when they were seated, he said, 'This meeting is now called to

318

order. Will the secretary please note and record in the minutes that we are starting at ten thirty-five.'

Although sorely tempted, Macomber resisted the temptation to rush the business of the meeting so that they could vote on the change of name before a possibly tardy Merton might arrive. So they listened to the reading of the minutes of the previous meeting, and to the reports of the several committees, and it was after eleven before they took up the motion to change the name of the school.

There was desultory discussion on the motion, largely by the opponents of the measure in an effort to delay the vote as they kept glancing at the door in the hope that Merton would appear. When Macomber finally called for a vote, Charles Dobson, true to his promise, moved that it be by secret ballot.

Macomber shrugged. 'I don't think there's any need to discuss this or to put it to a vote. If Mr. Dobson prefers a secret ballot, fine. The vote will be by secret ballot.'

The secretary passed out small pieces of paper, and then after a minute or two, collected them. Then he opened the folded pieces of paper and arranged them in two piles. He counted and announced, 'The vote is carried sixteen to four.'

Immediately, McKitterick, the man from

Bangor, moved that the vote be made unanimous. There was an interchange of glances from the opponents, then some head nodding, and the motion was carried.

★   ★   ★

Mark Levine had to run off immediately after lunch to take care of some business of his own downtown. But he returned to the college, to the president's house, early in the evening, so that he and Macomber could take a leisurely stroll to dinner. As they walked along, Levine asked, 'Did Merton call you to explain why he didn't come to the meeting?'

Macomber shook his head. 'No. I thought of calling him to inquire, but decided not to. He might interpret it as crowing over his defeat. I assume something important, some big business deal, must have come up and he was just unable to make it.'

'Maybe. And then maybe he knew the vote was going to go against him, and just couldn't face it.'

'That's not really in character. He's got plenty of guts. And I suspect if he had been present, he might very well have brought it off. I figured he had six votes and his own, would have made seven, which would have been just enough to have beaten us. I was surprised that only four voted to oppose.'

'I wasn't,' said Levine. 'I was canvassing

ever since I got here, Sunday. I didn't just call people and ask them how they were going to vote. I talked to some of them at some length. I thought there was a chance with this McKitterick from Bangor. He sort of hedged and kept asking me if I were sure it would be a secret ballot. I got the impression that while he would like to vote our way, he did not want to offend Merton, and that if it could be handled in such a way that Merton wouldn't know, he might come along. Another one—Bridges from Worcester, I believe—was involved in some deal with Merton, and wasn't about to take chances.'

'Like that, was it? Hm, I wonder if he might not take it so hard as to resign.'

'Would it bother you if he did?' asked Levine curiously.

'Well, except for this matter of the name, he was very useful. A college is more or less in the real estate business, you know, and he was good at it.'

Levine smiled. 'Then let's hope he doesn't take it too much to heart. In any case, we ought to celebrate. You'll be coming to dinner tonight, won't you? We'll have champagne.'

'Oh, I meant to talk to you about that. My old professor, Simon Cotton, is in town. He came to attend the Anthropology Society meeting that's going on right now, and I've invited him to dinner.'

'So what's the problem? Bring him along.'

CHAPTER FORTY-ONE

Macomber picked up his old teacher at the Harvard Club and then the two walked over to the Ritz Carleton, where Levine met them in the lobby and escorted them into the dining room. When they were seated, and a waiter brought over an ice bucket and a bottle of champagne, Cotton raised his eyebrows and asked, 'Is this your usual tipple, Mr. Levine?'

'Oh no, this is by way of celebration. When we place our orders, I'll select a proper wine for your meal.'

'And what are we celebrating?

'At the meeting of my Board of Trustees this morning,' Macomber said, 'it was voted to change the name of our college from Windermere Christian College to Windermere College of Liberal Arts.'

'I see. You mean you've cut your ties with the Church. And what church is it?'

'It wasn't any church,' said Macomber. 'Christian was inserted in the name when it was a ladies' seminary to indicate that it was a moral institution.'

'Donald thinks the vote today gives him greater control,' Levine offered.

'Believe me, it will,' Macomber asserted. 'A two-thirds majority was required, and I got it by gradually getting people on the board who were likely to back me. Now, perhaps I can develop a college that will be a real educational institution instead of an intellectual rat race, the sort of thing you have always urged, Professor Cotton.'

Cotton shook his head doubtfully. 'I wish you luck, of course, but don't be too sanguine about your chances. You'll be bucking the development of the American college for the last fifty or sixty years.'

'Why, what happened fifty or sixty years ago?' asked Levine.

'That was when college administrators saw that research was more profitable than teaching, so the focus of interest turned from student to faculty. The professor used to be someone who'd found satisfaction in the scholarly life and pleasure in imparting his knowledge to eager young minds. If he came across some special aspect of his subject, or some special problem, he might write it up for publication in a scholarly journal, or even a book. But he did it on his own time, because he wanted to. And when things changed, what he'd done for pleasure was now required as a term of his employment.'

'Publish or perish.'

'And XYZ University became the place where that fellow discovered a new planet or the new treatment for cancer. That also attracted endowments.'

'And I suppose,' said Macomber, 'when someone at ABC University was on the verge of publishing something that might be important, XYZ might approach him with an offer.'

'That's normal enough,' said Levine. 'It happens all the time in large corporations.'

'Ah, but in a corporation the inducement is a bigger salary, I suppose, and more responsible work. In the college, though, the inducement is apt to be a smaller lecture load, and in some cases the professor won't be required to teach at all. So while XYZ gains prestige, the ordinary student profits not at all.'

'But that didn't cut down on student applications, did it?' asked Levine.

'Quite the contrary,' said Macomber. 'XYZ couldn't accept all the qualified students, so they took only the cream—and then only the cream of the cream. And secondary schools gained prestige from the number or percentage of their graduates who were admitted to XYZ.'

Cotton said, 'In general, students come to XYZ because they want to know morc about themselves, about society, about the world, about the universe. But in truth such colleges have become a professionals' camp where rookies come to compete for the few available positions on the team. The result is a rat race. We produce a bunch of superbly trained young people with second-rate minds.'

'Why would they have second-rate minds?' Levine demanded.

'Because they compete with grades. And when you're intent on grades, you quickly learn that the way to get them is to suppress original thought and give the professor's thoughts back to him. You spend learning years doing that, and you'll go on doing it for the rest of your life.'

'Where did you get your Ph.D., Professor?' asked Levine.

'I don't have one,' Cotton said simply. And then, arrogantly, 'Who could grant me one?'

Macomber laughed while Levine blushed in embarrassment.

The waiter removed dishes and served coffee. Levine lit a cigar and asked, 'Are you going to be here for a few days, Professor?'

And Macomber said, 'If you are, I'd like to talk to you about some of the changes I'm planning.'

'I was planning to,' said Cotton, 'but my wife called me earlier this evening and asked me to come home. Nothing wrong—she was taking care of the grandchildren while their mother was in the hospital, and they did a job on her; she's a soft touch—but I told her I'd take the morning plane out.'

'I'm flying, too,' said Levine. 'What time is

your flight? The reason I ask is that the company I'm doing business with here has put a limousine and chauffeur at my disposal.'

'My flight is at eight o'clock.'

'Mine is a little later, but if you like, I'll pick you up at seven.'

★   ★   ★

As they drove along next morning, Professor Cotton explained, 'My wife is a nervous sort. I warned her that taking care of a couple of kids at her age was silly. And it isn't as though my son-in-law couldn't afford to get someone in for the two weeks. But no, it was a grandmother's duty.' He shook his head in annoyance at her obduracy. 'On the other hand,' he went on, 'I've been away almost two weeks, and I'm tired of eating in restaurants. I was planning on spending a few days with my cousin in Barnard's Crossing—oh, good Lord!'

'What's the matter?'

'I told them I'd be out today. They'll be expecting me there.'

'Well, you can call him when we get to the airport,' said Levine.

'No . . . he's at the temple for the morning service at that time.'

'Oh, observant, is he?'

'He's the rabbi of the congregation,'

'Of Barnard's Crossing? Rabbi Small is your cousin?'

'Oh, you know him?'

'He gave a course at Windermere one year, a few years back. And he's your cousin?'

'That's right. Second or third cousin. Let's see, my grandfather and his great-grandfather were brothers.'

'Then how do you happen to have different names, Cotton and Small?'

The professor smiled broadly. 'Do you know any Hebrew?'

'Well, I went to a Hebrew School when I was a youngster.'

'Pronounce my name, but accent the last syllable.'

Levine looked at him doubtfully and then said, 'Cot-ton.' Enlightenment came. 'It means little, small.'

'That's right. His grandfather translated the name; mine transliterated it. I think the original was Cottonchik, either because he was short or perhaps because he was very tall, in the same way the we might call a fat boy Slim.'

'You can call him when you get to Chicago, or if it's important, you can even call him from the plane.'

'Yes, I could do that, couldn't I? Actually, it isn't terribly urgent. He's leaving the rabbinate, at least the job in Barnard's Crossing, and thought he might like to try

327

teaching for a while. I met somebody from Iowa who thought there might be an opening at his school.' They had reached Levine's airline and the chauffeur was handing his bags to a porter.

He shook hands with Cotton and said, 'Well, it was nice seeing you again, Professor.'

'Yes, and thank you for the dinner and the ride.'

Levine had his baggage checked in and then made his way to a phone booth. He called President Macomber. 'Don? That Rabbi Small you thought so much of, the one from Barnard's Crossing. He's a cousin of Professor Cotton. And you know what? He's leaving his job and is planning to go into teaching for a while.'

'Hm, he's just the man I think we want. I'll write to him.'

'Don't write to him, Don. Call him.'

'Perhaps you're right.'

The call from Simcha came while the rabbi was having his breakfast after his return from the minyan. 'That was Simcha,' he said. 'He's not coming today. He's not coming at all. He's on his way back to Chicago. In fact, he was calling from the airplane. Imagine that. He thinks he might have something that would interest me, in Iowa. He said he'd write me.'

It was while he was having a second cup of

coffee that the call from Macomber came. 'Well, well, well,' he said in response to Miriam's inquiring glance, 'that was President Macomber of Windermere. It's not entirely clear, but somehow he heard through one of his trustees, who got it from Simcha, that I might be interested in a teaching job. He wants to see me.'

CHAPTER FORTY-TWO

As the rabbi drove into Boston he thought about the call he had received from President Macomber. Rabbi Small did not think that it concerned a teaching position, unless it was to take over the three-hour course he had taught some years before when Rabbi Lamden, who normally gave it, had asked him to substitute for him. He had enjoyed teaching it, to be sure, but if that was what Macomber had in mind, he would not accept since it would preclude his taking a full-time job if one came along. Certainly, if it was anything more than that, Simcha would have mentioned it when he had called earlier.

Macomber greeted him cordially, almost effusively. 'I had no idea that you were related to Professor Cotton,' he said when they were seated, he behind his desk, and the rabbi in the visitor's chair. 'I was one of a coterie devoted to Professor Cotton.' He chuckled. 'In fact, we were called Cotton-tails. Naturally, when I heard he was going to be in town, I got in touch with him. We had dinner together Tuesday night, he, I, and Mark Levine, who is a trustee of the college and one of my closest friends. We sat and talked until it was quite late, about education in general and Windermere in particular.'

Macomber recounted the gist of the conversation, and then said, 'Well, that's what I want to do here, make Windermere a real college. I want to educate rather than train. I want to develop a faculty that will be devoted to teaching students rather than to writing papers for publication in learned journals. Learning for learning's sake.' He broke off as the rabbi nodded vigorously. 'You agree? You approve?'

'It is our traditional view of learning. We have a saying: Do not use your knowledge of the Torah as a spade to dig with.'

'I don't—yes, I think I do. It means one should not use his knowledge of the, er, Torah for practical purposes, to make a living. Yes, I see, it's learning for learning's sake. But—But don't you—I mean, don't rabbis in general go contrary to that principle? Don't they make their living from their knowledge of the Torah?'

The rabbi smiled. 'Yes, they do, but the

rationalization is that they are being paid for the time they are taken away from productive work. There is another tenet in our doctrine of education. It is to the effect that the father who fails to teach his son a trade is teaching him to be a thief. That is, we distinguish between study that one does for oneself and study that is to be used in the service of society and by which we make a living. You might say it is like the distinction between undergraduate, liberal arts study and graduate study.'

'I'm afraid that distinction with us has become rather blurred of late,' said Macomber sadly. 'All study nowadays seems to be directed to getting ahead: from the high school to a good college: from college to a good graduate or professional school; from the professional school to a good job, and from a good job to a better one.' He had been leaning back in his swivel chair. Now he straightened up and, hitching the chair closer to his desk, said in a businesslike voice, 'Rabbi Lamden, for whom you substituted a few years ago, is retiring next year—'

'And you think I might be interested in taking his place?'

'No. I don't intend to continue the course he gave.' He smiled.

'To be perfectly frank, Rabb, that was instituted for public relations reasons. Since the name of our school was Windermere

Christian College, it was intended to reassure the parents of the Jewish students we had attracted. It was a snap course that all the Jewish students took because it meant an almost certain A.' As the rabbi started to protest, Macomber held up a placating hand and added, 'Oh, I know it wasn't that way when you gave it, Rabbi, but that was the way it was under Rabbi Lamden.

'Well, we are no longer Windermere Christian; we are Windermere College of Liberal Arts—as of Tuesday, when our Board of Trustees voted on it,' he added in response to the rabbi's look of surprise. 'And I would like to make it a real liberal arts college; not just a fall-back school for those who have been refused admission elsewhere, but a college of first choice, for those who want an education rather than training for a job. That entails an understanding of the society of which they are a part, of its origins and history. We've always acknowledged the Greek and Roman influences, but the Judaic only as it filtered through Christian doctrine. Well, I'd like courses in Judaic thought and philosophy, either as part of an enlarged Classics Department, or even as a separate department. Would you be interested in taking charge?'

CHAPTER FORTY-THREE

The rabbi did not attend the board meeting on Sunday. When his letter of resignation was read by the secretary, the immediate reaction was that the committee had somehow been at fault.

'What did you guys say to him?'

'We didn't say anything to him,' declared Ben Clayman. 'Levitt said he was surprised the rabbi didn't have a life contract—'

'Yeah, but I didn't push it,' said Levitt. 'When he said he preferred it that way, I dropped it.' With a touch of malice, he added, 'And I didn't make fun of his car by calling it a jalopy.'

'You think he'd resign because I called his car a jalopy?'

'Look, fellows,' said Al Bergson. 'I know why the rabbi resigned.'

'So tell already.'

'If you'll all pipe down. I stayed on after Clayman and Levitt left, and the rabbi told me he wouldn't accept any of the expensive gifts that were suggested because he was going to resign. Why? Because he's fifty-three, so he can still try something else. He's been here twenty-five years, so he's eligible for his pension—'

'Yeah, but it means a big cut in his salary.'

'Twenty-five percent, but as he explained, his daughter is getting married and his son will be getting a good job. So with the kids off his hands, he figures he'll be able to manage.'

'What kind of job is he looking for?'

'Why doesn't he just stay on until he gets the job he's looking for?'

'I suggested,' said Bergson, 'that he take a leave of absence, even for as much as a year, that we could hire a substitute for the year and then—'

'I don't think that's such a good idea. What happens if the guy we hire turns out to be a real hotshot? Do we tell him he's got to go at the end of the year?'

'Yeah, and if we say it's only for a year, what kind of guy are we likely to get?'

'You know, the guy is right. Twenty-five years! Enough is enough.'

In the end they agreed to accept the rabbi's resignation and to write him a letter to that effect.

'Make sure you say "with regret." You know, "We accept with regret—"'

'Make it "with deep regret."'

'Then in the fall we can throw him a big party and give him a nice gift like a silver kiddush cup or—'

'How about an illuminated address? You know, on parchment, in this old-fashioned kind of print and with fancy lettering at the beginning of each sentence. Something he can frame.'

'I think we ought to do the framing.'

'Yeah, you're right. We'd do the framing.'

★　★　★

After the meeting, Bergson stopped off at the rabbi's house on his way home. He described the meeting and ended with, 'They didn't appear terribly upset, David,' much to Miriam's chagrin. The rabbi was mildly amused.

'I wasn't even able to sell them on my idea of a leave of absence for a year, although one of them suggested that maybe you could stay on until you got another job and then resign. What's the story on a job, David? Got any leads?'

The rabbi smiled. 'Oh, I shall be Professor of Judaic Philosophy at Windermere next year.'

CHAPTER FORTY-FOUR

It was a hot, steamy day in July when Lanigan went to see Tomasello, the Assistant District Attorney, on quite a different matter. As he was leaving, he thought to ask about the Merton case.

'We're dropping it,' said Tomasello

shortly.

Lanigan sat down again. 'How come? New evidence?'

'The boss decided we didn't have a case, not one we could win.' It was evident that Tomasello was not happy.

'But why not? The guy came down Pine Grove Road, and he must have seen the wrecked car.'

'So what?'

'And he didn't report it to the police.'

'There's no law that says he has to.'

'So how about the watch? It was in his car, so he must have taken it off Joyce's wrist—'

'It wasn't in his car; you put it there.'

'Yeah, but when he saw it in his glove compartment, he didn't doubt that it had been there all along, and he even tried to bamboozle me into thinking Joyce had given it to him as security for the money he'd lent him.'

'We'd have a hard time introducing that in evidence. He hadn't been charged at the time, his rights hadn't been read to him.'

'So what? There was the watch. It was Joyce's and he had taken it from him.'

Tomasello's attitude softened. 'You'd have a tough time, Hugh, convincing a jury that it constituted theft. It had been his brother's watch, then his niece's. But most of all, it had a saint's relic, and any jury would accept the idea that a good Catholic—one who attended

336

Mass every day, mind you—would be apt to take it to prevent it being stolen. The main trouble with our case is that it depended on this doctor—'

'Dr. Gorfinkle? What's wrong with Dr. Gorfinkle?'

'What's wrong with him is that he's an eye doctor. He probably hasn't felt a patient's pulse in twenty years, maybe not since he completed his general internship. All we have is his word that Joyce was alive when he saw him. And this Gorfinkle—do you know him?'

'Sure, I know him.'

'Well, can you imagine him on the witness stand, trying to ward off the bludgeoning he'd take from a tough cross-examiner?'

'Yeah ... So Merton gets off scot-free. It's going to be kind of awkward when I bump into him in church or on the street.'

'Maybe if you should see him in the next week or two, but after that, no problem. I understand he's selling out, or had already sold out to a big Boston realty firm, and he and his sister are retiring to Florida.'

'And the girl, the widow?'

'I hear she's planning to go back to that Sisters' school in Ohio where she spent most of her life.'

'Did you see him, Luigi? Did you get to talk to him?'

'No, but his lawyer, the big shot, Elliot Bender, spoke to my boss, the D.A. They're kind of friendly. They were in the same law firm for a couple of years when they got out of law school—'

'You meant that's why—'

'The D.A. dropped the case? Oh no, but being friends, it was easier for Bender to get to see him. According to him, Merton was going to report it to the police, but he thought that they'd then call his niece, maybe wake her up if she were already asleep, and have her come to the hospital to identify the body. And that would be pretty traumatic for her. So he went to her house, planning to break the news to her and then call the police from there.'

'But she wasn't home.'

'Right, so he went to the Donut Shop to have a cup of coffee and then try her again later.'

'Why didn't he report it when he called the police to tell them his car had been stolen?'

'He figured they already knew,' said Tomasello.

*　　*　　*

It was an unhappy, troubled Lanigan who drove back to Barnard's Crossing. Had he been too precipitate in following Tomasello's suggestion of procedure when he knew the reason for his wanting to arrest Merton? Should he have questioned Merton further before going ahead?

As he approached the rabbi's street, on the spur of the moment he made the turn and stopped in front of the rabbi's house. He found him in the breezeway between the garage and the kitchen, sipping at a tall iced drink as he leafed idly through a magazine.

'I could use one of those, David, I've had a hard day.'

'It's a gin and tonic. Hold on and I'll get you one.'

He was back in a minute or two with a tall, frosty glass. They held up their glasses in a silent toast, and then the rabbi said, 'Crime increasing, or is it administrative detail that's getting you down?'

'Neither,' and he proceeded to recount his conversation with Tomasello.

When he finished, the rabbi said, 'That business on Gorfinkle is a lot of nonsense. He's probably taken his wife's pulse or his own countless times when she or he haven't been feeling well. There's no lawyer who's going to tell him he was mistaken and that when he felt a pulse there was none. The nub of the matter was the Joyce house on Shurtcliffe Circle.'

'Why, what was wrong with the house?'

'It was dark. When he turned into Abbot Road from Pine Grove, he turned right to go to Shurtcliffe instead of left to go to his own house on the Point because it was so much nearer, a couple of blocks instead of the several miles to the Point.'

'Why?'

'I don't think it was to tell the sad news to his niece, but because he had to go to the toilet—badly. And when he found that it was dark and no one was home, he drove another block or two to the Donut Shop. You remember, as soon as he entered, he headed for the men's room.'

'Then you think he did kill Joyce?'

The rabbi shook his head. 'I don't know what went through his mind at the time. He may have wanted only to secure the watch, and in taking it off Joyce's wrist he may have cut the artery accidentally. Or he may have removed it, and then in disgust at Joyce's drunkenness, have flung it down and cut the artery that way. Or, it may have struck him that here was a ready solution to his problem. I don't know the man except for what you've told me. Here, he'd built up a sizable fortune, to what end? He had no children and neither did his sister. The one hope of the family continuing was if his niece had children. That must have been important to him, else why would so devout a Catholic interfere with his niece becoming a nun? You would think it would be a matter of pride and joy to him that a member of his family had a vocation.

'But she was planning a Church-sponsored separation and a civil divorce. Since she was also devout, she would not remarry, at least not until her husband was dead. And he could bring that about so easily, by just pressing down for a moment.'

Lanigan nodded slowly. 'I see what you mean. Well, that's police business: a lot of work amounting to nothing much of the time.'

'Why do you say amounting to nothing? You cleared several people, Dorfbetter and Jacobs, of suspicion of murder, and maybe that coatroom boy, and maybe even Mrs. Joyce. You wondered about her not being home.'

'Yes, but the probable culprit gets off scot-free.'

'Just because you can't lock him up? He still has to live with himself, and he knows that his luck has run out. I wonder...'

'What?'

'In all the religions, there are those who disregard the basics while meticulous in observing the rituals, the externals. I met someone in Israel who was most scrupulous in observing every rule and regulation. He used two pairs of phylacteries. There's a dispute as to how the scrolls in the phylactery box should be placed, and he was taking no chances, he used both kinds. And then something terrible happened: his son was killed. And he stopped attending the daily minyan, and even going to the synagogue on the Sabbath. So I wonder if Merton, in whatever parish he finds himself in Florida, will continue to go to Mass every day.'

CHAPTER FORTY-FIVE

Some kind of party they simply had to have. After all, the guy had been there twenty-five years. What kind of party? As always, first suggestions were grandiose. 'Look, it's like the twenty-fifth anniversary of the temple, too, isn't it? All right, so he didn't come here the very first year the temple was started, but he came here the first year the building was put up. So why don't we combine the two, the twenty-fifth anniversary of the temple, or of the temple building, and the rabbi leaving after twenty-five years, and have like maybe a formal dinner dance at a ritzy hotel in Boston, and have a crazy door prize, like a Cadillac?'

'So how much would you have to charge for tickets to an affair like that? A hundred bucks apiece, minimum. And at that price, how many would come?'

'Yeah, and speaking personally, I'd have to rent a tux, so that would cost another thirty, forty bucks. And for that type of affair, I'm sure my wife would want to get a new gown.'

'Yeah, but the Sisterhood would have an ad book—'

'Ad-book, shmad-book, even if the wife didn't want a new gown, what with babysitter and parking, and tips, a couple would still have to shell out three hundred bucks, minimum.'

So sights were lowered. A Cadillac for a door prize was dropped almost immediately. 'That's all we need, to have a Boston newspaper report that a synagogue offered a Cadillac as a door prize at a party they were running.' And formal dress followed. 'What's the point? Everybody's got a dark suit, but how many of our members actually own a tux?'

The matter of location next came under fire. 'It would be on a Saturday night, right? Any of you guys ever drive into town to go to a show on a Saturday night? The traffic will kill you. And what's the point? Now, you take a place like the country club at Breverton—'

'But it's got to be kosher.'

'So you get a kosher caterer to take over. They come up with a couple of trucks with all the dishes, and they've got the food all cooked, and they've got these special like ovens in the trucks to keep it hot.'

'Look, if the idea is to avoid traffic—'

So it was finally decided to hold the party in the vestry of the temple, where there would be no problem with *kashruth* or traffic or tuxedos.

'You could have knocked me over with a feather, Rabbi. I sort of figured you'd always be here.'

'Like the electricity?' suggested the rabbi.

The other chuckled uneasily. 'Well, kind of. You know what I mean.' And moved on.

They came to the rabbi's table to express their surprise at his resignation, their regrets, their gratitude for things he had done for them, their good wishes. Most of them he barely recognized since they came to the temple, if they came at all, only on the High Holy Days.

Ira Lerner came over. 'You're still a rabbi, aren't you?'

'I guess so. Why do you ask?'

'Because I want you to marry my daughter Clara. She's marrying this Mordecai Jacobs, I think I spoke to you about it.'

'And when is the wedding to take place?'

'Oh, sometime at the end of the year, I expect.'

'Then don't you think you ought to have the new rabbi perform the ceremony?'

'You mean because it will be like in his jurisdiction? Normally, I'd agree. But it's like this: you married us, Myra and me. I don't know, it was like the second or third year you were here. Well, it's been a successful

344

marriage, and we'll be celebrating our silver anniversary in a couple of years. The point is, with all this divorce and separation going on, I'd like you to do for Clara and her boyfriend what you did for Myra and me.'

Fortunately, the rabbi caught the warning glance Miriam directed at him and managed a smile.

'I'm sure David will be more than happy to,' said Miriam sweetly.